The Summer of His Life

For Floyd, Violet, Barckley, and Bobby, who made the cottage an awesome and magical place. For Lloyd and Lois who instilled a love of reading.

Special thanks to Anne, Lisa, Stephanie and the ever patient Linnea for reading and re reading my books.

Chapter 23	Lessons, Life, Death and… Fishing	141
Chapter 24	Ultimate Power	145
Chapter 25	Horsing Around	149
Chapter 26	A Sailed	153
Chapter 27	Slick	159
Chapter 28	Fish Towel	162
Chapter 29	August Summer Sneeze Feels Fine	166
Chapter 30	Not a Ghost of a Chance	174
Chapter 31	Missing Life	178
Chapter 32	Life Saving	185
Chapter 33	Rowmance	194
Chapter 34	The Fall	201
Chapter 35	Pheasant Dreams	210
Chapter 36	The Tomb	210
Chapter 37	Narrows Escape	218
Chapter 38	Labor Day Weekend A-Head	224
Chapter 39	A Shot at the Future	231
Epilogue		236

Chapter 1   An Opening

I turn off the ignition with a melancholy sigh. I keep coming back. What has it been, fifty years? Every time I visit here, it feels... what? How can I describe the emptiness, that feeling you have when you walk into a room and forget why you are there? I sit in the car surrounded by Queen Anne's Lace that flowers at window level and I stare at the tiny weathered cabin. Its ancient white paint is molting snowy flakes onto the fading green trim. A soft chuckle escapes my throat as I realize that the greenest trim on the cabin is now the moss on the shaggy roof.

I shake my head and open the car door. Why do I come? There is no one here, nothing to see. With a grunt, I manage to exhume myself from the car and take a deep, deep breath. NOW. Now, I know why I come. My head swims. The smell of moist earth, leaf mold, and pine, caress my senses. Wind-directed leaf and water songs create a gentle music. Birds sing with glee, squirrels dance in delight at my presence, and chipmunks do a jig in celebration of my return. They cluck a greeting and duck away into that old hollow log between the cottages. Perhaps they have gone to make me some tea! Remember, I like three teaspoons of sugar. I make a grand bow of greeting to my small friends. When I straighten up, I see my uncle's favorite fishing lures, rusty hooks dug into the window sill so that they too, might dance in the wind. There's the shelf where the water bucket used to be. I look to the right and see where the red hand pump, that exhausted the younger me, once stood sentry duty. However, I save the best for last, and savoring each step, I slowly walk to the top of the hill to peer through the narrow opening of pine trees down to the lake. THE lake. I sigh again, this time with deep contentment. I could stand here for eternity... if my old back would let me.

I lick my dry lips and ease carefully down onto the moss-covered concrete steps that my mother helped pour in the energy of her maidenhood. I feel their reassuring roughness on my fingertips. I find myself rubbing my hands together as if they were cold.

A daddy longlegs waves a leg in greeting and continues on his way across the step. I close my eyes and take a deep breath through my nose. My brain nearly overdoses on these gourmet fragrances, visions from a half century ago, and eternal thoughts that power the spinning of the universe. It floods my conscious mind with visions of the past, that past which forms the very concrete steps of who I am. My mind runs across the concrete landing and I see that terrible, glorious summer with its joy, beauty and death. Though my eyes are closed, they begin to fill, as I knew they would.

Ah, here they are! I hear their voices, feel the coarse denim shorts, and I smell the bacon and coffee that formed the foundation of every breakfast. I grin in satisfaction. I knew they would come. I see them clearly. There are no cataracts here. No aching back. They were always here and they always will be here. Why didn't I see them when I pulled up? Joy washes across my face and my back muscles relax. My soul stretches out into its spiritual bathtub as a fire breathing dragon steps into the scene. Let's see... it was the summer of 1969...

The sun may have shone brightly on the tree tops high above, but far below the glitter, deep down upon the forest floor, anchored in the pine needles and last year's leaves, hung a gloom as dark as the evil nights that had birthed the dragon. Only one man dared brave the dark that resided here. He had trained for this moment for years, hungered for it and now he was ready.

The sword flashed red, reflecting the dragon's fiery breath which singed the air above his head, but the warrior held his ground and studied his opponent for an opening. He tossed his head and laughed. "Thinkest thou shall best me so easily? No man... uh, no wait... no man or beast has ever seen my defeat and neither will you, you foul smelling dealer of death."

The combatant held his sword with both hands, using it as shield and weapon, and waited patiently for an opening. His body glistened with sweat, highlighting his bulging muscles. His breath came hard in the smoky atmosphere, but he would wait until the moment was right. He resolved to fight all day and into the night.

"What are you waiting for? Shoot...I mean ...slay him before he burns my wings!" a fair voice cried.

"Quiet *girl*." *Girl* was his favorite insult. "I must watch and wait that I may kill him cleanly lest he escape and claim vengeance by destroying our village."

The dragon swayed and swung his hideous head towards the warrior, but the warrior jumped, spun in midair, touched ground for an instant, and then, doing a complete summersault he…

"Hey," the fairy exclaimed, "my mom's calling, I've gotta go."

"Then help me, you worthless pixy. I need a clean swing at his throat."

"About time you let me help. I'll fly up and grab his ears. Tink is tuff."

The fairy flew behind and over the monster's scaly head and pulled back with all her might on the hairy tuffs at the tips of enormous ears.

"Ahhh, now I've got you." The warrior pulled back his sword for the final swing that would spell victory. With a swoosh and thud the warrior fell on his back, slapped down by the dragon's powerful swaying neck. He jumped to his feet as the dragon's head swung back towards him.

"Oops," the pixy giggled, and she held up two handfuls of dragon's hair.

"Come on. You're supposed to help, Stinkersmell."

"Oh no! Look out for the dragon's fire!" the pixy shrieked.

Flames lashed at the warrior's feet. Too late did he leap. Safety was not to be had. He was thrown to the ground, and engulfed by the flames.

"Hey, that's not fair. Dragons breathe fire, not water." The drenched, almost 13- year-old boy, jumped to his feet just in time to be slapped with the dragon, which magically changed back to a swaying branch on the living pine tree outside the cottage.

The 11-year-old girl holding the wash basin giggled. "It's fairy water. I just saved your life. If you're wet, the dragon's fire won't hurt you." She began to gradually back away from him, her long black curls swung across her shoulders as she looked behind her to make sure the escape route was clear for the next part of their ritual.

"Here, Stinkersmell, let me save <u>your</u> life." The boy dropped his stick sword and reached for the yellow plastic bucket on the porch of the old cottage. As he reached for it, she slapped him with the pine branch one more time and took off at a run, giggling and shrieking with delight.

She headed past the '65 Rambler towards the dirt road a hundred yards down the two track through the beech woods. He was normally the faster of the two, but with the bucket banging against his legs and slopping water, he didn't have a chance. She cut to her right through the woods leaping over logs and brush like a deer, her long slender legs propelling her toward the parallel tracks in the dirt, where she doubled back toward her cottage.

This was his chance to cut her off. He cut through the woods at an angle calculated to cross her path before she reached the safety of her cottage. If she made it to the porch, she was safe. Her mother was very understanding, but Mike would not think of throwing a bucket of water at someone else's cottage.

He was just feet from the two track when she crossed in front of him. He swung the bucket. The water seemed to hang in the air as she passed underneath. He urged the water on, but gravity was not as eager as he was and not a drop touched her. She was several feet ahead of it as it splashed cheerfully to the forest floor.

"Missed me! Missed me!" she cried. She shot into the cottage, the screen door slamming behind her.

"You wait." He stood outside and frowned. He looked back at his aunt's cottage and then at Linda's. He had a thought. "Hey Stinker, I got a secret I forgot to tell you."

Two eyes framed by black curls appeared at one of the windows where she lay on the bed. "What is it?" she shouted back.

"You gotta come out here. It's secret."

"Just tell me.

"I can't. You got to come out here."

"Nice try." The back of the head replaced the eyes.

"Linda has to eat now." A much older version of Linda appeared at the screen door wearing an old apron and smiled at Mike

There was a rustle and Linda appeared at her mother's side, wrapping her arms around her mother's waist in demonstration of her safety. "What's for supper?"

"Macaroni and cheese."

"My favorite. See you after supper, Mickey."

"Mike. My name is Mike."

"Bye *Mickey*."

"Grrr."

A large red-faced man appeared at the door pulling Linda

roughly out of the way. "Quit making such a racket. Get off my property ya... kid!" He pulled his white Tee shirt down over his large, hairy belly.

Mike jumped back across the log that marked the property line. "Sorry." he said meekly.

He stalked back to the red handled pump, placed the bucket on the hook under the pump and started working the long handle up and down. After a few squeaky complaints water gushed out with each downward stroke. Soon the bucket was filled, and he stumbled clumsily along wrestling its lopsided weight back to the outdoor counter where they washed before dinner. The bowl that Linda had used lay upside down in the fine clay dirt surrounding the cottage. He picked it up and washed it off.

He had just straightened up, turned around and bumped into his 6-foot 2-inch uncle glowering down on him.

"You be careful with that or we won't have anything to wash with." His heavy black eyebrows frowned down as if they had an opinion of their own. "As long as you got water over everything else, you might as well take a bath."

"I just... Linda threw water on me."

His uncle just nodded sternly. "Wash up. It's time to eat."

Mike turned back to the yellow bucket sitting on the painted green boards that served as their outdoor washing counter. He carefully lifted the metal dipper off of the nail and dipped two cups of water into the blue enameled wash basin. The soap sat in a wire rack below the old mirror that uncle Vic used for shaving. The pale freckled face staring back at him looked sad and alone.

Aunt Lilly smiled and patted Mike's back as he walked up to the tiny dinner table on the enclosed porch overlooking the lake. "It's fun to watch you play so nice with Linda. Oh! I forgot the..." her voice trailed off as she hurried back toward the kitchen.

"She wanted to pretend," he rushed to say. His face burned. "None of the guys are up here yet. D'ya think they will come up this weekend?" He glanced at his uncle.

"Are you sure you wouldn't rather play with the girls?" His uncle smirked.

"There's just nothin' to do except..." He gave up and sat down and glared at his plate. He knew he shouldn't have come.

Mike had enjoyed visiting the cottage with his parents on weekends since he was born. So, it would be great fun for him to spend the whole summer with his uncle and aunt... or so his mother said. His mother started working this year and now both parents just seemed to work all the time. They were always too tired to do anything with him when they came home. Lately it seemed like dad was not home much at all. With school out for the summer, he knew his mom did not want him home all day by himself so here he was. Maybe she just did not want him home at all he thought and sighed.

As the lake was the heart of the surrounding woods, so the porch was the heart of the cottage. The front of the porch was waist-to-ceiling glass, and the sides were waist-to- ceiling screens. Only during storms were the shades pulled down and tied to try to keep the rain out. The nearest trees were only five feet away. Uncle Vic loved the trees, refusing to cut them down unless absolutely life or death. So, sitting on the porch was a lot like sitting in the middle of the woods. The best part was that the windows overlooked the lake, framed in by fragrant hemlocks, cedar and white pine. The dining table was pressed tight against the glass to ensure that the frail humans inside would feel as much as possible like they were outside. There was a larger table in the main room of the cottage, but it was generally stacked with groceries and other necessary but boring items. There was not much storage in the tiny cottage except for the battered pie cupboard. No longer a place to store cooling pies, it was filled with cereal, cans of beans, peanut butter, jelly and best of all, a most wonderful sweet musty smell that whispered "Welcome to the cottage, Mike." every time he opened it.

No one would want to sit huddled away in the center of the cottage when they could perch atop a throne on the ledge of the hill overlooking the lake. It was here in the fragrant heart of the trees, sprinkled with dancing sunshine, overlooking the sparkling lake that breakfast, lunch and dinner were eaten. Here, bills were paid, letters written, and laughter filled card games played. Here men shook their heads as they told war stories and women bragged about their brilliant children or whispered about Aunt Molly's plumbing problems. It was here that the next election would be decided and adults would consult Paul Harvey on the security of the nation. Here the sunset over the lake would be rated, night would be welcomed and prayers would be said. Mike was sure that a single prayer here carried more power than any ten he had ever heard in church. The pastor might have read about God, but Uncle Vic spent more time actually talking to God when they were in the hiking in the woods or fishing. Mike was sure of that.

"Lilly! Would you just sit down!" His uncle slowly eased himself into the creaky wooden chair. The slow deliberate maneuvering reminded Mike of a documentary he had seen demonstrating the docking of an aircraft carrier.

"I'm coming," Aunt Lilly called. "I thought maybe someone would like some strawberry Jell-O." She stepped onto the screened in porch bearing a melmac bowl. Her face shone as though she bore a Congressional Medal of Honor. "Here, I bet you'd like some." She placed the bowl next to Mike.

"Can we eat now?" His uncle grumbled.

"Certainly, unless you would like something else." She smiled sweetly. "Here, let me turn the radio down."

The big band music coming from the ever-present public radio station lowered to the volume of elevator music, reminding Mike that there would be no TV <u>for three months.</u>

"Let's pray," His uncle sighed and took his aunt Lilly's hand gently. Her small tender hand completely disappeared in his uncle's rough brown spotted hand.

"Thank you, Oh Lord, for the beauty of your creation and for this food which is such a delight to eat. Thank you for the hands that prepared it. And please watch over Buck. Protect him from those...Viet Cong. Amen." His uncle raised his head.

"And thank you that Mike could join us for the summer. Amen," his aunt added.

"Amen," his uncle completed.

Mike wasn't sure if he was supposed to say Amen, so he said nothing. He sneaked a look to make sure they were looking up. He released his breath and realized that he held it through the entire prayer and relaxed. He did not want to get hollered at.

"Have some Jell-O, Mike. I made you three hamburgers." Lilly handed him the bowl. "Is there anything else I could get you?"

"Thanks...uh, no," Mike muttered. He wished his parents could be here like Linda's. It was going to be long summer.

"What are you going to do after supper, Mike?" Aunt Lilly asked.

"I dunno."

"Don't you have anything you want to do while you're up here?"

"I want to go fishing and see *cool* stuff." Mike stuffed the last bit of his first hamburger into his mouth.

"What kind of *cool* stuff?" his aunt asked, delight sparkling in her eyes.

"Well, Buck said when he was a teenager up here, he saw the northern lights and found an arrowhead and watched the pheasants eat gravel from the road and milked cows and other stuff. I 've never done any of that. So, I made a list and I'm going to do all the stuff that Buck did since I'm going to become a teenager this fall."

"Makin' lists," Uncle Vic snorted. "Gotta do this, gotta do that. Sound like your father. Your whole life will be over and you'll have done nothing but make lists."

"Vic!" Aunt Lilly hushed him.

The rest of the dinner proceeded with Aunt Lilly talking about relatives that Mike did not know and an occasional grunt from Uncle Vic.

"May I be excused?" Mike asked.

"Oh, my cake!" Aunt Lil jumped up from the table and very nearly ran to the kitchen, returning with a chocolate cake with chocolate frosting.

"You have to have a piece of cake first," she said and cut two huge slabs. She placed the largest in front of Mike and the other in front of Uncle Vic.

It was easily the biggest piece of cake Mike had ever been given. Mike goggled at the monstrous hunk with a double layer of frosting. A family of four could have lived off that one piece of cake for three days.

"Cool!" Mike said. "Thanks." The word was barely out of his mouth before he forked the first mouthful in. He glanced up to see if Uncle Vic would eat his whole piece or, like most adults, protest and cut the enormous piece in half.

Mike furrowed his brow. To his shock, Uncle Vic was reaching his knife towards the big rectangular chunk of butter. A slab of butter larger than Uncle Vic's thumb smoothly slid onto the knife and a moment later was spread over two exposed sides of his piece of cake.

Mike paused in mid chew as Uncle Vic ignored his fork and lifted a piece of the cake with butter spread on it up to his lips with a smile as big as the cake.

"VIC!" Aunt Lilly scolded. "Remember what the Doctor said."

"A life you can't enjoy, ain't worth livin'."

Mike coughed as his own cake couldn't make up its mind which way to go.

"Have some more macaroni and cheese, Linda?"
"Isn't there anything else?"
"Not today dear. Your father still doesn't have a job.
"When will he get one?"
"I don't know dear. He doesn't seem... to want to look anymore. He is very ...tired."
"Maybe if he didn't drink so much, he wouldn't be so tired," Linda offered.
Linda's mother stood quickly and left the room.

The fighter pilot skimmed the treetops hugging the ground to avoid anti-aircraft guns that had been wreaking havoc with his squadron. He had been selected for this mission by his commanding officer to take out the rocket launchers threatening Washington D.C. Captured intelligence indicated a launch time only three hours away. He had one chance. He went in low and alone. The launcher would be difficult to take out. It hid on a rough rock wall on the side of a huge canyon. He would take advantage of the cover but it was incredibly dangerous. He slid over the edge of the cliff and dropped to the bottom of the river valley. His knuckles white, he held his course. The slightest movement of the stick would make the difference between life and becoming fast food for the hungry rock teeth reaching up from the valley. The river swung wide left, then wide right, and then left. *Look out for the pillar!* He jerked the controls back and the jet roared around it within mere feet of death. He should be coming close. There! He could just make it out. He would be past it in 3 seconds. Gritting his teeth, he flipped off the safety and fired his missiles. He was barely past the target when the world beneath him erupted in orange flames.

"Beehive this is Sting, missiles detonated on target, and we have secondaries." He swept back towards the target for confirmation. Suddenly, the controls were nearly torn from his grasp by a huge explosion. Smoke filled the cockpit. He fought madly to control the rocking jet. He could see the cliff wall flying up towards him but the jet refused to answer to his commands.
"Mayday, Mayday..." He pulled the handle on the ejection seat.
Scarcely had the chute opened when he slammed into the wall of the canyon, his chute tangled in a bush. He started to slide,

holding on with his fingertips; the rapids licked their lips 300 feet below. Air came in gasps. He was hundreds of miles from help. What could he do? Then he heard *the voice*....

"Hey, take it easy on that hammock. You'll tear it and we'll have to throw it out." His uncle squinted one eye at him.

"Sorry." Mike let go of the hammock and sat looking down the steep hill towards the lake. He sighed and picked up his book. He read a page sitting there on the hard packed earth and then got back into the hammock. "I'll be careful," he mumbled.

His aunt and uncle sat and watched the sunset over the lake. Mike glanced over at them to see if they were watching him. They sat next to each other holding hands in a glider; a sort of rocker made for two. If they were watching him, they hid it well.

This particular hammock was one of three best places in the world to read... until the mosquitoes come out. Mike slapped his arm and was rewarded with a large blood smear from a gorged mosquito. He grinned. Got it!

He swung back and forth in the hammock. The movement made it difficult for the mosquitoes to select a runway for landing. From time to time, he would look down the hill through the hemlock trees to the dock next door. Linda sat on the dock reading in the orange light reflecting off the lake waiting for her father to come back from fishing.

<u>The Jernil</u>
<u>A record of my sumer as told by Mike Anderson.</u>
Ok Mom I am writing this stupid jernil like you want me to. There is nothing to do up here exsept play with the girl next store. BLAH! I know Lewis and Clark wrote a jornel as they crost the west but I'm just sittin here bord to death. Can't I come home? I promus not to get in any truble when you and dad are at work. I'm going die of bordum up here without you or dad. Nothing else to write. Maybe the guys will come up tommorroww.

Chapter 2   First Friday

A soft light slid under Mike's eyelids. His eyes opened with the casual comfort found in the prospect of the three-month vacation before him. The sun wasn't up yet but the glow of its coming sat on the treetops across the lake. This was the first best place in the world to sleep, even better than his bedroom back home. The screened in porch with the old sofa which served as his bed, let all the wonderful smells and sounds of the lake in all night long. The chill on his face amplified the delightful warmth of the sofa piled high with 40 pounds of ancient homemade quilts. He snuggled deeper into the reassuring pile of historic warmth.

A movement outside the large screen caught his eyes. His uncle walked by the screened window carrying a fishing pole. He spoke to the boy through the screen. "Thought you wanted to go fishin' this morning!"

Mike sat up in bed. "Yeah!"

"Well, the fish are hungry now. You goin' to wait till noon? I am going now."

"I wantta go. Can't you wait a minute?" Mike jumped out of bed, pulled on his cold stiff cutoff jeans, and stabbed his feet into his beat-up Converse tennis shoes. As he ran out the cottage door facing the road, he grabbed a sweatshirt. He rounded the corner of the cottage, grabbed his pole and the old cigar box holding his tackle and began leaping down the 32 steps toward the lake. He had to slow down to avoid hitting his uncle who was still plodding down.

"What took you so long?" his uncle grumped.

"Well, I had to get dressed," Mike said exasperated. He missed the sly grin on his uncle's face.

"The fish don't care whether you're dressed or not."

"But it's cold!"

"That it is."

The air was colder than the water and a mist hung a few feet deep over the surface making it difficult to see across the lake. Looking down, the water surface was like glass and every stone and snail on the bottom of the lake was revealed.

"Look there's a crayfish," Mike cried.

"Grab him. He's good bait."

Mike looked at the one-inch pinchers. "I'm not grabbin' him."

His uncle laughed.

Mike looked up surprised. He didn't remember hearing his uncle laugh before. *Now he's laughing at me,* he thought.

"I guess we'll use the worms we dug yesterday."

Mike put on a life jacket, climbed into the boat and began to bail, while Uncle Vic studied the lake from the dock.

Mike paused from his bailing. "This sure is an old boat. Why don't you get a new one?"

"It doesn't leak much. Your grandfather made this boat. Look how each piece of wood fits tight against the other. It's a dandy. I wouldn't trade it for two of those noisy aluminum boats. They bang and clang anytime you touch 'em." He grimaced in disgust for anyone who could even think of such a thing.

"Like Linda's dad's?" Mike glanced over at the dock next door where the unused boat floated high in the water. "He *is* pretty noisy in it."

Uncle Vic just nodded.

Mike sat down in the bow and examined the boat. "How did grandpa get the wood to curve?"

"He had a little oven out beside the workshop. He would soak the board and then heat it up in steam until he could bend it the way he wanted. Then he nailed it to the boat. When it cooled it stayed in place. Heat and pressure shape it so that later it retains the desired shape. Not much different from how God shapes us, I guess," his uncle said and stepped into the boat with a grunt. The boat settled into the flat crystal-clear water.

Mike undid the ropes and his uncle started rowing toward the point. Mike sat with his face glued over the edge, looking down into the crystal-clear depths. Several small blue gills rushed here and there through the seaweed. Now and then he would see a bass. "There's a keeper. Let's fish here."

"If you can see them, they can see you. We'll go over to the bend, where they can hide and so can we." His uncle continued rowing slow and steady as a turtle's heartbeat.

They arrived at the bend and Mike awkwardly dropped the piece of concrete that served as an anchor. They didn't talk much. They caught a few fish. Some were small and some were keepers. The sun made its grand entrance and the mist evaporated. Mike peeled off his sweatshirt. The morning wind began to move the boat a little. Waves tapped the side of the boat.

A motorboat started up across the lake. Uncle Vic looked up and frowned. "Must be time to go, the hot-rodders woke up." He cast his line out again.

The motor boat tore across the lake and headed towards the narrows where they were fishing. It flashed by sixty yards away. Uncle Vic shook his head. "It's bad enough he has to make so much noise. He's got the whole lake and he has to bring his ruckus to us." About that time the wake from the powerboat hit the small wooden boat and both of them grabbed the sides to keep their balance in the rocking.

"Well let's go." His uncle reeled in his bait in disgust.

"OK." Mike pulled in the anchor.

On the way back, Mike could see Linda sitting on her dock reading. When they pulled up to their dock, she shouted over to him. Hey Mickey! What were you doing out there? You couldn't catch a fish if it bit you on the nose, even if you do smell like a worm.

His uncle looked at him and snickered. "Aren't you going to tell your girlfriend what you caught?"

Mike just stared at the bottom of the boat. He could feel his face flush.

As his uncle climbed out of the boat he said, "Remember to put the worms under the porch so they don't dry up."

Mike nodded and headed up to breakfast.

The sun was quite warm now. Mike lay on the dock reading a 5-year-old fishing magazine. The sun on his already browned back was just hot enough to require jumping into the lake to cool off every so often. The sun massaged his back muscles and stroked the back of his neck, as though attempting to teach him to purr. This was the second of the three best places in the world to read. Well, maybe the first.

For the mind to be able to read effectively it must be left alone by the body. Normally the body is constantly pestering the mind with things like "My left knee itches. Do something about that *right now,* fool." or "My word, but this chair is uncomfortable. Lay down idiot! The least you could do is wiggle some blood back into my toes." This last comment is most common in a school setting. Yes, school room chairs were the worst possible place in the world to read.

To really do some serious reading, the body must be in complete ecstasy so that it tells the brain, "I'm fine. Go away and leave me alone. I won't be needing you for a while." This is exactly the state that Mike's body was in right now, but it was about to get interrupted.

A car door slammed shut. Mike's ears perked up. A wild ruckus arose with the complicated composition of sounds that only two boys can make: sounds of feet running through dry leaves, a stick grabbed and broken against a tree, shouting, a chair knocked over and jumping on a porch.

"Yeah, we finally made it!"

"Look at the lake."

"I'll beat you to the dock."

"How high is the water?"

"Is Mike here?"

"Is the water murky this year?"

"Bet I see a fish first."

An avalanche of boys tumbled down the hill with a dog bouncing back and forth between them.

As they got to the bottom of the hill the competition got fierce. They were side by side when they reached the dock but the smaller boy shot ahead and stepped on the dock first. His brother pushed him, but the smaller boy's lightning reflexes saved him and he ran further out on the dock, the old white planks exploded with noise under their feet. Boom, Boom, Boom. Bluegills shot out from under the dock like torpedoes.

"Hey Slim Jim, Eric." Mike waved to the boys and ran toward their dock.

"How long you here? Did you catch any fish yet? I'm here for the whole summer, how 'bout you." The boy's sentences flew back and forth and blended together, in an indistinguishable mass like the worms in the bottom of the old coffee can.

When they slowed down, they discovered that Mike was there for the whole summer but the brothers, Jim and Eric, would only be coming up for weekends with the occasional holiday week thrown in. The brothers were near opposites. Intellectual Slim Jim was Mike's age and did most of the talking. Eric was built like a brick bulldog. A year and a half younger than the other boys and six inches shorter he was always trying to prove himself. Now he waded around in the water looking for clams, crayfish and other treasures. He was the shortest kid in the neighborhood and always seemed to get picked on, but it made him very good at fighting back.

Eric suddenly bent over thrusting both hands under water. He hooted and lifted out his trophy. "Wow, look at the size of this one."

"Wow!" Jim's eyes went wide as Eric waded back to shore holding out the huge brown-green crayfish, its pinchers extended menacingly.

"Cool," Mike said. "You should have seen the one I caught yesterday." He left out the fact that he had caught it with a net.

"You want to hold it?" He extended the crayfish to Mike eagerly.

"No thanks." Mike took a step back. Eric may be the youngest and shortest of the three boys, but he was definitely the most courageous.

"I found a new way to catch them," Eric boasted. "I never get pinched anymore. Well, almost never. Here, I'll show you." He dropped the crayfish into the lake near the dock. It scooted backward at an amazing rate until it was safely in the shadow. The other two boys lay down on the dock and peered over the edge.

Eric picked up one of the many sticks littering the sand and deftly maneuvered it from behind the crayfish until it was just above the creature's back. Eric quickly pinned it to the lake bottom and with it held in place, easily avoided the pinchers and picked it up by the carapace.

"Wow that's neat," Mike said in awe. They always scoot away from me.

"What shall we do with it?" Jim asked.

Mike glanced at the beagle on the dock that stared at the crayfish with a mixture of interest and suspicion. "I know. Give it to Dennis."

"Your uncle's dog?" Jim asked incredulous. "What'll he do?"

"Why, he'll eat it."

"Are you nuts? The dog doesn't have any teeth."

"I've seen him eat them before. Let's go find him."

Eric climbed out of the water and the boys headed up the hill looking for the old Springer Spaniel. They found him lying in a shallow gutter-like depression of dirt by the back porch. His tongue perpetually hung out of his mouth since the dog lost most of his teeth to distemper as a puppy. Uncle Vic said this made him a great dog, explaining, "he's never bit anyone." Usually, as he slept on the ground, his tongue lay in the dirt covered in dust and pine needles.

Eric looked at the crayfish with its large pinchers and then at the old dog. "That would be mean. Don't you feel sorry for the dog?

"'Course I do, but look at him."

The dog lifted its head and trotted over to Eric, his stub of a tail wagging in delight. Dennis' eyes never left the crayfish in Eric's hand.

"We're just giving him what he wants."

"Yeah, that's what the drug dealers say."

"Go ahead. Let the dog choose."

Eric gingerly set the crustacean down on the dirt.

This dog had spent years in battle against crayfish and was an expert in the martial arts of crayfish. Had he been a human, he would have written several books on the topic and traveled around the world as a consultant, giving lectures to people who have no clue what he is talking about. Never having to wage war on crayfish again, he ultimately would forget everything on which he proclaimed to be an expert. Fortunately, for his skill set, he was not a human and cursed to become a consultant.

The dog assumed his standard stance, studying his opponent to determine what school of defense this particular crustacean had studied. Once the analysis was completed, he shifted position, faked with his right front foot and lunged.

The dog jerked back with a yelp. Maybe it was not too late to be a consultant.

"Ooo."

"See!"

"He can't get it."

"No, he is just lulling the crayfish into a false sense of security."

The boys took on the roles of every set of sports commentators since the beginning of time.

The crayfish backed up slightly. Then stopped and posed, its open pinchers extended like fencing swords.

The dog's head nodded as if accepting the challenge of a fellow master. He sucked his tongue in to escape the weapon. The dog shifted position and lunged.

The crayfish deftly shifted position too and spread its claws menacingly.

Yelp! The dog cried jumping back.

"Oh man."

"Git him, boy."

The dog lunged again, but this time, just before he made contact, he pulled back and came down on top avoiding the pincers.

The boys sucked in their breath in unison at each lunge and then watched wide-eyed as Dennis scooped up a mouthful of pain, tipped back his head, bit down quickly and swallowed.

"Wow."

"Cool."

The long dirty tongue wrapped itself around the outside of the mouth to make sure no crunchy morsels had gotten away. Then looking with distain on the fighting ring, at the lack of challenge, the dog went back and dropped into his depression where his blackened tongue was once again flung back into the dirt.

"I don't believe it," Jim said. "Why would a dog inflict such pain on itself?"

A door slammed next door. Linda's dad tramped down the steps toward the lake carrying his fishing pole and a six pack of beer.

"Hey is Linda up this weekend?" Jim asked.

"Yeah." Mike shrugged. "I guess she is up for the whole summer or something. Her folks sold their house in the city. They live here now."

"That's weird."

"Her dad lost his job."

"That's still weird."

"Hey! I got a plan how we can make some money," Mike said to change the topic. He felt uncomfortable talking about Linda's family.

"We'll look for treasure."

"Right. I hate to tell you, Mike, but there weren't any pirates or gold in Michigan." Jim shook his head sadly at this poor idiot.

"No, not gold, Indian artsy facts. I talked to Buck before he shipped out and he said when he was my age, he found an arrowhead up here and Dr. Jacobson bought it from him for *ten dollars.*"

"Ten dollars? That's nothin'. I had fifteen dollars once."

"Well do you have it now?"

Jim shook his head.

"Well, I think with all of us looking all summer, we should be able to find a whole mess of 'em."

"Where do we look?"

"Why anywhere there was Indians."

"But that's everywhere."

"Yeah, I figure we just keep our eyes peeled all summer and we're bound to find some. Remember all the cool stuff we found last year?"

"Yeah, but nobody's going to pay us for a snakeskin or a sun-dried possum."

"Hey that possum was pretty cool. I still got that." Mike grinned.

"What did your mom say?"

"She doesn't know, but I had to move it to the garage. She complained that my room stunk and she was gonna make me clean my *whole* bedroom."

"Jim! Eric! You come help unpack." Jim's father shouted from the next cottage.

"See you later Mike!" The brothers ran off.

Mike strode quietly across the pine needles toward the lakeside of the cabin. As he approached the porch, he heard his aunt and uncle talking. Something about their voices made him stop before he came within sight.

"Harold needs to get a job, any job," His uncle stated in disgust.

"Now Vic, times are tough and he can't get a job."

"But he won't find anything up here fishing."

"Luann said they had to sell their house in town. She inherited the cottage, so it was paid off."

"He needs to get off his high horse and take a job that is less than perfect. I worked at a job I hated for 20 years after I lost my job at the railroad. A man does what he has to." A chair slid across the wood floor noisily and Uncle Vic stood up. "I'm going to cut some wood."

Mike heard his uncle stomp out the back door. Mike practically ran down the steps to the lake, not wanting to meet his uncle in mid stomp.

He threw himself down on the dock and picked up the magazine he had been reading earlier. He watched as Linda's dad, Harold, rowed out to the drop off. His angry strokes were choppy and short, sending up a splash as the oars struck the water. It looked very different from the smooth deliberate strokes with which his uncle caressed the water.

At least Linda's dad comes up here, he thought. He looked back to his magazine as a cloud drew across the sun.

Joranl

Ok Mom I'm trying to rite again but I don't know what to rite. I wish you were coming up. I am so home sick, I can't stand it. The boys are here finaly but just for the week end, then it's back to me by myself. Dont forget to feed my hamster Stinky. What is Pual doing this summer without me? Bet he's as miserable as I am. Oh I forgot to mention the peple next store are living here year round. Isnt that weird? He needs to get a job. What happens if he dosnt get one?

I hope you come up this weekend. Oh weather suny, water kinda cold didnt do nothin, but tomorow look out!!! the guys are here!

Chapter 3   The Great Design

"Mike Angelo, you have made so many great and glorious statues. I want you to make the masterpiece to sit outside my castle in da Vinci."

"Yes, but only if I can have the freedom my creative talents require. I can have no one tell me what to do or it would spoil my creative genius."

"That is fine. You name your price. I will give you my castle in Florence and my daughter to marry."

"I have no time to marry."

"You are indeed the wise man. So, what masterpiece are you making now?"

"I have made so many glorious things they could fill the world, so this time I am making... The World." The master artist held up a round globe and examined it closely for flaws.

"Hi Mike. Whatcha doin'?"

"Little John!" Mike looked up at the large pudgy boy on the dock from where he was wading in the shallow water. Little John was only a year older but much larger than Jim and Mike.

"You're a mess. You been rolling in the mud?" Little John asked.

"It's clay." Mike wiped a brown hand across his forehead adding another light brown streak to his already striped form. I'm gonna make stuff. You want to help?"

"Make stuff? Sure. What do I do?

"Get down here and feel around the lake bottom until you get something really gooshy." He reached down and pulled up a handful of the treasure from under the water.

It wasn't long before the two boys looked nearly identical even though little John was a full head taller than Mike.

Soon the plastic yellow mop bucket was full of the slimy brown mass.

"Ok. What do we do now?" Little John wiped a clay-covered hand through his thick brown hair.

"Watch." Mike pulled out a thimble-sized chunk and began to roll it between his hands. He then walked out of the shade to a sunny part of the dock and placed the less than perfect sphere gently on the edge of the dock as if it was the Hope diamond. He stood back to admire it. After a couple of seconds of study, he turned it precisely a quarter turn, set it back down and nodded knowingly.

"There. The sun will bake it until it's hard as rock. Uncle Vic says he used to make marbles this way when he was a kid," Mike said with a bit of a swagger.

"Wow, that's neat. Let me try."

Soon the dock was covered with a hundred irregular balls of clay.

"They look like little cannonballs," Little John said. "Hey, we should make some soldiers."

"Yeah, that would be cool, then we could shoot the cannonballs at them."

Several attempts at soldiers lay on the dock when they heard steps coming up the dock.

"Hello *Mickey*," she sang. "Hi John," she said in a normal voice.

Little John looked at Mike. "Mickey?"

"What do *you* want stinker?" Mike asked without looking up.

"I came to see if you wanted to do something."

"No, we're busy." He said continuing to study his project.

"Oh. How fun! You're making dolls! Can I do it?"

"WE'RE NOT making DOLLS!" Mike glared, "We are making soldiers."

"Not very good ones. Here. Let me try." She picked up a chunk of clay rolled it between her palms. After repeating this process several times making different diameter cylinders, she began to shape them.

"Those are looking great." Little John stopped working to watch Linda skillfully shape the clay into a figure holding a bow.

"That's Robin Hood." A short time later she added another figure to it. That's a fairy." She looked at Mike and smiled.

Mike glanced at it. "Stinkersmell." He snorted. Then he

grudgingly added, "They're not bad."

"Here." She handed him a couple of her cylinders. Soon several, at least recognizable, soldiers joined her two characters on the dock. Linda helped them make several more.

"What are you guys going to do with them when they dry?"

"We are going to have a great battle."

"Not with these two. Tink doesn't like to fight."

"We'll set yours aside," Little John said.

Linda looked from the clay figures to the two boys. "You look like clay people yourselves. Don't stay out in the sun too long or you will turn to stone."

"We'll turn you to stone." Mike picked up a handful of clay and flung it at her. It missed her mostly. She squealed and ran down the dock. Mike ran after her but the water slowed him down.

"How come you're so mean to her?"

"I'm not mean. She likes it."

"Missed me," she shouted down from the top of the hill.

"Linda, you come in now," her mother called.

Mike and Little John spent the next hour setting up clay men and shooting them down with their cannon balls. Battle after battle left fewer and fewer clay soldiers in one piece. Some fell victim to the cannon fire. Some fell in the water and disappeared back to the soil from whence they came. Eventually they were down to the last two soldiers.

"Let's keep these two."

"Why?"

"They are the only two left. That makes them the best. Besides I want to show one to my mom."

"OK. Which one do you want? Did you make one of these?"

"Neither, Linda made them both."

Little John looked around at the scattered legs and arms, the carnage of the imaginary war. "These things are sure a lot easier to break than they are to make."

Jouranl

I hope you didn't let Pual borrow my bike. He broke it last time. Mom guess what? The Swanson's buought up a letter from Buck. He says it stinks in Viet Nam. It smells like someone burning down the outhouse becuz that's what they do. And he was actualy in a battle, but he said it wasn't like he expected. He couldn't see anyone even though there was lots of shooting on both sides. All he could see was a few guys on his side. I guess some got hurt. He said there was lots of screeming. Then the hellecopters came and hauled them away. He said he is glad to serve his country, but watching people die is awful. There was more to the letter but aunt Lil had to quit reading, to take care of something in the kitchen.

Chapter 4   Picture This

Mike looked glumly out the window. "Is it going to rain all day?"

"Well... this is Michigan, so you don't know, ...it might snow." Aunt Lilly squeezed his shoulders.

Uncle Vic had taken advantage of the bad weather to run "to town" to pick up some tools and the mail.

"It's not fair. It rained all day yesterday."

"Would you like something else on the radio? I want to hear Paul Harvey at noon but you can change it until then. There are some Reader's Digests here. I think Buck left some old books under the bed..." Off she went to probe the deepest darkness under the bed in the lone bedroom. Mike shuddered at the thought of reaching under there.

"That's ok, I am tired of reading."

"Would you like to play Canasta after I get the kitchen cleaned?"

"No, we did that all day yesterday."

"We could walk around the lake."

"In the rain?"

"I have some jackets. We could pack a snack. I have some of that good strawberry jam."

"No, that's alright."

"Well let me know if you think of something you would like to do."

"Okay." Mike just stared at the wall, and picked up his journal notebook.

Jouranel

It's raining again. Nothing to do today. Wish I was home watching TV. Nothing to watch here but the rain and the pictures on the wall.

Mike stared at one of the old black and white pictures looking for inspiration and something caught his eye. "Aunt Lilly?"
"Yes dear?"
"Who are these men and what are they doing?"
"That is your grandfather and he is building this cottage."
"Cool."
"He hauled all the wood up here in his Model T truck. It took him two days."
"He built the whole cottage in two days?"
"No," she chuckled, putting a hand on Mike's shoulder. "It took him two days to travel the 80 miles to get up here. He had several flat tires and going up the hill outside of Shelby, all the lumber slid out the back of the truck."
"That's nuts. Why didn't he buy the wood up here?"
"It was used lumber that he got from tearing down other buildings. We didn't have much money so we used whatever we could find cheap. It was your mother's job, after she got home from school every day; to straighten and sort the nails he pulled out of the old buildings so your grandpa could use them for something else."
Mike's wide-eyed silence proclaimed his awe. "Straighten nails?"
"Would you like to see 'The Book?" She said, The Book, in a tone usually reserved only for the Bible. "I kept a diary of the building and of the cottage and people coming up."

The woodsman threw off the worn and tattered blanket and climbed out from the weather-stained piece of canvas that served as a tent. The scattering of snow would be gone by noon but he would have good tracking until then, and a couple deer hanging from the buck pole would come in handy as he worked on this cabin. He had brought a couple of other men with him, but they knew it would be his skill that would fill their bellies tonight.

"Boy, they stacked up deer like split oak in the woodshed, and lookit all those ducks."
Aunt Lil sipped her tea and then put the cup down. "You should ask Uncle Vic about those. Those are a few years later when his first sons came up here." She pointed to the next page. "That's

Bob and Tom and those are your uncles, my brothers. They rode the train up and Vic picked them up after work."

"What train?"

"It was pretty wild up here yet, there was no highway and the easiest way was to take the train up to Scottsville. The winter was hard and we seldom came up then. It was best if we could have a horse drawn sled. But that was hard to arrange."

The engineer knew it was up to him to get the …to get the… Mike scratched his head. Oh …serum to the hospital. It had been a long winter and brutally cold. Snow piled up on the tracks forcing him to back the train up several times and hammer his way through enormous drifts taller than the train. He could hear the wheels slipping on the icy tracks so he dumped more sand under the wheels and was rewarded with a new surge forward. He burst through the last drift; there, up ahead, he could see the station a few miles away, up the hill, across the valley but the train was slipping again. He tried to dump more sand on the track but there was none left. The wheels spun and the train stopped moving. He knew if he tried to walk the entire distance to the station through the chest deep snow and across the ice choked river, he probably wouldn't make it, but he had to try.

The engineer supported himself on his hands and knees and rapped on the door with what little life was left in his frozen body. The beautiful nurse that opened the door gasped in horror at his blackened frostbit nose. Even as he gasped out his last breath, he held out the serum that would save the town.

"You'll be remembered forever," she said as she gently pulled the serum from his already frozen hands. She climbed into the horse drawn sled and looked back in sorrow on the handsome engineer, a tear frozen on her cheek.

Aunt Lil set down the plate of cookies and pointed to another photo. "Here is a picture of your mom and me, putting in the concrete steps that go down to the lake."

"MY MOM! Pouring concrete!?"

"We did what we had to."

Several hours later Mike put the well-worn photo album reverently back up on the shelf. He looked around the room differently now. Reading the dates on the old banners and the Pine

Tar shampoo calendar saved for the beautiful woodsy picture. There was a lot of his family wrapped up in this old cottage. He had not realized how much.

"Hey how come there's no picture of me on the walls or in the book."

"You're too new."

"I'm almost 13!"

Aunt Lilly chuckled, "Look around. Most of those pictures are black and white. I don't get around to things like I used to. Your mother was always so much better at that than I was. I've taken several pictures of you over the years. Which one would you like to put up?"

"I don't know. Maybe in the fall you can put up a picture of me and Uncle Vic with a mess of ducks like that picture, or maybe with a couple deer. That would be cool."

"It should be something very special. Remember people will probably be looking at it for the next 40 years. What do you want people to remember you for?"

"Me with a whole lotta ducks…no wait… with one of Uncle Vic's deer. No, it should be my deer…but I'm too young. Hey, maybe I'll catch a big pike. That would be cool. A picture of me with a big pike!"

"You have to catch one first."

"I… oh… yeah."

"How about I just surprise you at the end of the summer. I will put a picture up of you with a *real* trophy."

"Uh… Ok. Don't forget?"

"You'll remind me." She laughed and hugged him tightly.

Journale

Today flew by real quick. I got to see lots of pictures when you, I mean when mom was young. That's really weird. My Mom poured concrete. Aunt Lil showed me lots of cool stuff. I always thought being with old people was boring but Aunt Lil can be a lot of fun. Uncle Vic likes to lecture but I guess he's ok too. He was gone most of today. Aunt Lil is more fun when he is gone. We had a party with lots of coookies and I drank my first tea! Aunt Lil was amazezd at how mush shugar I put in it, but she didn't scold, she just laughed.

Chapter 5   Indian Fever

Eric, Jim, Little John and Mike sat on the porch facing the road. The cool breeze in the shade of the hemlocks felt good. It was a warning of the heat to come later in the day.

"When do we start lookin' for arrowheads, Mike?" Jim asked.

"Why? Haven't you been lookin' this weekend?"

"Yes, but not going out and looking just for them. I mean where do we look? You said we would make some money finding arrowheads. It seems like we should look some place special."

"Hey, ask your uncle. He's been coming up here forever. Maybe he even knew the Indians!"

Mike looked at his uncle raking leaves behind the barn. It seemed like he was always working, just like Mike's dad. Mike hated asking his uncle questions. He always had to run through a gauntlet of questions himself.

Mike swallowed hard. "Uncle Vic? Do you know where we could look for arrowheads?"

Before he could answer Eric piped up, "Did you ever fight any Indians?"

Uncle Vic leaned down and squinted one eye at Eric. "None that ever lived to tell the tale," he said grimly.

Eric's eyes bugged out and his mouth dropped open.

Uncle Vic chuckled. "Sorry to disappoint you. I never fought any Indians. Fought with a few Irishmen though, and one *very big* Swede." He rubbed his chin in memory of the occasion.

He looked back at Mike. "There could be arrowheads anywhere here abouts. They used to hunt around here. There are some old Indian mounds down the road, but it wouldn't be…"

"There are some what?" Jim asked.

"Some Indian mounds. Where they used to bury Indians, but that wouldn't be appropriate to look there."

All of the mouths dropped at that. "I'm not goin' to no cemetery," Little John whispered.

"I don't think you should go there. That would not be right. I am just telling you there used to be Indians all around here. Maybe you want to talk to Sam McCurry across the road. He's part Indian. Maybe he can tell you where to look."

The boys stood in front of the door and stared.
"Who's gonna knock?"
"Mike should knock. It was his idea."
"It was Uncle Vic's idea." Mike protested.
"He's your uncle."
Jim pushed Mike to the door.
Mike just stared at the dark house. "I don't think anybody's home."
Eric reached around him and knocked on the door.
The door opened suddenly and a thin tough looking teenager a few years older than them stood in the doorway.
Mike looked at the boy's black ponytail and could easily imagine a feather braided into it.
"What can I do for ya?"
Uh… is… uh… your uh… father home?" Mike stammered. He hoped he wasn't.
"Yeah, just a minute." The boy started to turn.
"Are you really an Indian?" Eric asked.
"Yeah, what of it?" The boy said defensively.
"Do you know how to Indian wrestle?" Eric's eyes widened.
"I wrestled in high school." The older boy grinned proudly. "I took third in the state in my weight class."
"Really? Could you teach me?"
"I suppose. What's your name?"
"Eric."
"My name is Paul. I can show you a few moves some time, but I have to work today, and you have to promise to be careful and not hurt anyone."
"I will. Can I come back tomorrow?"
Paul grinned. "I s'pose. I'll go get my dad."

The two Indians paddled their birch bark canoe silently down the Pere Marquette River. Something wasn't right. They had seen no squirrels since the last rough water. These lead scouts held the lives of every member of their tribe in their ability to read the sights and sounds of everyday life in the woods.

The big fish that come up the river every year were becoming fewer each year and the tribe depended on them to make it through the winter. Last Fall these two braves had traveled to the mouth of the river and found them plentiful. During the long hungry winter, the chiefs decided that in the spring they would move the tribe.

They slid their canoe noiselessly to a sand bar and stepped ashore. The rest of the tribe would soon be coming down river behind him. They crept stealthily inland, keeping the river in sight but looking for sign of enemies.

There. The tall swamp grass was matted down. The pattern was too big to be any animal except the great bear but there were no pad marks. A man had passed this way. It was difficult but the skilled tracker followed the track. Soon he saw the path lead up a hill. They knew this would be where the ambush was planned. The taller one motioned with his arm and then pointed at his eyes and up the hill. They must circle and see who was there, but his people would be coming down the river soon.

They ran back the way he had come, leaping like a deer over logs in his way. The short one sped ahead but stopped near the top of the hill. The taller came up the hill from a different approach circled to the east and there they were. Should they go back and warn the others?

The decision was made for them as an arrow came whistling by, its flint arrowhead missing the taller one's head by scant inches. He fired back and soon the air was filled with deadly arrows. It wasn't long and the shorter one was out of arrows. With a whoop he went charging in, swinging his war ax, heedless to the hail of arrows. One struck him in the arm. He pulled it out and threw it to the ground and then jumped on the nearest adversary, a huge Indian nearly a foot taller than himself. He leapt and plunged his knife deep into the belly of the man, turned and slashed at the next, but even as the first man fell, he could hear the shouting.

"That's not fair! I shot you about a gazillion times!" Jim shouted.

"All but one missed and I pulled that one out. I can't help it you're a bad shot. Besides, I shot you just as many times and you're still standing, so I had to finish you off the hard way."

"Oh, come on," Little John protested. Let's just keep playing.

Jim and I can try and sneak up on you two this time."

"Oh alright. Say, do you think it really happened like this. I mean like Mister McCurry said. I'd think Indians would all get along and fight the cowboys. Why would they fight each other?" Jim asked.

"Cuz there weren't any cowboys in Michigan," Little John suggested.

"Why does anybody fight each other? You and your brother were just fightin'." Mike asked.

"We were not. He just wasn't being fair," Jim said.

"I was too."

"It just seems like the Indians had enough problems without one group attacking another."

"I don't know," Little John said. "Sounds like they spent most of their time hunting and fishing. Doesn't seem like problems to me."

"Can I play?" Linda came running up. "What did you do to your faces?" She wrinkled her nose as she looked at the black mud on their cheeks and foreheads."

"This is war paint and no you can't play," Mike stated fiercely.

"I don't care if she plays," Little John said calmly.

"She'll want to talk all the time. How can you sneak up when you're talking? Why don't you go play with your clay dolls," Mike said looking at the ground.

She looked away. "I don't want to. Besides I can't. My dad broke them." She dug her toe into the ground. "He knocked them off the table and stepped on them last night when he came home."

"Oh, let her play, Mike," Jim said.

"You got to promise to be really quiet," Mike said.

"I will." Her eyes shone like sunlight on the lake. "Oh, just a minute." She ran back in the house.

"Now what?" Mike made a great show of rolling his eyes as his dad did when waiting for his mother.

Jim and Little John headed down to the lake to get in the rowboat for the next round. This time Eric, Mike, and Linda would hide, if Linda ever came out.

Less than a minute later the screen door slammed and she ran back toward the boys.

"Hey cool! She's got her face painted!" Eric said.

"I put on lipstick for you, Mickey." She pointed to the red streaks on her cheeks.

"Grrr. Just be quiet," Mike said sternly, his face as red as her lipstick.

Chapter 6   Heading to Glory

Mike thought the week would never pass. The boys had all gone home for the week and he spent the week raking and cutting wood.

"Uncle Vic, why do we have to rake so much? It's boring."

"Because we have so many trees. You don't mind cutting wood, do you? What difference does it make?"

"Cutting wood isn't boring, 'specially when you drop a log on your foot." The day before a freshly severed log attempted to perform the same trick on Uncle Vic's right big toe. Mike had learned several interesting new words. He wasn't sure what they meant but maybe some might have been Celtic.

Uncle Vic frowned. "You thought that was funny, eh?"

"NO!" Mike nearly shouted in dismay. "I just mean it's not boring. It's like something is more exciting if there's a chance you might get hurt." Mike spent a great deal of time and energy seeking out activities where there was a high probability of leaving with fewer body parts than he had when he arrived.

Uncle Vic chuckled. Well, let's rake for another 10 minutes and then we'll cut some wood.

"Anyone want a brownie?" Aunt Lilly called.

Mikes eyes lit up and he dropped the rake.

His uncle cleared his throat. "In ten minutes," he called back.

Mike looked at his uncle who looked down at the rake. Mike sighed, picked up the rake and returned to his tedium.

Ten minutes later he and Uncle Vic washed their hands in the blue porcelain coated wash basin.

"Can I have two brownies?" Mike pleaded.

"Have as many as you want, dear." His aunt replied with a smile.

He grabbed two and headed down to the lake. "Hey Stinkersmell, look what I got," he hollered.

Linda was sitting on her dock reading. Her eyes flew open wide when she saw the brownies.

"My aunt gave me two and I only want one. You want the other?" He sat down on the edge of the dock next to her.

"You sure you don't want it?" she asked."

"Yeah."

"Thank-you." She took a big bite. "MMM. This is good. Tell your aunt she makes the *best* brownies." She looked over at Mike. "I had a big surprise this morning." she said timidly. She watched him closely.

"Oh?" he said cautiously.

"Yes. When I woke up, there, on the window ledge of the bedroom, was a new clay Robinhood and fairy staring in my window." She watched his face.

"Oh…uh did your dad fix them?" he said studying the remains of his brownie.

"He couldn't do that; they were smashed to dust."

Mike shifted his weight. "Hey, did I tell you I caught a bass this morning? It was this big." He held his hands about a foot apart.

"You must have gotten up before I did to catch a fish that big."

"Yeah, Uncle Vic likes to be on the lake before the sun is up. He says that's when they're hungry." His voice tapered off as he realized he had taken her bait.

She beamed at him. "They're a lot nicer than the ones I made. Thanks, Mike."

Mike kicked the water with his feet. "You're welcome," he mumbled into his brownie. "They didn't turn out as good as yours."

They were silent for a minute. Finally, Linda broke the silence and very quietly asked, "Why are you so mean to me around your friends?"

Mike held his breath. His mind froze. His whole being locked up. He was surprised ice didn't start forming from his feet and spread over the whole lake.

"I…I dunno."

The world stopped moving as each both silently willed the other toward… they did not know what.

"I know…" Linda finally practically whispered. "It's just our little secret."

Mike wrinkled his forehead.

"What?"

"Nothing." She shook her head.

Girls confused Mike on the best of days and this interchange was too much for him.

"Mike," his uncle called coming down the stairs to the lake. "Time to get to cuttin' some wood."

"I'm coming," Mike called back, eager to show how important he was.

His uncle carried a small pruning saw instead of the usual six-foot crosscut saw that Mike loved. With Uncle Vic on one side and Mike on the other, the crosscut made quick work of just about any log. It thrilled Mike to see the sawdust fly with each pass.

"What are you going to do with *that* little saw?" Mike asked. Disdain fairly dripping from his words.

"We're just going to cut a cedar branch."

"A *cedar*?" Mike was incredulous. The cedars, which grew along the lakeshore drawing their life water from the lake itself, were practically sacred. Uncle Vic never ever pruned or cut them even though many of his relatives suggested he would have a better view of the lake. To him they represented the wildness of the way the lake used to be. Uncle Vic had been coming here since he was two years old. There were no other cottages on the lake then. Now, with the shores of the lake littered with cottages and their manicured lawns, his cedars were the only wildness still along the shoreline.

Mike too had grown to love the smooth brown trunks and the fragrant greenery.

"Are you going to clear out a place to pull the boat up?" Mike stepped around the tangle of roots that stitched the land to the lake.

"Nope." His uncle spent several minutes examining branch after branch. Mike just followed him around confused.

Finally, Uncle Vic handed him the saw and said, "Cut right here."

Mike took the saw, but he was still confused. "Are you sure? That branch is still alive." Mike's bewilderment grew. Uncle Vic never cut live wood.

"Yes. Just cut it right there." Mike had learned better than to ask for an explanation on previous chores. He nearly had to stand on his tiptoes to cut the branch but was soon rewarded with a three-foot long straight cedar pole with a big knot on one end.

"Now what?" Mike asked covered with the wonderful sweet-smelling sawdust.

"Follow me."

They walked up the thirty-two steps to the top of the hill around the cabin to the small storage shed where his uncle kept his tools.

"Here start cleaning the bark off that," his uncle commanded.

Mike dutifully pealed the bark off while his uncle rummaged around for tools. When he finally got down to picking off the smallest leftover strands of bark, Uncle Vic handed him a rasp. "Here, just take the rough edges off that big knot on top."

Uncle Vic dug around some more and after a while came back with some sandpaper. "That looks good. Now make it smooth."

"But what am I doing?"

"You're doing what I tell you," he stated flatly.

Mike cringed inwardly but his mind chewed on various uses with curiosity.

Mike set to work making the pole as smooth as his own skin. He thought it was cool, watching the rough wood take beauty under his touch. The knots he had cut off the branch left bumps and irregularities on the straight pole but under the sandpaper they became eyes looking back at him from the heart of the limb. What was at first a flaw in the uniformity, now defined the wood as ornaments define a Christmas tree.

He laid down the sandpaper. "It sure is pretty."

His uncle leaned in and inhaled deeply. "And don't it smell nice." Uncle Vic took it from Mike and ran his rough old hands along the smooth softness of the wood, caressing it as a father gently touches the cheek of his first newborn. He looked it over carefully. Looks like you did a good job." He tossed it back to Mike, and slowly strode back to put the tools away in the shed.

"But what are you going to do with it?" Mike asked.

"It's your shillelagh."

"It's what?"

"That's an Irish walking stick or swinging stick. I think really a shillelagh is shorter and used for self-defense, like a club, but we always called walking sticks shillelaghs. You can still use it for self-defense. It is good to carry it when you walk in the woods."

"This is mine?"

"Well, you made it, didn't you?" His uncle turned and walked back to the shed.

"Hey, I did." Mike marveled that he had made a thing of such incredible loveliness, beautiful to the eye, delightful to touch, unique from any other walking stick ever made and he, himself, had crafted it. "Thanks a lot, Uncle Vic."

Mike was still sitting on the porch admiring the stick when Uncle Vic came back. Uncle Vic inhaled deeply. Mike could always tell when he was about to say something special because he would slowly inhale through his nose in a noisy way and the slower he inhaled, the more important his words would be. This one was a particularly long and reflective sounding one.

Uncle Vic put his leg up on one step and reached into his back pocket for his pipe. This was a sure sign that a story was coming. He tapped the pipe on a handy tree to clear out the old ashes. The fragrance of cherries from his uncle's pipe tobacco wrapped around Mike and carried him into the story.

"When I was your age, most people still used kerosene for light. They had glass lamps."

"They had what?"

Glass lamps with wicks, like candles but instead of burning wax they burned oil--- like those two on the old dresser in the cottage. Every Saturday night I had to wash the black soot off all the chimneys." He paused in reflection. "Gad, I hated that." He shook his head. "We had a peck of these lamps.

"The chimneys were blown by hand. There was a factory in our town that employed... oh, probably a couple hundred men who took a gob of goopy molten glass on the end of a long pipe and blew air into it, to form the lamps. When they had a bulb at the end of the stick, it almost looked like a walking stick. Well, these men were real artists and someone had the bright idea to have a competition. So, every Fourth of July we would go downtown to watch the parade and here they'd come." Uncle Vic used his pipe as a pretend walking stick and stuck his nose in the air and strutted. "All the men from the glass blowing factory, paraded down Main Street with their walking sticks. The heads of each were all glass, shaped into the most glorious shapes; dragons complete with scales, women's heads with long flowing hair, boats, everything you could imagine. They were so fine... so *elegant*." He closed his eyes in the ecstasy of the memory. "Gad! I wished I was one of them." A long inhale. "After the parade they would have a judging. We always had to hang around to see who would win. Usually, it was the same few men." He was silent for a while. "Of course, they closed the factory." He shook his head and looked toward the lake. "I don't know what happened to the men."

He inhaled noisily, abruptly his expression changed, and he

grinned down at Mike, leaning into him with his shoulder he said, "Shall we go *strut* down the road?"

Mike grinned. "Yeah! Let's go see Billy."

"Sounds grand to me." Uncle Vic reach into the tool shed, grabbed his own shillelagh and they swaggered down the road.

Mike closed his eyes. Crowds of people cheered and waved. Men waved their straw hats. Small children in knickers stood gaping as he paraded by with his shillelagh. Young girls in dresses down to their ankles, with large bows in their hair waved and threw flowers. The entire world stopped and stared. He just walked on; his head held high. The glory of the universe shone on him. He knew what it was to strut. God winked, and angels gaped in awe.

Mike opened his eyes at a small noise and saw Linda watching. He flashed her a smile and a benevolent nod, then grinned up at his Uncle Vic. The smile on his uncle's face matched his, but his uncle's eyes were closed and the crowd cheered their elegance.

Chapter 7 Armed and Dangerous

"Hiya Billy. You like my new shillelagh?
"Well, whatchya'll got? Let me see it."
Uncle Vic waved at Billy and headed home. He still had chores to do.
Billy sat in a wheel chair in the yard facing the road. He was about 12 years older than Mike. He talked funny because he was from Indiana. He liked to talk... a lot.
"Ah, don't know. That looks purdy dangerous. Your parents know you're walking around here armed?" He squinted one eye at Mike.
"What?"
"Your cousin Buck came over with his shillelagh one time and was explaining to Carl Phelps... You know them. They live on the other side of the lake. He'd be about two years older than Buck, brown hair, crew cut. Anyway, he was explaining how they used them for self-defense. Well, pretty soon Buck is swinging the thing around his head hollering some old Gaelic phrase and the thing slips out of his hand and hits Carl on the head. Well, Carl picks it up and starts swearing at Buck and runs around the yard chasing him. They're going back and forth around the house and trees and Buck steps in some dog crap, slips and lands on his butt right in the crap. Carl starts laughing so hard he drops the shillelagh and doubles up. Then he sees these red drops on the grass. He turns toward me and says, "Am I bleeding?" His face was just covered in blood. I called for Ma and she came out and put a butterfly bandage on it. It took six stitches. Buck was in the doghouse for a while with Carl's mom, but Buck brought over some fudge he made and pretty soon things were back to normal. Carl wasn't one to hold a grudge, and no one could hold a grudge against Buck for long. In fact, I think Carl was one of the guys Buck talked into

helping to paint the Miller house one summer.

"You know the Missus Miller?" He did not wait for a response but kept going. "She was old and didn't have any money, so he said they'd paint it for fun. From what I can tell it looked like they had a lot of fun. When they would walk by here on their way home, there was usually more paint on them than on the house.

"So, what do you hear from Buck?" Billy asked.

"Oh, nothin' much. The last letter said he made it to Vietnam and he has gone out on a couple patrols. He says it stinks like somebody burning house 22. Uh... That's the number on the door to the outhouse at the cottage."

Billy laughed, "Oookay, I'll bite. Why is there a 22 on the outhouse door?"

Mike shook his head in confusion. "That's not a joke. Grandpa used a door from some building he tore down. When he put it on the outhouse, it still had a room number on it. So, it's always been house 22, but... you can use it for number one or number two."

Billy chuckled, "You got me after all."

"It's a two-seater!" Mike stated with a pride only a kid could show.

"That's in case you have company, right?"

Mike stared at Billy in confusion.

"Well, you don't have an upstairs, do you?

"Uh... No."

"Well, you wouldn't want them to use the downstairs, would you?"

Mike grinned, "No, I guess not. But there is the dog house right next to the outhouse."

"What number is that? Say, did Buck ever tell you about the time a raccoon kept eating the dog's food?"

"No."

"Well, it seems that every time they would go to feed Dennis, Dennis would eat only a little of it and save the rest for later. Maybe that was because he lost his teeth. Well, before he could eat the rest, this big ol' coon would come down and eat the food. Your Uncle Vic was going to shoot it but it wasn't in season and Buck was all for trying to catch it. So, he borrows a live trap from Jacob's. They live next to the bait shop down here." Billy pointed down the road, "You know the ones with the good-looking blond girl." Billy winked, "Marsha is her name."

Mike shook his head.

"How old are you? I can't believe you'd miss her. Anyway, shor' nuff Buck catches the raccoon and takes the cage and throws him in the trunk and off we go. That was back when I could walk and off we go, down this old two-track, up toward the swale. We get back in there a mile or so and we all get out and Buck hauls out the trap. Well, that coon wants nothing to do with us. Judging by its expression it called us low-down no good mother's sons of communists. It growled and hissed, showed its teeth and made all sorts of noise. Buck opens the trap and it charged out of the cage like a bull. Buck levitated about 8 feet up in the air and came down on the car hood. He might have jumped higher if'n I wasn't on his shoulders. As soon as it saw we were out of the way, it runs *right under* the car. Well, with the way the two track humps up in the middle, if we try to drive off, we'll crunch it for sure. After ten minutes of cussing, Buck decides the raccoon is a better cusser, so Buck goes gets a stick to try and persuade it out but he can't seem to get it to budge. Finally, he wallops it good and the thing goes and crawls up into the wheel well.

"That's no problem, Buck says, we will just ease the car forward and as soon as the tires move, he'll be gone. Buck gets in the car while I stay outside to see what happens.

"Well, he eases it forward and the raccoon starts running on the wheel staying on top. I'm all tired out running alongside of the car trying to keep up but the raccoon seems to be doing fine. So, Buck stops and starts to back up. Well, that raccoon just turns around and starts running the other way. I'm watching the raccoon and not watching where I'm going."

Mike let out a snort.

Billy shook a boney finger at him, "Now, don't ya'll get ahead of me," he scolded Mike with a wink. "Ah ran smack into a small beech tree. It was like being hit with a 2 by 4. Buck sees me run into the tree and thinks it is about the funniest thing he has ever seen. He starts laughing and forgets that the two track turns just short of the crick."

Mike laughed out loud.

"Now," Billy held up a finger in mock sternness, "I tole ya'll don't get ahead of me. The car jumps out of the two track ruts and heads down the slope to the creek. Fortunately, it was… uh, brought to a stop before it got stuck down in the muck. At least that is how Buck phrased it when he explained to Uncle Vic why the bumper was all bent up and the tail light was busted."

We got another letter from Buck. Aunt Lil would only read part of it to me. He is making friends but he says the woods will probably never seem quite as friendly as they used to. That is sad to me. I am hopping to get the guys walking in the woods tomorrow. Jim says he knows these woods real well. I hope we don't get lost.

Chapter 8   Saturday Morning Walk

The morning sun shone sharply with the threat of a hot day coming, but behind the cottage in the shade of the many beech trees, the light breeze was still refreshing. Better yet, the breeze kept the mosquitoes and biting flies grounded in their hangers.

Mike was putting the finishing touches on a triple-decker crunchy peanut butter sandwich. He chopped up the second layer of grape jelly, used a forty-year-old knife to trowel it smooth and set the bread with the peanut butter on as carefully as if he was disarming an atomic bomb. He had studied peanut butter and jelly with some real masters. For example, Jim maintained that to keep the jelly from seeping into the bread and making it soggy, the best approach is to have peanut butter on both slices of bread with the jelly isolated from the bread by a layer of peanut butter on either side. However, Larry believed the best peanut butter sandwiches had a layer of butter underneath the peanut butter to keep it from being too sticky. Mike believed that to truly experience a PB& J you needed to make it a triple layer. So today he was combining all three principles. Unfortunately, it took about 20 minutes to make a sandwich this way. He finally got it assembled perfectly, gently wrapped it in wax paper, placed it in a paper bag and dropped an apple in on top of it.

Light footsteps on the porch caused him to snatch up the bag and turn but it wasn't whom he expected.

"Hi Mike," said a perky voice through the screen. "I hear you're up for the whole summer." Buck's 22-year-old girlfriend stepped into the kitchen and gave Mike a hug.

He squirmed uncomfortably as her shoulder length blond hair brushed his face.

"Oh, you have to let me hug you once in a while. Buck isn't here for the summer and I have to have someone to give me hugs.

Buck wouldn't mind." She made a show of hugging him again. "Is your aunt around?"

Mike's face flared like summer's first sunburn. "Uh...yeah she's..."

"Grace!" Aunt Lilly hurried into the kitchen to give a tight hug. "Are you up for the summer?"

"Between summer jobs. I thought we could trade news from Buck."

Aunt Lilly wiped her eyes. She seemed to do that a lot, Mike thought. The two females quickly settled in to talk and Mike saw it as a good time to sneak out. He unobtrusively grabbed the paper bag, holding it in a manner not easily seen as he headed out to find the boys.

Uncle Vic tightened his leather gloves and grasped the rake. Mike was afraid for a moment that he would be trapped into helping, but he boldly headed down toward the two-track behind Uncle Vic's cottage along with the guys that had been waiting outside.

"Where you boys off to now?" Uncle Vic asked squinting one eye down harshly.

The boys looked at each other before answering. Each boy had a paper bag. Jim had an old canvas Boy Scout back pack.

Mike finally spoke up, "You were right." This seemed to be the proper lead in to anything else he said. Grownups loved to hear young-uns state this obvious truth. "Mister McCurry told us about a great Indian battle over on the Pere Marquette. One tribe ambushed another as they came down the river. The battle lasted for days, according to Mister McCurry. Mike vibrated with excitement as he told the story.

"He is not sure where the battle took place, but such a big battle would cover a whole lot of area and mean a lot of them lost arrowheads. He even said *he* might buy a couple if we find any."

"He showed us a couple he had found," Jim added.

Uncle Vic looked from boy to boy. Each one looked ready to wet his pants with excitement. He couldn't help but smile. "How you gonna get all the way over to Pere Marquette? I'm not driving you and that's a lot of road walking."

"Mister Sam showed us a railroad track by his house that will lead us through the woods right to it. Did you know there used to be a railroad through here?" Mike asked.

Well, they had the narrow-gauge railroad track for hauling out trees back when they were lumbering off this area. But that was many years ago and all the tracks have been pulled up. Now it's just a mound of dirt that runs through the woods, and not much of a mound in many places. It's all grown over with trees and such. You sure you want to try that?"

"We'll be real careful and if we can't see where it goes we'll just turn around."

Uncle Vic squinted down at Mike and said the words Mike hated, "Did you ask your aunt Lil?"

Mike rolled his eyes and shook his head at the ground. "I'll never get out of here. Can't *you* just tell me I can go? The others are all going." Mike looked up to his uncle with his best pleading face.

Uncle Vic rubbed his chin and looked really hard at Mike without saying anything.

Mike let out a long sigh and started walking toward the cottage.

"I'll tell her I gave you permission otherwise she'll make me go with." He winked. "You stay out of trouble. I better not have to come after you that's all I have to say."

Mike hurried off before Uncle Vic could change his mind.

Uncle Vic shook his head and went back to his raking. As they headed down the road, he stopped raking and watched them jostle and joke with each other. Mike carried his shillelagh on his shoulder. Maybe he should go with them... It sounded like a pretty good time. He chuckled lightly, tightened his gloves and sang softly to himself.

I don't know Mike, I think we should turn around," Little John said softly, almost in a whisper.

"The track goes right through here. You can see it plain as day," Jim stated a little too loudly.

"I don't know. It seems to go that way."

The sun was nearly directly overhead but in the dense woods the gloom of shadow and the camouflage of bushes made distant objects hard to distinguish.

"What's that black thing over there?" Little John whispered tensely.

"Where?"

"There!"

"There?"
"No there."
"That?"
"No that."
"That black thing?"
"Yeah, that's what I said. That!"
"What about it?"
"What is it?"
"What's what?"
"I think it's a bear."
Long pause.
"It would have moved by now."
"That's a stump."
"That's not a stump."
"What is it?"
"It's a bear," whimpered Little John.
Mike and Eric looked at each other.

Mike picked up a stick and threw it at the bear. It bounced off the stump and fell into the leaves.

"It *looked* like a bear." Little John tried to regain some dignity.

Mike leaned over and whispered, "It was a bear. I hit it with a magic stick and changed it to a stump."

"Tinkerbell give you the stick?" Jim snickered. "Or did you sprinkle your own fairy dust on it?"

Mike glared at Jim. "I don't think that's the railroad bump."

Eric sat down calmly and opened up his lunch. As the smallest and youngest no one would listen to him so there was no point to talking. He took out his sandwich and ate half of it. The other boys continued their discussion.

When Eric finished, he tore the wax paper in half and wrapped his lunch back up. As he stood up, he grabbed a branch and broke it.

"I say we go this way. If you want to go home, go," Jim practically shouted.

Eric stuck the wax paper on the broken branch and followed Jim. They all headed off in a line following Jim.

"See there's the river!" Jim cried triumphantly.
"Yea!" Mike cheered.
"How will we find our way back?" John asked quietly.

"I can find our way. There were only a couple a tough spots and I memorized those," Jim stated. "Let's start looking for arrowheads. Hey, look at that log. It goes almost across the river. I bet I can make it all the way to the other bank."

"Bet ya can't," Eric shouted.

"You think the water's deep?" Mike asked suspiciously

"Not here," Little John said." You can see bottom. Over there by the bend I bet it's deep. Look how dark the water is."

"It sure looks cool," Mike said. He crawled down by the bank and watched the water striders.

The brothers, Eric and Jim, were jumping on the log going across the river trying to knock each other off.

Meanwhile, John sneaked up behind Mike and pushed.

"Arggg!" Mike appeared to attempt to crawl up into the air as he tumbled into the water.

He came up sputtering." What are you doing? That's dangerous!" he shouted.

"It's only knee deep," Little John said apologetically. "It doesn't matter that you can't swim. Here you can push me in." He grinned and fell face first into the water.

It was impossible to stay mad at little John. Mike laughed and splashed him as he came to the surface.

"Water fight!" Eric shouted and the brothers jumped from the log and joined in.

Soon they were each stripped down to their blue jean cutoffs, walking along the bank dripping wet, pretending to be Indians. From time to time, they took a break to look for arrowheads but, of course, the sight of a turtle or frog interrupted all other activities until any hope of seeing it, let alone catching it, was long gone. Most of the time, they just played.

Late afternoon, while the other boys took turns sliding down the clay banks into a swimming hole, Mike, who didn't bring his life jacket, made a great show of studying the flora and fauna of the river. He was appalled to see the great abundance of long-legged, thin-body spiders hanging over the river ready to pull men and boys out of any passing canoe. It was amazing any Indians ever survived. He was deep in thought, studying one especially large spider that nimbly spun a web, while practicing Kung Fu. Mike didn't hear Jim come up close behind him.

"Boo!"

Mike jumped, barely missing the spider; he landed in the deep pool. Popping to the surface, he shouted at Jim, "Help me!" He commenced his best dog paddle. "Idiot! Why'd you push me?" The current pulled him down river. He spun and twisted his legs bumping invisible branches. His mind screamed; HOW DO YOU KNOW THEY ARE BRANCHES? Maybe it was one of those huge catfish that eat people whole or it was a huge snapper. He had never felt such terror in broad daylight.

"I didn't push you. You jumped in," Jim shouted. "You're fine. You're already to the sand bar. Stand up!"

Mike felt the sand bump his toes and he stood up.

"What a scaredy cat. We been doin' that all day."

Mike was boiling with anger but he was too ashamed to say any more.

"Aw let 'im be," Little John said. "Come on. Let's look for turtles."

Long about supper time Little John looked around at the lengthening shadows and said, "I'm hungry, shouldn't we be heading home?"

"We haven't found any arrowheads yet," Jim countered.

"I don't think we're gonna find any today." Eric made it a point to disagree with his brother just on general principal. But he generally went along with whatever the older kids decided.

Mike looked at the darkness under the trees. After spending all day in the sunshine near the river, the black shadows of the woods looked ominous. The arrow shaped ferns lined the inky blackness like ragged teeth of an enormous mouth ready to swallow them alive. "I think we should get going. My aunt will wonder where we are."

"Oh, all right," Jim made a great show of kicking the dirt. "If you guys are too scared, we can go."

They spent about twenty minutes finding their shoes and shirts.

"Where did we come out at?" Little John wrinkled up his brow.

"I think we came out right over there on the other side." Jim said studying the woods on the other side of the river.

"No, we came out right here and there is the tree we walked on. Eric pointed down to the tree and to a lump in the woods that marked the railroad."

"No, the mound is over there. See?" Jim said obstinately.

Little John shaded his eyes and looked over to the other side of the river. "Yeah, I see the mound over there."

"But right here is where you pushed me in. See my footprints."

Mike said agreeing with Eric.

"Oh yeah, you're right," Little John said looking at Jim.

"I'll bet the railroad crossed the river here and the trail continues over there. You want to follow that for a while?"

"I think we should go home," Mike said softly.

"Awww, come on."

Eric started walking into the woods with Mike in the direction they had decided. Little John followed and after a few more steps Jim came along. Soon Jim was in the lead. They followed the rail mound fairly easily most of the time but there were a few times it just seemed to fade away and once, when it ended, they saw two lines of mounds in the distance. Did the railway split? They studied it for a long time. The longer they studied, the darker it got. Then Eric pointed. There is my lunch wrapper. They fairly ran to the wax paper. Little John tripped over a grapevine as the growing shadows made it more difficult to see. Mike grabbed the wax paper like a lifesaver. They continued to follow the railway, but they were walking slower as it became more difficult to see and they walked closer together. They walked slower and slower, each afraid to be in front.

As if by mutual consent, they stopped walking and stood still.

"Something's here," whispered Little John.

"I...I think you're right," Mike stammered.

They knew he was right, though how, they couldn't say. Their fear erupted into terror as the woods exploded with noise. Bodies rushed by them on both sides.

"AHHHHH."

"Maaaaa"

"EEEEE"

The boys pushed and shoved each other trying to get away, but the bodies were on both sides of them.

"Deer!" Mike gasped at last.

The deer ran and leapt seeming to glide in an effortless flight through the crowded shadows. They plunged past and stopped fifty yards away to examine the intruders into their woods. The largest doe flicked its tail to unlock her legs and walked off looking disgusted that she had wasted all that effort on these harmless human fawns. The rest followed.

Only then were the boys able to pull in a shaky breath.

"Wow. That was cool," Mike whispered.

The abundance of wild excitement around them shaped the

current darkness all the more into a terrifying unknown. Each looked in every direction desperate for a sign of any kind of which way to head. In the silent gloom, the sound of their hard breathing was an anchor. It was the only thing that gave them any comfort.

Reluctantly Mike took a slow step forward. The others tentatively followed suit.

"How long do you think it would take to starve to death?"

"We won't starve."

"I know. I'm just talkin'."

"Weeks."

"What do you think it feels like?"

"Like I feel now."

"I don't want to die."

"It takes lots longer."

"I can't see a thing."

"We've walked too long. We should have been home by now," Little John whispered.

"No, we're all right," Jim said.

"I think we passed it. We took a wrong turn. See there is a mound over there." Little John pointed. "Wait. There is another one and another one."

"There are some over there, too." Eric pointed in another direction. "What do you think they…?"

"The Indian mounds!" Jim interrupted.

"It...It's the Indian graveyard," Little John whimpered. "Let's get out of here!" He took off running without another word.

"Wait! Where do we go?" Mike shouted, but by then he was standing alone. All alone. Alone in a graveyard… in the dark!

He just about caught up to the others when Little John came up on a flock of partridge resting quietly.

Now, it should be noted, for those not familiar with partridge, that it is a brown and black speckled bird, perfectly matching last year's leaves sprinkled on the dirt. It is better camouflaged than any other animal in the world, making it nearly invisible at any distance. In the darkness of dusk, they are as invisible as the wind. They are about the size of a Cornish hen and when they take flight, they sound like a Huey helicopter with a full load of Marines taking off. Their wings make a tremendous booming sound that can be heard for quite a distance. They also have a tremendous sense of humor, preferring to wait until your foot is directly above them to take off. The booming sound of their take off can be heard for a quarter mile, the screams of the hiker, about two miles.

The first one took off just before John would have stepped on it. The noisy boom stopped Little John like a gunshot. Even so, his heart kept going for another six feet. Each bird in the flock waited for an open runway, so there was a near continuous booming through the woods as bird after bird took turns scaring the boys to death. Every boom was echoed by several shrill screams. The birds, satisfied they had scared their victims to death, landed only a few yards away so presumably they could feast on the dead prey, or at least repeat the spectacle.

Little John stopped all forward momentum immediately at the first takeoff. On the second take off, he was turned around and by the time the third bird took off, he had leapt over two boys and headed for Mike.

Darkness and trees obscured Mike's vision. Mike heard an explosion and all of a sudden there was a huge wide-eyed monster heading straight for him. It attacked the boys in front of him and now it was heading straight for him! He screamed and ran in the other direction. Eric soon caught up with him but each boy was reluctant to be in front. They couldn't see more than a few feet in front of them. If they were going to be eaten, they wanted to be able to watch someone else be eaten first. After all, how often do you get to see someone get eaten?

Several glances back and they realized they had outrun the monster, and it even looked like Little John and Jim had escaped also, although it was a while before anyone had enough oxygen to talk.

"Where... gasp... are we?" Mike panted out.

He was answered by a distant low moan.

They stared at the whites of each other's eyes shining in the dusk. "I don't..."

"Quiet..."

"Was that..."

"I don't think we..."

"Moammmm"

"Oh momma, there it is again," John groaned. "We're gonna die. Oh, why did we come? Oh, why did we come?"

"Why did we wait so long to leave?" asked Jim.

"Let's get out of here," Mike said, but they remained frozen, staring in the direction of the sound. Afraid to go back, afraid to go forward, a brief glance in various directions confirmed they were lost and had no clue which way to go.

"The dead are going to c...come and haul us back to their graves so we'll be their slaves forever in the other world," John whimpered.

Eric took a couple steps forward.

"Don't go toward it!" Jim grabbed at him, not quite able to reach him and unwilling to take another step.

"Moanmmm."

A large white apparition appeared in front of them.

"URGhhha. A ghost," John groaned.

"That's a cow," Eric said.

"A cow ghost?"

"No, it isn't."

"Go see," Mike whispered.

"That's no cow," said Jim.

"You go," said Little John.

Eric sneaked forward.

Jim pushed John.

"AGHH," John jumped.

"Why would a cow ghost haunt us?"

"All those hamburgers you eat."

"You said cow not pig."

"Hamburgers come from cows."

"Then how come they're not cow burgers?"

"That makes no sense."

"Shut up!"

The others followed timidly. The woods thinned, the dark oak leaves on the ground gave way to lighter colored beech leaves and here and there a wild apple tree. Soon he could clearly see a field. The sun was just setting, and the tops of the trees in the distance shown with green glowing brilliance to the boys stepping out of the darkness. The field stretched on to a row of old maples marking the road. The crown of light on the tops of the trees gave the trees the appearance of candelabras set on a table of green. The table was decorated with a brightly painted red barn, old battered brick silos and a white house. The fields of corn in the distance edged the table, while plenty of black and white salt shakers were heading toward the barn. It was one of the grandest sights Mike had ever seen. The creek that ran through the bottom of deep green meadow disappeared into thick green grass so lush, that Mike was tempted to eat it himself. An elderly man was opening a gate for the cows heading to the barn to be milked.

They were saved! Mike ran toward the farmer, but the farmer did not look quite as happy to see them as they were to see him.

Chapter 9 Strange Scents of Fun

Woods, out buildings and fences blocked the passage from the fields to the road. The easiest way to the road and safety was past the farmer. The boys ran across the field toward the road on the other side of the barn intending to bypass the white-haired, angry farmer who looked quite as scary as and certainly older than any Indian ghosts that might be lurking in the woods behind them and beside them.

The farmer had different ideas. As they ran around the far side of his barn, he headed around the barn their way. Eric was fast but he didn't have Jim's endurance. It was a long run across the field and as Jim approached the corner, he could see freedom on the road. He vaulted the fence just as the farmer came around the corner and in midair Jim had to choose between landing on the farmer or shifting to the side. He flung himself with all his might to the right of the farmer.

The other boys slid to a halt on the other side of the fence.

The farmer glared at them. "What in thunder do ya think you are doin' in ma fields?"

He looked hard at each one in turn. Eventually his glare came down on Jim. The farmer started to chuckle. The other boys turned their gaze to Jim. The farmer laughed out loud and soon the other boys joined in. Jim had flung himself face first onto a small mountain of very fresh manure. He gradually rolled over wiping his hands on his filthy cutoffs. He tried to wipe off his face but with his filthy hands it was ineffective. He was covered. It was even tangled in his hair.

"Ewww. I'm glad you went first," Mike said.

The farmer comforted Jim." It won't hurtcha. It's just good clean manure from healthy cows."

"I always did like the smell of manure," Little John piped up.

"Me too," Mike added. "It makes me think of coming up here."

"You like it?" Jim asked acidly. "Here." He flung a hand full of the soft greenish goo at John. It landed square on John's chest and *stuck*.

The farmer chuckled again. John just stared down in horror as the glop, shifted like a live thing and oozed down his shirt and landed with a plop on his right tennis shoe.

The farmer slapped his leg and cackled loudly.

Jim threw a heaping handful the size of a small pumpkin at Eric. Eric jumped aside and most of it missed him, but Mike was standing behind and got a face full.

Mike couldn't let the attack go unchallenged. It being a barnyard, there was plenty of ammunition handy. The air was soon filled with flying manure.

The farmer laughed until tears came. He laughed until he had to sit down.

Little John hesitantly bent over to delicately pick up some of the greenish brown mass. He was reluctant to touch it but wanted to retaliate. Little John was significantly larger than the other boys were. Bending over away from them, his huge bottom presented a temptation the Pope couldn't have resisted. Several large clumps slapped his rear and slid down his bare legs before he could straighten up and fire back. Jim ran around the far side of the barn for cover. Little John chased Mike around the meadow. This left Eric out in the open, an easy target for Jim, who would hide until he was ready and then throw from cover.

"Here," the farmer said handing Eric a firm handful. "You wants ta git a fresh clump with just the right consistency. Then pack it like a snow ball. Them old ones are just hard flyin' saucers." He demonstrated and when Jim's head next appeared, a more or less smooth packed ball of manure slammed into his face. "See that's how ya does it." The well satisfied farmer grinned as wide as any kid and wiped his hands on his dirty bib overalls.

"Argghhgh." Jim stood in place wiping his face. Now it was Eric's turn to laugh. He ran up to Jim and start flinging handfuls at him.

Pretty soon they all looked and smelled the same. As if by mutual understanding they finally quit. Little John and Mike walked over to the barn where Eric and Jim were trying to clean themselves off.

The grizzled old farmer stood with his hands tucked into the front of his worn bib overalls chuckling and shaking his head. "So, what were you boys doing out in my field?"

After their long explanation about getting lost in the woods, the farmer introduced himself. "I'm Axel Vanderkooi, and this is my farm. I would appreciate it if, in the future, you'd come in through the front yard. Don't go out in the fields when the cows are out there. Sometimes they're unfriendly."

"You mean we can come back?" Mike asked excitedly.

"Why sure! I haven't laughed this hard since my brother and I had our last cow sh... uh... manure fight fifty years ago." He rubbed his scruffy chin. Has it really been fifty years? No... probably more like sixty years. Well anyways if you're the Malloy nephew, they live on the lake a couple miles away. I better give ya a ride back, but you'll have to wait until I finish with the cows. Hmmm... Maybe you could help." He looked at them sideways.

"Sure!" The boys could hardly believe their luck. The chance to play on a real farm.

They stepped inside the barn and Mike's stepped onto another planet. A world where the air is so moist and thick with smells that you can chew them. The low ceiling and earthy fragrance made Mike feel like he was underground, yet the scent of green hay was so strong it felt like sunshine you could taste.

The cows were each held in place with metal bars with their rear ends over a gutter with an all too obvious purpose just as the black and white cow in front of Mike lifted its tail and dumped a small bucket load of ultimately fresh manure into the trough.

"Oh gross."

"Here give them each a couple forks full of hay and shovel of this here silage."

An hour later, they were exhausted, sitting with their backs to the barn examining the interesting collection of new scars and red marks on their arms from hauling hay bales. Each boasted his scars were largest and each had hauled twice as many bails as all the others put together.

The pooka pooka sound of a tractor came around from behind the barn pulling a hay wagon. Its lights attracting moths of every kind, even the large green Luna moths that Mike loved.

"I'm not lettin' you in my truck like that. So, you're gonna have to ride on the wagon." he shouted down to them.

The boys fairly flew onto the trailer. All the way back they lay on the bare boards and watched the stars float past the treetops.

Mister Vanderkooi dropped them off on the road. The narrow two track to the cottages would not be wide enough for his hay wagon.

At the sound of the tractor Uncle Vic came down the road with a flashlight. "Where you boys been! The womenfolk were worried sick. Mister Swanson is out driving around looking for you boys."

"This was the best day of my life!" Mike shouted from the wagon.

"We'll talk about it when you…" Sniff…sniff. "What in thunder have you been rolling in? Whowee. D'cha fall in an outhouse?"

"We had a manure fight!"

"It was cool."

"We saw the burial ground."

"I hit Jim in the face with a manure ball!"

They all talked at once. Each convinced it was the best time in their life. Uncle Vic played the light from one to the other. He unconsciously took a step back. Little gobs of pre-eaten grass stuck all over their skin like small pox scabs.

"Where did you find theses hooligans, Axel?"

"They were in ma hay field. Sorry I didn't get them back earlier but I got to take care of my girls."

"Girls?" Mike said.

"He means his cows." Uncle Vic wagged his head. "Thanks for bringing them back. We'll try to keep them out of your way in the future."

"They're welcome back anytime." Axel shouted over the engine. "It was the best time ah had in years. Especially when one of the girls sprayed the big one." He slapped his knee and cackled.

"Yeah, Little John got nailed," Jim hooted.

Uncle Vic shined the light on John who was grinning ear to ear. "I was just walking behind it when it raised its tail. How should I know the thing could spray ten feet? It was horrible." Yet the grin remained, despite his remarks.

Axel just shook his head. "City boys… I hosed them all down but I don't know how much good it done."

"We're much obliged to ya," Uncle Vic said still looking at John and shaking his head. You boys head down to the lake and get cleaned up I'll tell your folks and see if I can get a change of

clothes. You'll just have to skinny dip for a while."
"Really?"
"We can *do* that?"
"Cool!"

Chapter 10 In De Scent

The boys scrubbed and soaped off as best they could with only minor distractions of water fights.

They heard something on the dock. Instantly they went to a crouch with only their heads above water. Only Little John's eyes were above water, which was quite a chore for the large boy in the waist deep water.

Aunt Lilly stood on the end of the dock with a platter. "I thought you boys would be hungry so I brought you some sandwiches and chips and dip, cheese and crackers some apples and a banana. We only had one banana left. Oh, and I forgot the cookies. Do you want some pickles? I brought some mustard and mayonnaise down. Oh, I forgot the catsup. Do you need pickle relish? I think I might have some pickle relish. I'll go look. I'll just leave this on the dock."

A chorus of thanks and cheers erupted from the boys.

Little John forgot himself and lunged for the dock not quite keeping himself decent. The others continued to crouch.

Aunt Lilly acted as though she did this every night. "If you boys want anything else just let me know."

As soon as she was off the dock, the boys dove for the sandwiches.

"Mmm' your m'aunt mis m'real mice Mike." Little John said through a mouthful. "My mom woulda hollered for a half hour and then made me get my own food."

"Ours still will," Jim said nodding.

Eric added his nod.

"Hey Eric, you missed a spot," Jim said pointing to his shoulder. "I'll help ya."

"Hey! Not near the food."

"You need help rinsing off?" Little John asked, pushing Mike's head under water.

Of course, Mike grabbed John's legs, pulled him under, and on it went.

Mike jumped up and pushed Little John's head underwater.

"Why are you guys swimming so late? What smells so bad?" asked Linda from on the dock where their discarded, manure-soaked shorts were.

They all dropped instantly, just their heads above water.

"It's ...uh the egg salad sandwich," Mike said." Why don't you go home? Aren't you supposed to be in bed?"

She sat down on the dock. "I'm waiting for my dad to get back."

The boys looked at each other in alarm.

"Hey, do you hear a car?" asked Mike.

"Yeah, I did. I bet he's home now," Jim rushed to add.

"Silly. He is out in the boat fishing. Isn't the water cold this time of night?"

It was not... until she said it was. Now that they were no longer playing and splashing and the sun was down, they were each suddenly freezing. Mike shivered involuntarily. "It's fine," he said abruptly.

Little John jumped to one side. "Something touched me. Where is your uncle?"

Mike pointed. "Here he comes."

Uncle Vic rounded the cabin into the light from the porch loaded down with towels. Little John's father followed behind.

"I'm in trouble," Little John grumbled.

"Hey Mike, do you think the crayfish come out at night more?" asked Jim.

"You know they do," Mike answered without a thought.

"Well, I think I just saw one by your foot."

"WHERE?" Mike squinted into the dark water. It did not occur to him to wonder how Jim could see into the water and he could not.

Eric had been sneaking up from behind. As soon as Mike said where, Eric reached forward and pinched Mike's calf.

"GGGAAAAAAAAAAA!" Mike exploded out of the water. "It's got me! It's got me!" He leapt toward the dock to escape.

"Mike!" Linda shouted, the whites of her eyes shining like spotlights, "Where's your swim suit!"

He dove back under the water, then remembered the killer

crayfish.

It has been said that panic is a virus with a gestation period of 0.01 seconds.

"WHERE IS IT!" John screamed, running away from Mike. Running in waist deep water is tricky. Once away from the play area the bottom got soft. It grabbed his feet and down he went. "Somethin' got m....glubble bub." Followed by more splashes.

Of course, during Mike's explosion, he pushed Eric underwater and he came struggling up coughing and splashing and knocked Jim backward. Soon they were all coughing and screaming.

"Linda your mom said to come up now," Uncle Vic said.

Linda, walked down the dock slowly glancing back from time to time. At the end of the dock, she disappeared into the nightshade of cedars between the cottages just as Mister Swanson appeared at the top of the hill, bearing clothing for his sons.

Little John went up the stairs, his father leading him by his ear. The Swansons dressed leisurely, now that Linda left; it was no longer cold. It wasn't until they left that Mike finally got out of the water.

"Uncle Vic, how long have you known Mister Vanderkooi?"

"Oh, I don't know about forty years I guess."

"Has he worked on the farm forever?"

"Yep, he was born on that farm. He told me once he left it only two nights in his life. Cows got to be milked you know."

"Man, I really feel sorry for him. Would it be alright if we go help him sometime?"

"As long as you let us know where you are this time and no more manure fights."

"Awww...."

"Linda! Time to come in!" Her mother called down from the cottage.

Mike's head snapped toward a rustle in the leaves on shore. He heard the feet pounding up the steps and his eyes flashed to the light on the porch at Linda's cottage where she just now shot into the house.

Jernal

This was the coolest day ever!!! We went over to the river with just the guys. No adalts. And we saw the indiean burial grounds and were just about run over by a ton a dears. We met this real farmer. Jim fell face first in a pile of cow plops and we had fight with

Mike paused in his writing.

hay and stuff. And then we got to feed the cows and he gave us a ride home on the trailer be hind his trackter. When we got back we were so dirty Uncle Vic made us go

Mike paused again.

swiming in the dark. I think someone was watching us.

He paused again. This seemed like an odd statement when he left out the skinny-dipping. Was Linda watching them? That was kind of a weird thought. Guys might peek at girls but girls do not peek at guys, do they? He put the pencil tip to the paper to write something else but what? His mind swirled through a series of thoughts, none of which did he want his mother to read. He put the pencil down and decided to finish writing his journal after he had figured out what to say. He lay back on the sofa to sort out his thoughts and soon fell asleep.

Chapter 11   A Case of the Milk Shakes

The sun shone brightly out on the lake, however, up behind the cottages the morning shade kept a sweet coolness. The boys stood in a semicircle behind Uncle Vic's cottage looking from the girl to Mike.

"How are you gonna help carry hay?" Mike glared at Linda.

"If you can do it, I can too," she stated firmly with her hands on her hips.

"You won't like it. It's dirty and it smells funny." Mike shook his head and looked from Linda to the guys.

"You're dirty and smell funny and I like you," she grinned.

Mike's face burned.

"Awww! Let her come Mike," wheedled little John.

Mike just turned away. "Ooh alright, but don't you come whinin' later about wantin' to come home."

"Thanks! I got to go ask my mother." She shot off into the cottage.

Mike kicked at the dust. "Mister Vanderkooi said we could come. He didn't say we could bring the whole world," he said to no one in particular.

"She'll do fine. If she needs help, I'll help her." Eric grinned at Mike.

Mike's head snapped around to Eric but he said nothing.

Presently Linda came out carrying a little bag with some lunch like the boys. They started off to the farm. Mike led the way with his shillelagh.

"Hi Mister Vanderkooi. We all talked about it and we felt sorry for you having to work from sun up to sun down, so we came to work for you."

"You did? I can't afford to pay ya anything," he said gruffly.

"They all looked surprised. We didn't expect to get paid."

"Oh... Ah...well that's real nice of ya, but I got a lot to do and I can't be watchin' ya all the time. Can any of ya drive a tractor?" He looked at each one of the shaking heads. " Humph. By the time I was your age I'd been drivin' fer fifteen years. Well, let's see." He took off his John Deere cap and showed off the tan line between the hat and his hairline while he rubbed off the sweat. "You did real well with the manure the other day. You can shovel out the barn," he said brusquely.

"Really?"

"Cool."

"Oh, look, baby cows." Linda peered in the barn at the calves.

The farmer's head snapped around. For the first time he noticed one of the kids in cutoffs and a T-shirts, was a girl. He brightened up. "Hey, you weren't here last weekend, were you?"

"No, I wasn't," she said quietly. "This is my first time seeing a farm. I hope it's all right."

Mister Vanderkooi's face softened. "Why sure it is, sweetie." He paused, looking into her deep brown eyes. When he spoke again his voice was soft as a newborn calf's nose. "You look like my daughter when she was your age. She's a veterinarian down state now. Com'on into the barn and I'll show ya how we feed the calves. What's your name, honey?"

"Linda."

"Well, Linda, let's go see if the calves are ready for some breakfast."

They spent the rest of the morning cleaning the barn (shoving scratchy hay down the back of each other's shirt), feeding livestock (playing with animals) and fixing fences (running around the field).

By noon they were pretty well whipped. They ate their lunch and sat in the shade watching the chickens eat grasshoppers.

"I'm never eating chicken again," Linda said shaking her head.

"Why, you gonna cut out the middle man and just eat grasshoppers?" Eric asked.

Mister Vanderkooi came out and sat down with them to eat his lunch." I don' have anything else for you to do today. Thanks a lot for helpin'. You're welcome to come back anytime."

"You must have had a great time growing up out here as a kid."

"It was a lot of work, but I love being outside and the animals don't give me any back talk, even though they are in charge."

"What do you mean they are in charge?" Linda asked.

I got ta milk 'em and feed 'em make sure they got good water every day. Even when I'm sick and even in the blizzards."

He looked off into the distance and rubbed his chin. "Why, one time we had a ferocious blizzard. I got up in the morning to milk the cows and the snow was so deep I couldn't open the front door. Well, I had ta milk 'em so I opened the upstairs window to get out. You know it had snowed so hard and the wind had blew so long that I could actually step out from that upstairs window onto the snow. But the wind, she was still blowin' so that I had to walk sideways just to keep from being blown over. I could just barely make out the barn. It was a dark patch in the white. Well, I make for the barn but how am I going to open the door with all the snow piled in front of it, I wonder? Well to my surprise, I tugged on the door and it popped right open. I went inside and closed it, but the animals were all gone!"

"Where were they?"

"Did they freeze?"

"Were they out in the blizzard?"

"Those thoughts went through my mind. It was kinda dark in there. The drifts covered the windows, so I took a few more steps forward to look around and... suddenly felt myself flying through the air. I fell ten feet to the barn floor..." He looked at each of them and shook his head at the memory. "I had entered the barn through the hayloft and thinking it was the main floor walked right off the ledge. Fortunately, I landed in a pile a hay I had thrown down the night before."

"Wow! Did you break anything?"

"Nothing important, but I had wasted my time."

"What do ya mean?"

"Why, it was so cold, the cow's udders had froze right up. I couldn't get anything out, they was as solid as an icicles. It was a week before I could get anything out of them but milk shakes," he winked at Mike.

"Really?" Little John gasped.

"So, if we got a big refrigerator and put the cow in it, we could get milk shakes?"

"I dunno I never tried." He scratched under his hat.

"Vanilla or chocolate milkshakes?" Linda asked.

Mike pushed her. "Silly... you can't get chocolate milkshakes from a cow. It had to be vanilla, of course."

"Hay lofts can be a lot of fun. I used to pretend I had a fort in this one and make tunnels in the hay."

"Cool, can we do that?"

"No, not anymore. There are too many rotten boards up there. The center is still pretty strong but I don't trust ya up there yet. Too dangerous. I got a bunch a reject lumber from the sawmill down the road to fix it, but I decided I don't need the loft anymore."

"So, what are you gonna do with the wood?"

"Nothin'. Why? You want to buy some? I ain't going to *give* you all my lumber."

"I just had an idea. It would be really cool to build a tree fort over on the other side of your pasture."

"Why over there? Yer gonna have to haul all the wood you need way across the pasture"

It will be a great view. We would be able to watch enemy soldiers coming over the field."

"The only enemy soldiers you're gonna see over there are the da… darn deer coming over to trample, plunder and steal my corn. If ya wanted to ambush some of them…" He paused; a sly grin formed on his face. "Here boy…. let's go look for a spot ta put your hunting blind…uh... your tree fort."

They cheered.

He stood up and strode across the pasture. "But'cha got to build it accordin' to my directions. Right?"

"Sure."

"You bet."

Mike hammered a two by four to the trunk of the tree for a step. "That was a great idea of Mister Vanderkooi, showing us those deer trails so we can pretend they are enemy soldiers."

"Yeah." said little John handing him another board. "But why do you think we had to build it out of sight of the road?"

<u>Jornal entry</u>

We went to the farm with the girl next store. It was really cool. You might remember her name is Linda. I call her Stinkersmell. She really earned her name today. We sat down to eat lunche and she didn't look at the ground before she sat down. She wore a cow pie the rest of the day. She was a prety good sport about it though. The farmer let us build the most amazeing tree fort ever buildt in the western hemesfere on his land. He made some funny rules but taght us about shooting lanes, camoflashe, feeld of view and other militry stuff. I didn't think a farmer would no such stuff.

Next weekend I 'm going fishing in Turtle bay. Uncle Vic says that is where Buck caught the biggest fish they ever saw. Everyone says there is a humongus big snapping turtle over there but I'm not afraid. What could happen?

Chapter 12   Fishing for Excitement

It was late on a warm afternoon and the waves made by the boaters made the raft bob up and down like a toy in a child's bathtub. Mike and Little John sat on the end of the dock kicking the cool water and watched the raft dance with the waves.

"Fishing in Turtle Bay? Are you nuts?" Little John lowered his voice to a whisper, "Old Ironsides lives there." He looked around as if afraid the legendary snapping turtle might hear him.

"Have you ever *seen* Old Ironsides?" Mike asked.

"No, but Alex, down the road, he says he seen him. They were fishing for the big bass that everyone knows live over there under the lily pads, and he throws his lure too far and hits a *big old log* about 6 feet long. His lure got stuck on the log so he gives it a tug," he lowered his voice to a hoarse whisper, "…but it's not a log. And it starts movin'." Little John's eyes bulged like turtle eggs.

"It was old Ironsides and he pulled them along in the boat fast enough to pull a water skier. He pulled 'em round and round. Finally, the line broke. They headed back to the main lake as fast as they could, but before they got to the mouth, they see something rushing at their boat like a torpedo. It was the snapping turtle. He hit their boat and nearly knocked them in. He said it was a good thing they were in an aluminum boat or they would a bin goners fer sure. They got a big dent in the boat and made it to the mouth of the lake but just barely."

"Oh, those are just made-up stories. I been fishin' there with Uncle Vic a couple times and it's real cool lookin'."

"But if we get caught there after dark…"

"We won't be there after dark. There're no cottages over there and there's lots of lily pads for the fish to hide. We seen some big ole bass in there too. I've seen lots of turtles but never Old Ironsides. Come on. We'll leave before dark."

"I'm not afraid of the dark. It's just... Alex says a fisherman disappeared over there, and they found him a couple days later and he was half *eaten*."

"They just make up those stories to keep people from the best fishin' spot on the lake. We'll stay near the mouth and we can leave when you want. I'll let you use my "Silver Minnow""

This was just too much temptation for Little John. All the boys knew Mike's dad had actually caught a 23 and ¾" Northern Pike on that Silver Minnow.

"Oh, all right, but we leave when I say. Give me the lure."

"Not until we get there. If we see that old snapping turtle, we'll just hit it in the head with an oar and bring it back for dinner."

After supper Little John met Mike down at the dock. Mike put on a life jacket and climbed into the old rowboat. He handed Little John a life jacket.

"I don't need that. I'm a good swimmer. I can swim across the whole lake. You know that." He said flippantly.

"Ok." Mike tossed it back on the dock, and studied the bottom of the boat.

Little John loaded his fishing pole into the boat along with the red Coffee can filled with the fattest and tastiest worms the boys could find. Significant debate occurred on how to determine how they taste. Mike suggested Little John take a bite of each since he likes to eat so much, he must be a good judge. When John protested, Mike argued "It's not like you got to swallow." But in the end, they decided if Dennis was willing to lick them it was good enough. Of course, Dennis' tongue covered a lot of ground and he ended up licking all of them in one swipe.

Mike untied the boat. Little John looked at the sun then back at the dock and then towards the bay. "Say, hand me that life Jacket. I'll use it as a head rest."

"Ok."

"I got another one!" John shouted. His pole bounced and danced as John eased the large bluegill to the boat.

"He's a dandy," Mike nodded. "Put him on the stringer with the others. Boy since the sun hit the trees they really went nuts. It's like a switch turned on." Mike said.

Little John glanced uneasily at the sun. The trees on the far side of Turtle Bay obscured most of it. "We probably should get going pretty soon. My mom will worry."

"But we got lots a crawlers left and the fish are going nuts. We've never had 'em hit like this. As soon as we can't see any more of the sun we'll go."

John struggled with another night crawler.

"Hey!"

Mike's pole bent in half. Fifteen feet from the boat there was a huge splash and a bass bigger than anything either boy had ever seen shook his head and spat Mike's crawler back at the boat. Then with a wave of his tail as though thumbing his nose, he disappeared back into the lake. Mike's pole went slack. He reeled as fast as he could but there was no resistance.

"Man!"

"WOW"

"Did you see that?" They both talked at once, going a mile a minute; they spent the next ten minutes shouting back and forth about what had lasted less than ten seconds.

"He's still out there. I got to get a new hook on." Mike scrambled to tie on a new hook.

"He won't be out there long!" John threw his bait right to where he had seen the last splash."

"Hey no fair!"

"You had him once and missed him. It's my turn."

Neither boy noticed that the sun had set and the first stars began to appear in the dark blue sky. The darkness under the trees crept its way onto the lily pads and groped its way out to the sides of their boat. Gradually they caught fewer and smaller fish. It had been a long time since they kept any, but the fish they had already caught reminded them of their presence from time to time by bumping the boat.

Silence slowly descended on the boat as the enthusiasm of the huge bass subsided and darkness enveloped the lake. They could no longer see into the weeds underneath the boat. Their bait disappeared when they dropped it into the water. The lake had become a black pit of invisibility. The darkness poised on the edge of their boat and leapt into Little John's throat, forming a tight ball, making it difficult to breath.

The boat creaked in the evening silence, as Little John shifted uneasily. "I think it's time to get goin'."

A splash in the distance radiated ripples out across the mirrored smooth lake. Mike made a great show of grimacing. "Oh, just a little longer." But as soon as he said it, he regretted it. He felt he was supposed say it but...

The fish on the stringer hit against the side of the boat again. It was louder now that the lake was silent. Darkness must be denser than sunlight. It carries sound better. Mike shifted his pole to the other hand. He wondered how fast he could get the anchor up if he had to.

"What would we do if we fell in? We wouldn't be seen by anyone. We could be out here for days!"

"We'd just swim to shore." Mike whispered, unsure why he was speaking so softly.

"But I can't see anything under the trees. What if someone is there?"

"Who could be there?" *Aliens*! The thought jumped into Mike's mind as soon as he said it. *They could see us easily from space and see we are alone. No one would notice if they came now. That's what happened to that fisherman! They did some weird experiment on him and then dumped him back in the lake.* He began to reel in his bait. His eyes flashed from the darkness under the trees to the stars starting to appear overhead.

"Something moved over there." Little John said shakily pointing to an old log.

"Where?" Mike turned slowly to look, in a forced nonchalance.

"Over by that big log. You don't think that log is really..." He couldn't finish the statement.

"That log has been there for..." It was just dark enough to make colors fade and edges blur. Was that the log he thought it was or... "It *did* move! No... Yes, it *did*!" Mike finished reeling in his bait in a blur of movement, never taking his eyes off the log. Neither said a word but Little John put down his pole and began to put on the extra life jacket. He seemed to have some difficulty.

Just as Mike's bait was about to the boat something hit it. His pole bent double. Both boys' eyes went wide.

"What do you think it is?" Little John stammered.

Mike didn't answer but kept reeling grimly. Soon a nice bass appeared beside the boat. "Hey look at this. He held it up proudly. "I think it's the biggest fish I ever caught. Get out that stringer."

Little John let out a long exhale." It's a beauty. Wait till everyone sees all these fish."

Yeah, and you were worried about the dumb old turtle."

Little John lifted the stringer of fish into the boat while Mike worked on getting the bass off the hook.

"M...M...M...Mike!" John stammered, holding up the stringer.

Mike lifted his head and gaped.

Both boys stared in horror at the bodiless heads of the fish, their entrails hanging below their gills like a grizzly necklace.

Little John's mouth moved like the fishes, but nothing came out.

"Whassa ...I... Lesge'outtahere," Mike mumbled.

There was another bump on the bottom of the boat this time followed by a high pitched screeeeeee, like claws scratching at the bottom of the boat.

Little John dropped the stringer in the bottom of the boat and grabbed the oars.

"Don't throw them in here! He'll come in after 'em!"

"AHHHH." Little John threw them back over the side.

"Don't throw them over the side. He'll follow us!"

"Eeee." Little John threw them back in the boat.

"Not in here! Weren't you listening!"

But Little John already grabbed the oars and they were moving before the anchor was off the bottom. Mike hauled the anchor such that it fairly flew out of the water and fell into the bottom of the boat as it came back down.

"Here give me and oar."

Mike grabbed for the oars only to knock the right one out of the oarlock and into the water.

"ARGuhg. What are you doing!"

"Oh help"

They both motioned toward the oar but neither could bring themselves to reach down into the water and grab it. Meantime their forward momentum carried them further away from the oar.

Little John rowed furiously with the left oar to try and get back to the floating right oar." Getitgetitgetitgetit!"

Mike grabbed his pole and flung the line at it. The hook caught.

As soon as it was within reach John grabbed it, all the while unintelligible sounds poured out of his mouth at high volume.

He started rowing but not fast enough for Mike who jumped onto the bench next to him and grabbed one oar. With one boy on each oar, they were soon underway at high speed. However, with Little John being so much larger and stronger, they were soon going at high speed ...<u>in circles</u>.

"Slow down." Mike hollered just as he pulled with all his might to make them go straight, but the oar missed the water and he fell over backwards.

Eventually they made it back to the main body of the lake. They slowed their rowing slightly and stayed very close to shore just in case their parents were looking for them. They stayed so shallow that twice they scraped bottom. Both times the screeching on the bottom was echoed by the screeching from the boys.

"Hey did you catch anything," Eric called from his dock as they rowed up to it.

"We saw Ole Ironsides!"

"Yeah, he was 6 feet long and nearly knocked the boat over."

Eric's jaw dropped. "Were you scared?"

"Naw. Little John tried to hit him with the oar. Nearly had 'im too." Mike said proudly as he tied the boat up to the dock and jumped out of the boat barely ahead of John.

"Aren't you going to tie the boat up at your dock?

"No, yours was closer and I uh… gotta go to the bathroom," Mike said backing away from the water.

Mike sprinted up the stairs, almost... but not quite beating Little John to the top.

Chapter 13   Strawberries and Melons, Birds, and Bees

Mike stood on the dock and admired the old wooden canoe for the work of art it was. Each hand-stained rib and plank joined and spread like the veins on a leaf. The canoe sat on top of the water, indeed belonging there like a newly fallen leaf, as much a part of its surroundings as any tree, insect or branch.

"Get in back."

"In back? But I don't know how to steer."

"'Bout time you learned," Uncle Vic sighed a long and noisy sigh. "Put your paddle in first. Then step lightly in the center of the canoe," he commanded.

Mike hugged the dock and felt out with one foot into the beautiful old wood plank canoe. It moved and he drew it back to the dock with his foot.

The canoe bobbed and wobbled on top of the water. It felt like a living thing, a wild horse that roamed the plains of the sea, but he would tame this horse to his will and drive it wildly across the hills.

"Put your hand on the opposite side of the canoe for balance."

Mike settled into the sunken leather seat and the bow popped up out of the water as the stern sank under his weight. His uncle stepped into the bow and the boat sank down in front. His uncle pushed off from the dock. The craft slid through the water completely silent. Mike just watched the water slip by as though he sailed through the air above the water. Uncle Vic slid his paddle into the water at the same rate that the water moved by. He thought his uncle rowed a boat silently but here there was no creak of the oar, nothing to show movement but the dripping of the oar as he lifted it from the water.

This must be what it is like to fly! Mike thought.

"You've got to steer you know."

Mike was jarred from his awe to realize they were going to hit the raft. "WhatdoIdo, whatdoIdo?"

"Paddle on your left," his uncle rumbled.

Mike dug his paddle into the water with a loud splashing and the canoe turned.

"Cool."

His uncle chuckled. "You paddle when I paddle and we offset each other."

They spent about 20 minutes together. His uncle showed him the basics of steering and moving silently.

"Okay, let me off at the dock," his uncle said.

The front of the canoe popped up as his uncle stepped out.

"Okay, now you get in the front and face the back."

This made no sense but Mike did it.

"Now paddle. You're closer to the middle now so the other end won't stick up so much."

Mike paddled and found that it worked very well by himself.

"Boys, let's go!" Aunt Lilly called from the top of the hill.

Mike looked around, "Is she calling you a boy?"

"Well, I ain't a girl."

"Oh... well, where we going?"

"We're going to the market."

"The one with the clear bee hive?"

"Yep."

Mike fairly jumped out of the canoe. Together they pulled it up on the shore. Mike caressed the smooth wood sides. "Thanks a lot Uncle Vic that was cool. What are we getting at the market?"

"Strawberries are in season. Aunt Lil wants to see about getting some to make jam."

"Not short cake?" The horror on Mike's face forced Uncle Vic to chuckle.

"Well now, she didn't say anything about shortcake, but I bet if we ask her real nice, she might consider it.

Mike unconsciously licked his lips. "With real whip cream?"

"Is there another kind?"

Uncle Vic pulled the old green Rambler into the gravel parking lot, and Mike popped out before Uncle Vic put it into park. The market was little more than a big garage. They could probably get six or seven cars in it if they took out the fresh flowers, huge mounds of asparagus and crates of strawberries.

"They still have the bees!" Mike shouted and ran to the clear glass windowpanes surrounding the honeybees busily making their honeycomb. A plastic tube led from the hive to an exterior wall of the market.

Below the beehive, huge hand-labeled jars of honey and honeycomb shined with a golden glow. Last year Mike's dad had bought him some honeycomb on one of his rare free weekends. The honeycomb was disappointing but he could taste the honey with a slab of butter melting down the sides of one of his aunt's homemade rolls.

"Aunt Lilly are you going to make your rolls sometime?" He looked back toward the car where she was just now closing the door.

She smiled that sweet smile. "Not today but I will have to make some baking powder biscuits for the strawberry shortcake. Oh, wouldn't some honey be good on them. I will have to make a double batch."

"Really? Wow, that would be great."

Mike nearly ran through the market from one pile of crates to the next. The musky sweet smells of melon, onions, and fresh flowers were so solid he thought he could taste them. He closed his eyes and inhaled deeply. He could see the fragrances! He walked down the aisle with his eyes closed one step at a time. The melons hit him like a two by four, sweet bowling balls of smooth flavors melted inside his nose. He was buried in their scent. He couldn't climb out of a barrel this deep. He took three more steps and he was still buried. The bowling balls of scent rolled over him as he pushed his way through the musty fragrance that was so much a part of the living cottage smell. But a new lusty perfume called to him. At first it was just a tickle, a sly touch of sweetness through the musty melon scent, two sweet fingers under his chin, leading him forward. The mustiness diminished and the fingers became a hand to the side of his neck, stroking yet tickling in the sweet tart smell of fresh--- ripe--- strawberries. These weren't cold refrigerated berries picked half white and sold next to white Styrofoam coolers. Not the stiff lifeless, tasteless Frankenberries picked by machines. These were handpicked in golden sunshine by loving young farmers' daughters. These were full, red, tender berries still warm with life. No white tips, no large hollow center, just sweet red joy. The least touch of these berries left a red kiss on your hand and a stamp on your brain to last a lifetime. Surely this was the fruit Adam and Eve had been tempted with in the garden. The living warmth of the fruit carried the fragrance up into the sinus cavities in such a way that they penetrated all the way to the brain stem, wrapping individual brain cells in chemicals so powerful they could make shy, young boys brave any terror...any terror, that is... but one.

"You like strawberries?" asked a voice sweeter than the sweetest strawberry ever grown.

Mike's eyes flashed open. A girl about fourteen or fifteen placed another quart of gorgeous strawberries on the display. *A junior high girl was talking to him*! A very CUTE junior high girl. Her piercing blue eyes and sun-bleached, blond hair contrasted with her well-tanned face like a model out of a magazine. She was a little taller than Mike but not much. Her thick blond braids hung down the front of her shoulders to where her plaid cotton shirt bulged quite pleasantly.

"Uh... what?" Mike's senses, already on overload, swirled into a hot summer tornado.

She stepped closer to Mike and held out a large deep red strawberry.

"Here have one of my berries."

"Oh...thanks." He gently took the berry from her and for the briefest moment, their fingertips touched, or... was it a caress? The electric spark flashed from his toes to the roots of his hair. Mike's face instantly flushed as red as the berry. His heart roared like an outboard motor.

She wiped her red stained hands on her short cutoffs, prompting Mike to look down at her athletic, tanned legs extending from the short, frayed, blue jean cutoffs.

He swallowed hard. WhadoIsay? WhadoIsay? His mind screamed. This is important! Alarms rang in this head. Say something quick! "Uh...Did you pick these?" he asked. He bit into the berry as an excuse to try and think, but explosions of flavor crashed through his senses as his tongue crushed the sweetness to the top of his mouth. "Mmm."

"I picked some of them. Don't you love the smell?" She bent over the crates and inhaled deeply, then straightened up. "Aren't they great? I wish this season lasted all year."

He bent over to smell them as she had. She bent over also, so their faces were close together--- very close. She was so close that he felt her breath. Her eyes locked on his like a guided missile. Her armor piercing blue eyes crashed through the back of his brain into his skull.

"I love strawberries," she licked her lips.

He stared at her moist red lips. The strawberry juice made those lips a deep juicy red, brighter and more fascinating than any lips he had ever seen. He wondered if her lips tasted like strawberries. Hormones splashed through his brain in buckets. He couldn't stand it. Mike straightened up and swallowed. He swallowed again, his heart flopping around in his stomach like a freshly landed blue gill on the dock.

"You live around here?" she asked, her sly eyes taking measure of her captive.

"No." Mike shook his head dumbly. *WhatdoIsaynow???*, his mind screamed. "I'm staying at..."*where do I say I'm I staying?* "Uh... at the Lake." Deep gulp. "...for the summer." Breath came in shallow, hesitant gulps as this poor fish worked its gills outside its natural environment.

The cashier called out, "Lisa! Quit flirtin' with that boy and get back to work."

"Maybe I'll see you later, but I have to work until 4:00," the girl said and bit the right side of her lower lip. She hesitated for a second before she spun around and walked toward the back door of the store.

Mike stopped breathing. Every other body function crashed to emergency stop as the only other creature in God's creation walked away from him. Yet, he savored even her walking away. It seemed she was still speaking to him through her simple body movements and, of course ...she was.

Uncle Vic walked up. "When you said you like to come because of the bees... I didn't know you meant the *birds and the bees*." He placed his hand on Mike's shoulder. "Time to go." He chuckled as Mike continued to stare after the girl.

Mike's lungs unlocked and he let out a long breath. He walked shakily toward the car and didn't say a word until they were back to the cottage.

After unloading the car, Aunt Lilly repacked some of the items. "Mike, would you take this bag of things over to Linda's folks."

"Why?" Mike peered into the bag. Two quarts of strawberries

sat on top.

"The prices were so good we could buy a lot at the same price as a little but we can't eat it all and Linda's Dad isn't working. Don't you like to get presents?"

Mike winced. "Yeah, but are you sure we have enough strawberries?"

"Well, if we run out, I guess we'll have to go get some more." She hugged him.

"Okay." He snatched up the bag and ran off.

"Hi Mickey! Whatcha got." Linda opened the screen door.

The hormones must have still been screaming at Mike and he found himself looking at Linda differently, comparing her to the girl at the store. Linda was younger, but she was very pretty. Her shirt didn't bulge as much, but... he realized he was staring at her chest and looked away.

Linda smiled pleasantly, opened the bag and looked inside.

She inhaled quickly "Strawberries... Mom!"

"Shhh...your father is sleeping. Hello, Mike what have you got?"

Mike was suddenly aware of loud snoring coming from the other room. "Aunt Lilly got a bunch a stuff cheap but she said it was more than we could eat."

"Ohhh, how thoughtful." She looked inside.

"Mama, there's strawberries!"

"Don't get too excited," Mike said making a face. "They're on top of a pile of asparagus." He stuck out his tongue.

"Fresh asparagus is my favorite." Linda's mother appeared to struggle with her words. "Be... be sure to tell your aunt thank you." She took the bag and quickly walked into the other room.

"Mike!" his aunt called.

"Seeya, Stinker."

She stuck out her tongue." Bye, Mickey"

"Hey!" Her dad shouted. "Be quiet out there. I'm trying to sleep! Stupid kids."

Linda winced. "Sorry."

"Mike, would you feed Dennis?" Aunt Lilly asked as Mike stepped back into the cottage.

"Sure."

Mike readied the food and brought it out to the doghouse. He looked down at the dog lying in the shade asleep. "How come you get to sleep all day and have someone wait on you?" he asked the dog. The dog just lifted his head and licked his mouth with his dirty tongue.

"Here Vic, take this to Axel. We should repay him for bringing the boys back."

"Mike come on along. You have to give this to Mister Vanderkooi."

"Why are we giving him some shortcake too? We won't have any strawberries left!"

"He doesn't get it much since he lives alone. And he was pretty nice to you boys the other night."

"Yeah, I suppose. He's a pretty cool guy. I used to feel sorry for him 'cause he has to work all the time. But now I think he's got one of the neatest jobs in the world. I mean he can be outside all the time and he gets to be with the animals. No one tells him what to do and he can wear dirty jeans all the time."

"You think you'd like that?"

Mike shrugged. "More than I'd like being inside some old factory all day, I guess."

"I know what you mean." Uncle Vic nodded in resolute agreement.

Mike snapped his head to look back at his uncle. Grownups were never supposed to agree with a child's opinion. Here was something new.

Paul Bunyan sized up the monstrous tree. "No Babe, I don't need you for this one. In fact, I don't even need my ax. I been feelin' a mite restless lately. I need to stretch my muscles. Paul leaned his body into the ageless giant. It shuddered and groaned but held its ground. Paul dug in his toes and grunted. The tree wavered and then with a mighty snap it fell over. The boom as it hit the ground shook the earth as far away as St Louie. Babe snorted in admiration.

"A few more trees and we'll be all the way to the Pacific."

"Hey Paul! Paul Bunyan! That's enough."

"Okay Uncle Vic." Mike ran out of the cat tail swamp. His sockless shoes squishing with every step. "You were right Mister Vanderkooi! Did you see me? I could push those old dead trees right over. Why are they dead?"

"The swamp kills 'em I guess."

"We need to let you get back to work." Uncle Vic stated to mister Vander Kooi and moved towards the car.

"Well, thanks for stoppin' by. Tell Lilly she still makes the best strawberry shortcake this side of heaven." He stood up. "Hey, I got somethin' for you to try. You like beef jerky?" Without waiting for a response, he trotted into the house.

"What's jerky?" Mike asked.

"Dried meat. It's pretty good if the meat is taken care of. In the old days, Indians and mountain men didn't have refrigerators so they would dry their meat to make it last. That's what jerky is."

Mister Vanderkooi reappeared with a worn paper bag. "Here take it with ya. I got plenty." He reached in the bag as he handed it over and took out a stiff six-inch long chunk of something and handed it to Mike.

To Mike it looked like part of the opossum he and the boys had found along the road last year. He peered at it sideways, and turned it over, trying to find a reason to refuse. Still, if the Indians use to eat it…

Uncle Vic and Mister Vanderkooi chuckled. Uncle Vic reached in and grabbed a chunk and without hesitation bit off a hunk. After working his jaw a couple times, he nodded. "Say, that's pretty good Axel. You make that yourself?"

"Yep. It comes in pretty handy workin' on the farm."

"Say that reminds me," Uncle Vic asked," is it okay if I were to come out and hunt deer on your farm?"

"Shore. When ya coming? Tomorra?"

Uncle Vic chuckled, "Well… I thought I'd wait 'til deer season in November."

"Oh, hell, they'll be all gone by then. Why don't ya come out this week? Them da… darn rats are eatin' half my crops."

"Just the same, I'll wait till November."

"Well, when ya come, bring the boy with ya. The more a them rats that are killed the better."

"I'm too young to hunt." Mike said.

"What? Can'cha hold a gun?" the farmer squinted in disbelief at Mike's arms to see what sickness he might possibly have.

"No, I mean I'm not old enough to get a license…. But I'd like to hunt here when I'm older."

Mister Vanderkooi just shook his head and waved his arm.

"You can hunt here tomorra for all I care. Just don't shoot my cows or you'll have to buy me a new one." He walked off muttering. "Too young to hunt! Never heard of such a thing."

Mike's head swam. He could hunt here!

Journal entry

I get to go hunting! Not this year but wow! Mister Vanderkooi said I could hunt his farm and Uncle Vic even said I could use one of his guns. I wonder if I can use small one on the wall of the cottage. Wow. Oh mom, you should come snorkeling with me up here. The water is real warm it's just like those specials we watch on TV. Well, it is if our TV reception isn't very good the colors are washed out and the fish are small. I go almost every day now.

Chapter 14   Underwater Exploration

At five thousand feet down, the ocean bottom looked strange. The first man to scuba dive so deep, the world-famous diver Jack Cloostow, knew he was viewing sights never before seen by man. He was so deep that the only place he could see anything was in the narrow cone of light thrown forward by his small flashlight. He was traveling right along the edge of the weeds. He must avoid the weeds. They were slimy and thick. No telling what lived in there. If you went into them, you would get tangled, twisted and probably drown. Something moved in the murky distance. Was that his diving buddy or... he just couldn't see anything. He turned each way looking for his partner but he was nowhere to be seen. He swam back the way he came pausing to look at the strange patterns in the sandy bottom. What kind of an animal would...? Something brushed his ankle. He jerked back and spun but it grabbed his leg. He spun his body and tugged at his leg, to no avail. He reached for his dive knife but when he spun the squid must have cut his airline, for he took in a mouthful of water. Now fighting to control the panic rising within him he plunged his knife deeply in the giant squid. The beast released him, and he headed to the surface.

It was 10,000 feet up but he made it. He took a big gulp of air and headed back down. There was something to finish. The squid had followed him to the surface but now apparently had second thoughts. Shooting out a cloud of black ink it headed toward shallow water looking for a place to hide. There was nowhere to go and soon Jack was running through shallow water.

"Come back here you low life invertebrate squid."

"Man, did you jump!" Jim laughed over his shoulder, but he didn't slow down. When he got to shore, he ran up the steps and stood looking back.

Mike stayed at the water's edge. He knew going up into the shade, covered with water meant Jim would soon be attacked himself. Sure enough, within a few seconds, Jim started slapping as the mosquitoes and flies began dining on the tasty morsel in the security of the shade.

Jim could stand it no longer. He howled and ran down the steps waving his arms around his head. "Truce... truce..." He shouted and ran past Mike and dove into the shallow water seeking relief.

Mike ran out to join him.

Jim surfaced." Truce?"

Mike slapped a handful of sandy brown mud on Jim's head and nodded. "Truce."

"Oh man..." Jim rinsed it off and came up sputtering. "Why are you such a scaredy cat when it comes to water?"

"I dunno. I guess cuz I don't know what's out there that you can't see and I can't swim."

Jim looked at him in surprise. "Yes, you can. We've been swimming all afternoon."

"With mask and snorkel. That's different."

"Why?"

"I don't know. With the snorkel I can breathe and the mask I can see."

"That doesn't make any sense."

"Hey, let's swim out to the raft. I bet we see lots of fish out there."

"I'll go get my life jacket."

"What for? You just said with the mask and snorkel you were okay."

"I feel better with it."

"That's dumb."

Mike ran up to the boathouse and got his life jacket on. He made a point of not looking at Jim when he came back, but out of the corner of his eye he could see Jim shaking his head.

Mike heard a powerboat go flying past the front of the cottage. He looked up to see Uncle Vic coming down the steps with a hammer and some nails to fix the dock. Mike could almost feel the anger in his uncle's glare at the boat. "They tear up the silence and the lake. The waves wash away the shore." The expression on his uncle's face changed and Mike heard the powerboat slow and head in their direction.

"Hey, Mister Malloy!" a joyful man's voice bellowed.

Mike spun around, and realized Buck's girlfriend, Grace, was in the back of the boat waving. He stiffly waved back. Mike vaguely recognized the crew cut on the driver and remembered the guy as Buck's buddy. Another blond girl, in a bikini sitting next to the driver, smiled at Mike.

Grace was wearing a one piece with a sweatshirt pulled over it.

Mike smiled back and nervously looked away. His eyes quickly slid back to the girl and her bikini. He hadn't seen many bikinis and this one looked particularly interesting from an engineering standpoint. He couldn't determine how the top stayed up without straps, and indeed this one looked like it might give way at any moment, like a dam bursting due to an over flowing flood. He thought perhaps he should study the device in detail, just in case… say, he wanted to build a dam.

"Hello, Patrick." Uncle Vic waved back.

Patrick shut off the engine and the boat coasted toward the dock.

"Whaddaya hear from Buck?"

"Not much." Uncle Vic walked out on the dock." He's gone out in the boonies a couple times but he says it's not much like the camping he's used to. They have had a couple of mortar attacks but so far, he's doing fine."

Patrick reached across the water and shook Uncle Vic's hand. "I only got one letter from him. It sounds like the living conditions are pretty uncomfortable, but I bet Buck is having fun. He always seems to make everything a game."

"Yes. Well, I wish he would play his games here. How long you home for?"

"Next week I go back and get ready to ship out."

"Best of luck to you." Uncle Vic said, sadness in his voice. "I wish those SOBs in Washington would make up their mind to win this war. At this rate we will be there forever."

Patrick nodded. "I hope it's over soon. I've got too many friends over there. I bet it's been pretty quiet this summer with Tom and Buck gone. Remember when they built the high diving platform on Tom's folk's raft?"

Uncle Vic snorted a laugh. "Yep, and the three of you got it rocking and tipped the raft right over."

"Don't include me in on that. I was on the shore laughing at them. It seemed like we spent that whole summer water skiing and playing." He sighed. "Things change. Hey Mike, do you slalom ski like Buck? I got some water skis right here." He reached down inside the boat and pulled up two well used water skis

"Uh... no."

Grace jumped up from the boat onto the dock and hugged Mike. "Mike will do it. He's tough like Buck," She made a show of squeezing his upper arm. "Look at these biceps!"

Now she's mocking me, Mike thought.

She hugged him again.

This time Mike did not squirm while she held him close and whispered in his ear. "I know you can do it. You look just like Buck did at your age."

"Huh?" Maybe she was not mocking him.

"He's afraid of the deep water," Jim chided.

"We'll work on that," Grace encouraged.

Patrick grinned. Yeah, old Buck was always nervous about the deep water till he started skiing.

"Really?" Mike's jaw dropped, "I don't think..."

"Oh, come on Mike..." The blonde whispered leaning her bikinied body against his. "It really impresses the girls." She winked and glanced over to Linda's dock where she sat with a book in her lap watching them.

Mike who was now convinced beyond a shadow of a doubt that bikinis were worthy of great study could only stammer. "Uh....Uh....Uh..."

"Go ahead Mike," Jim nudged him. "Can I go too?"

"Sure."

"Are you going water skiing Mike?" Linda shouted from her dock.

"He sure is!" Grace shouted back. "You want to go for a ride?"

"You bet!" Linda dropped the book and ran over to their dock.

Before Mike could say anything more, he had his feet shoved into the skis and Patrick was telling him something about hand signals, slack rope, and keeping skis together, which was just too confusing. Then to his amazement, he was bumping along on the skis behind the boat.

I'M SKIING! His mind shouted in amazement.

The line jerked, yanked, went slack, then jumped ahead again but he maintained his balance though many times he was sure he was going to fall. Every muscle in his body was rigid. If he had known he looked like a jockey on the back of a racehorse bent forward at the waist way too far for water skiing. He did not care.

He was on top of the world. He was water skiing! The boat full cheered and hooted as he made a shaky loop around the lake.

They were coming around to the dock and his muscles were clenched into a perpetual pucker. His entire body had been shaking from the exertions since he stood up. He knew he could not make it around the lake again, but how do you stop? They had not covered that. Buck would come sliding up on one ski spraying everyone on the dock and calmly walk up to the shore as though he was just getting out of a car.

The boat swung out into the center of the lake. Mike didn't dare go down out here where it was deep. Who knew what was out here in the deep water? You can't see into it. Even now there might be giant turtles or huge fish that have lived here for a thousand years, waiting, just waiting, for the right food to come along. And here he was, bobbing around behind the boat like bait; one of those noisy spinning surface baits made to attract big fish. He now knew he would die out here.

There might even be alien space ships under the water, hiding their huge space ships in lakes all around the world, waiting for the day they would receive the signal from their home world when they would all attack. Here he was out skiing above their ship and he would fall into the water and hit their vessel. So, to prevent him from discovering their nefarious schemes they would haul him into their ship and keep him captive. That is what would happen to him if he didn't slide into the shore easily. He glanced into the water and was almost certain he saw several green faces grinning up at him.

Buck had made it look easy but Mike would have to cross over the rough wake thrown up by the boat. The cottage was approaching. Time was almost up. He would ease over it slowly. He eased the nose of the right ski into the wake.

In reflection, Mike could still remember the smiling face of Linda cheering him on. He saw her wave and then his ski caught the wave from the wake. Exactly what happened after that was difficult to remember. First his right ski tried to separate his leg from his body. Not able to accomplish that, it settled for slapping him in the back and leg several times. He knew that Buck would drop one ski and continue on the other. Mike figured if he shook his leg, the ski should drop off and he would slalom like a pro. He lost balance and both skis flew off while he skidded along the surface on his back. Mike skipped across the top of the water for what seemed like a half mile.

Why don't they stop? He finally determined he should let go of the towrope. The water slapped and tore at his flesh like meat hooks. The whole fall lasted about 0.5 seconds but when he finally stopped skipping and entered the water it was like being hit with a four by four. How could water be so hard? It took forever for the life jacket to finally float him out of the depths back to the surface. He coughed and hacked and spit up water. The people in the boat cheered wildly.

Don't they realize I'm dying? He wallowed in the waves, content to let the life jacket support the red ragged chunks of flesh still attached to his body as it could. In his blurry mental state, he knew he should apply a tourniquet to those extremities that had been torn off, but how? He knew both his arms were gone. He did a mental inventory and was shocked to find that all his body parts were still attached. He expected large chunks to be missing. Next, he checked for function. He could wiggle his toes and his fingers. He coughed again. Laughing waves slapped his face as he coughed again, nearly gagging.

The boat stopped to pick up the skis and then stopped again.

Why didn't they come to get him so he could die on land?

Finally, the boat pulled up. Jim shouted, "Hey Mike, that was so cool! You made it all the way around the lake before you fell. Was that really your first time? You were great!"

Mike was silent for just a moment, his eyes locked on Jim who was still laughing. Mike's brain finally kicked back into gear. "Yeah, it's not as hard as I thought. *Jim*, you should try." Mike barely managed to keep the evil smile off his lips.

"Can I?" Jim asked.

Patrick grinned. "Sure, just remember to tie the string on your swimsuit. Right Mike?" He held up Mike's swimsuit.

Grace bit her bottom lip and made a show of looking away while Linda covered her mouth and laughed out loud. Her black curls bouncing with the waves.

Journal
I nearly died today. I went water skiing! It was horrible. They were all laughing at me. You should have seen me mom. I think I know what I have to do next time so it is not so hard. I can't wait to do it again.

I hope you are coming for the 4th of July. You can't miss the picnic. Everyone comes.

Chapter 15   Fourth of July Bike

Mike sat on the back porch of the cottage Saturday morning whittling on a stick. He was making a sharp stick. Over the past few weeks, he had made several. Each one started off to be a barbed fishing spear but the more he worked on it, the more it began to resemble a hot dog stick. This morning he was examining the spear wondering if he should use it to spear some fish. It just needs a little more work. Ah, but then he would need something to roast the fish on. Something like a hot dog stick. He immediately began to make some more cuts, when he heard a mechanical noise and looked up.

"Hey that's not fair!" Mike shouted.

Jim and Eric each rode up the two track to the cottage on a brand-new stingray bike. Their long banana seats and high handlebars looked like something off TV.

"Man, those are neat! I wish I had a bike up here." Mike looked longingly at the fancy new bikes. One was a bright green apple, and the other was a deep purple.

Jim's face shown with pride. "We just got 'em. The folks said we could bring 'em up, but only for the fourth of July weekend. The best thing about them is we can each carry a passenger behind us on the banana seat. Here hop on."

Mike slid in behind Jim on his bike. Jim stood up on the pedals and the big knobby tires dug into the soft earth, throwing enough chunks of dirt up into the air to delight any kid.

They sped up and down the dirt road practicing sliding sideways and Eric showed Mike how easily the bike did a wheelie. After they exhausted all their tricks Jim said, "We thought the bikes would make it easier to go back down to the river."

"Cool, I'll go tell my folks,"

"Oh. Are your folks here for the fourth?"

"Oh, uh…No. I meant Aunt Lil and Uncle Vic but my folks are supposed to come tomorrow."

They spent much of the day looking for treasure along the river. At times they even remembered to look for arrowheads. With the bikes they were able to go further and they found riches beyond their belief.

"Hey look at this chair. We can put this in our tree fort at Mister Vanderkooi's."

"There's no webbing," Eric said.

"I can't get that in my back pack," said Jim. "It's full of bottles and the saw blade we found. You'll have to carry it."

Mike considered the aluminum frame of the chair. Thick black muck dropped on his shoes from one of the hollow tubes. Shreds of what might have been green nylon weave or maybe seaweed blew lightly in the wind. It was a great find. Mike hated to leave it.

I'll just hide it by the road and maybe Uncle Vic will drive me back for it."

"Good idea. Say, how far do you think we are from the farm."

Mike screwed up his forehead and calculated the distance.

"About 2 miles." He stated confidently. He had no idea how far a mile was but then neither did Jim.

"Sounds good. Let's go see him."

It was a while before Mike was convinced, they had found a safe place for his chair. He covered it with pine branches and leaves and then they headed for the road. He insisted that he go first and make sure there were no cars coming before the brothers brought up their bikes. Mike didn't want someone else to see where they were coming from and go looking for their treasure.

"Do you really think you'll catch fish with that frog?" Eric asked Jim.

"Sure, why not?"

"Well…" Eric pinched the flat disk between two fingers. "It looks like a Frisbee with legs." He handed it to Mike to examine.

"It *is* kinda flat, Jim," Mike said as he picked out a piece of gravel that was imbedded in what one could only speculate was the frog's belly.

"So? It's just like that new expensive freeze-dried bait I read about. You get him wet and he'll taste just as good as he would when he was fresh. Just drop him in my backpack." He turned and presented his backpack to Mike.

"Just don't forget which is your sandwich and which is the frog," Mike chided.

"I'm beginning to feel like that frog," Eric said as he wiped sweat from his forehead and climbed back on his bike. "We've been riding forever."

"Look!" Mike pointed through the heat waves coming off the asphalt. "There it is."

A light wind blew their way. "Hey, I can smell the hay."

Eric wrinkled his nose. "I don't think that's hay you smell. Maybe today isn't a good day to stop and see him."

" We have to at least go up to the fort he let us build and see if my chair will fit in it."

Mike practically flew up the two by fours nailed to the trunk that served as a ladder. "Wow, cool."

"Will it fit?" Jim called up.

"Never mind that... look what I found." He held something over the side of the platform for the other two boys climbing up to see.

"What is it?" Eric was up next. "Cool, can I have one?" "Yeah, there's one for each of us. I wonder what they're from."

Eric examined the brass cartridge in his hands. It's a lot bigger than the .22 that dad lets us shoot.

"Let's go ask Mister Vanderkooi."

They found the old farmer working on his tractor.

"Whatcha doin'?" Eric asked.

"Oh, the da... dern tractor quit workin'."

"Can we help?" Mike asked.

"No! I need to go to town to get a part but ma truck isn't workin' either and I don't feel like walkin' to town."

"Why don't you buy a new one?"

The farmer cackled. "That's what I like about you boys, you can always make me laugh."

"You want us to give you a ride?" Eric offered.

"Yeah, we could do that. We have room for two," Jim added.

Mister Vanderkooi looked at the bikes for the first time. "You know... that might work. I haven't ridden a bike in 50 years. When I was a kid, I went everywhere on my bike. 'Course it wasn't fancy like this one. I don't need anyone to ride me. I can ride the bike by myself."

Eric got off his bike and offered it to the farmer.

A big smile began to grow on the farmer's face. He ran his hand over the smooth plastic seat. "It looks real nice."

Eric pointed to the gearshift. "It pedals real easy too because it's a three speed. It's…"

"Eh… It's got a transmission? Well, never mind that. I can figure anything out. They say you never forget how to ride. Let me see."

He climbed on the bike and pushed off. "Whooo wee. This is great. Whooo, whooo!" He went around the circle in front of the barn. The bike was too small for him and his knees and elbows stuck out at odd angles. He had a grin on face so big it looked like his face would split.

"Go Go GO! You didn't forget," Mike hollered.

Mister Vanderkooi sped down the drive way and onto the road. He picked up speed as he started down the hill. The farm being at the top of the hill, the boys had a good view across the field.

"Boy, he's goin' real fast," Eric said

"Yeah, he's a lot braver than I am. When he gets to the turn, he's gonna have a tough time staying on the road."

"I wonder if he knows about hand brakes?" Jim asked.

"You don't think…?"

"I don't think he does!"

"Loooook OUT!"

"Owww." Mike sucked in between his teeth.

"My bike!" Eric shouted.

The boys were silent for a minute.

"Lucky for him it's all swamp," Mike observed quietly. "If he had gone off the road like that into the woods, he would hit at least five or six trees.

Mike looked at Jim. "Do you think we can find Eric's bike?"

Jim nodded to his brother who looked worried. "Yeah, I think the bike is ok. Only Mister Vanderkooi made it all the way to open water. The cattails and brush probably stopped the bike. You *know* it couldn't have gotten through all those briars."

"I gotta get my bike!" Eric shouted in a shaky voice, and headed down the drive at a sprint.

"What do you think Mike?" Jim looked worried.

"I think we should go get Uncle Vic."

"I think we better go see if Mister Vanderkooi is still alive."

"Well, something is splashing around out there. Let's go see."

Mike and Jim followed Eric down past the edge of the road and started into the brush. Before they got down to the edge of the swamp, Eric was already shouting back at them. "Everything's alright. I was pretty worried... but look! I found my bike and it still works."

Mister Vanderkooi slogged out of the water, covered from the wisps of hair on his head, to manure encrusted boots, in thick black gooey muck. "Everything ain't alright. I can barely walk. I'm all busted up." He stepped back on some more stable hassocks of grass, and pulled his way through the brush toward the boys, muttering and swearing. "I ain't never ridin' a bike again and if I ever get my hands on that bike I... I... well looky there." The farmer moved some brush away and lifted up an old rusty single speed bike. The front wheel was bent a little but the rest appeared intact, though encrusted with rust and enough vegetation to contain its own ecosystem. "Looks like I'm not the only one who's done that. You know..." he paused and scratched his muddy chin. "I could clean this up. Bet it would be good as new. You boys wouldn't be able to keep up with me then. You wait. Let's get 'er up to the barn and see what we can do." He started walking the bike down the road back to the farm and the others followed. Eric brought up the rear, looking over his bike for any significant injuries.

"What about your tractor?" Jim asked.

"Eh? What's that?"

"What about your tractor being busted?"

"Oh, well I guess we better get that taken care of first."

"Look out, a car is coming!" said Mike, "Hey it's Uncle Vic."

The car stopped with a jerk.

Uncle Vic looked again and his jaw dropped. "Axel, are you alright?" He asked, looking around presumably for the truck that must have dumped its full load on him.

"Never better." Axel grinned back, his milk white teeth contrasting to the black goo covering his face and the rest of his body. "Why do you ask?" A black glob dropped off his right ear onto the car door.

"Uh...You're a might dirty."

Axel looked a bit surprised that anyone would notice. "Oh, you know how it is working on a farm. Say... look what I found. I'm gonna fix it up and then I can go for a ride with the boys." He beamed like a six-year-old with his first two-wheeler.

"As soon as he gets his tractor fixed," Jim added.

"Hey Uncle Vic, could you pick up a part for him?" Mike piped in.

The farmer nodded his head. "Yeah, great idea. I'll just ride into town with ya." He handed Mike his bike and opened the passenger side door.

Uncle Vic's eyes flashed as he stared at Axel in horror. "But Axel, I uh…"

"What?" Axel looked back at Uncle Vic with the innocent eyes of a child.

Uncle Vic's eyes were fixed upon a glob of black debris resembling a cow pie hanging from his elbow, poised to leap upon his immaculate car seat.

"Ah… don't you want to clean up your new bike while I run to town. You just tell me what you need."

"Say that's a good idea… still…" he said, his black crusty boot, poised above Aunt Lilly's clean carpet. Something within the black goo squirmed. "Yeah you write down what I need and I'll clean up the bike."

"You might want to clean up yourself."

"Here's some money." Axel reached into his pocket and handed Uncle Vic a handful. A couple of presidents peered out from under the handful of mud.

To Mike, it looked as though Abe held his nose.

The boys helped hose off the bike and offered to hose off Mister Vanderkooi also. Unfortunately, while hosing him down did get rid of most of the big chunks, the scent bloomed.

They were just about done when Mike stuck his hand in his pocket and remembered the shell casings they found in the fort. "Hey Mister Vanderkooi, we found these in the fort. Do you know what they are from?"

"Oh, you found those didjya. I… uh… I thought you'd like 'em. I had to shoot a cow. It had a busted leg. I thought you'd like to use 'em to play war."

"Gee thanks! You climbed up in the fort just to put those there for us? Thanks!" Mike looked at the cartridge with new respect. It seemed to burn into his fingers. He didn't know whether to be afraid or to thrill in its power.

"What kinda bullet is it?

"It's a 30.06 cartridge."

"Cool." Mike turned the shell over in his hands. The boys all gazed at it in awe. This was a shell from a gun that actually killed something.

Uncle Vic pulled into the driveway.

"Say that reminds me." He went back into the house.

When he returned, he had a small grocery bag. "Here Vic, I don't have enough room in my freezer for all this beef. The meat is good, but I suspect she'd been eaten' down in the swamp, the meat tastes a little like venison."

Uncle Vic bit his bottom lip and said "Uh… Thanks."

Mike continued to turn over the cartridge in his hands. It whispered to Mike, but what did it say? "I am death. Fear me," he heard. Then "I can feed you and protect you. Care for me." Then it tried to say, "I am a toy. Play with…' but Mike shook his head and stuffed it in his pocket.

Chapter 16   Fourth of July Raspberries

Early morning was one of the best times for lying on the dock. The sun shone brightly but it wasn't hot yet and the wind hadn't come up enough to cause waves. Looking into the lake was like looking into a zoo in your basement. You could watch through a plate glass floor where crayfish danced and turtles made special guest appearances.

Small fish hung suspended above the bottom at the end of the dock waiting for handouts like a pack of hungry dogs. Many mornings they were rewarded with left over crusts of toast from breakfast or pea sized balls rolled from stale bread, but today they just hung there, an audience for the floorshow on the stage above their heads.

The dock was shaped like a capital T with the cross section in the deepest water. Jim dealt the battered cards, lying on his stomach on the dock, his feet stretched out toward the shore, a sleepy beagle spread out at his feet. Mike, Little John and Eric all sat cross-legged at the top of the T. Eric had the least room, his back toward the fish but being the smallest, he was used to it.

It was a beautiful scene of incredible peace and tranquility that could make an excellent garnish to a lifetime of memories. A gifted artist might paint such a scene. A poet would easily expend a thousand words on the serenity expressed by each layer of nature from the still unmoving green leaves, the lazy circles of gliding hawks to the patient, peaceful sleep of the multicolored hound. Into the peace slid the sounds of the cards sliding into a casual pile in front of each boy, but with each card Jim dealt while lying on his stomach, he extended some muscles in very awkward positions. The inevitable happened and a very loud, very rude sound ripped from his posterior.

Mike snickered, followed by light laughter all around.

The beagle stood up and sniffed.

Fresh laughter.

The beagle walked up to Jim's rear and sniffed hard.

Eric snorted and snot shot out his nose.

Uncontrolled laughter, tears and choking. Little John made gagging noises; Mike slapped Eric's shoulder.

The beagle then did the unimaginable. His long pink tongue flicked out and the dog... licked Jim's butt.

Laughter exploded in gushers. The dock shook and rocked on its saw horse base sending out ripples in the water.

Little John pounded on the deck with his fist.

Mike grabbed his stomach. He laughed so hard he couldn't get air. He thought he would die.

"Ewww," Little John groaned through his alternating coughing and high pitched, "Hee hee hee"

Eric rocked back and forth, tears rolling down his face.

Mike couldn't get enough air but it didn't matter. He coughed, choked, wheezed, hacked, laughed and did everything but inhale. He realized one might actually die laughing but he didn't care. His stomach hurt from continuous contraction so badly that he wasn't sure he could ever make it work right.

Jim rolled back and forth on the dock.

The bewildered beagle looked from one boy to the other trying to decide what was wrong with them. In the end he went back and lay in the sun.

Every time one boy started to get control of himself, one of the others would make a rude sound and off they went.

It was inevitable, Eric rocked too far back and over he went with a splash. This, of course, triggered a new peak of uncontrolled hilarity.

When Eric emerged, Jim was on his hands and knees on the end of the dock looking in. "You alright?"

Eric reached up, grabbed the dock with one hand, Jim with the other, and pulled his brother in.

None of the boys could utter a complete sentence for an exhausting eternity without laughing.

"I have to go up and eat," Little John gasped. "My stomach hurts." He bent over rubbing it.

"If it was a little smaller, ...ouch ...ouch, it wouldn't hurt so much." Jim giggled.

"Heee... Hee... Ouch, ouch, oh it hurts, don't make me laugh it hurts too much. My jaws ache from smiling," Mike laughed and groaned.

Little John made his way slowly up the hill heading toward home.

"Come on Jim. Let's go."

Mike made his way slowly up the hill still giggling. He glanced over at Linda's cottage. Someone was shouting. Mike stopped giggling and then stopped walking.

SLAM! Something crashed down on a table. CRASH! Something else banged down.

The back door flew open and Linda shot out obviously crying. She ran toward the road.

"Linda?" Mike wasn't even aware he spoke.

She turned and ran toward him. She flung her arms around him and sobbed.

Mike's arms hung at his side. He was an only child. He had never had anything like this happen before. It seemed like he was supposed to put his arms around her and say something, but he was so startled that nothing came to mind. His body rocked with each of her shaky sobs.

He slowly and awkwardly put his arms around her. His arms felt like the stiffest of oak branches. He just held her while her body shook. A long shaky breath followed each sob. Her hot face pressed against his shoulder while tears drenched his neck.

He had wondered sometimes what it would be like to hold her but this wasn't what he expected. His hands started to shake and his eyes burned, but he didn't know why. Finally, he wet his lips and said, "It's all right, it's all right, you're gonna be fine." That's what his mom always told him. "Are you hurt?" She shook her head and pulled away from him.

His arms opened but remained extended, reluctant to let go of Linda, yet wanting this uncomfortable situation to leave.

Without a word she walked down toward the always waiting lake.

Mike was still breathing hard. He felt something on his cheek and touched it with his fingers. A tear had sneaked out and trickled down his cheek. Linda reached the top of the hill and Mike didn't know what to do so he headed over to the hammock to watch her. He swung in the hammock slowly as she trod down the long steps wiping her eyes. It looked like she might be limping. Maybe she hurt herself?

Mike looked over to her cottage. Maybe he should go tell her mother that Linda was crying. But it occurred to him, she came out of the house crying, so her mom must know it. It made no sense to him. Why didn't her mom come out to comfort her?

He swung back and forth watching Linda sit on the dock for a long time. She didn't read or anything. She didn't even sun bathe. Odd, as he thought about it for the first time. He had never seen her in a bathing suit. She usually wore long sleeves and pants even when it was hot. Her mother almost never came out of the house either. What is wrong with this family?

The miner adjusted the straps on his backpack as he headed up the side of another rocky hill. The sun beat down on his browned forehead and great rivers of sweat flowed down the sides of his head. He wiped his eyes with the back of his arm and continued his journey. He had wandered this mountain range 25 years looking for gold but never found more than enough to keep him going. He was hot. He was tired. It took a passel of gold to feed both him and his mule and today the hot sun just made it worse. He had to keep going or he wouldn't make it through the winter. He looked back toward his faithful comrade and crested the hill pulling on the reins of his mule. "Come on Esmerelda…" With that he peered over the top of the hill. "Glory be. We hit the mother lode." He slapped his mule on the back and the mule slapped him back.

"Hey," the mule hollered as he set down the pack and became Eric. "Raspberries everywhere!"
"Wow."
"I saw 'em first."
"Oh, there's lots for all of us." Little John sauntered up last of the group as usual. He reached past the others and grabbed a few sun-warmed berries and popped them into his mouth.

Two hours later, covered with sweat, dirt, and red raspberry juice, they dragged their feet along the dirt road heading back to the south side of the lake. Each carried a small pail of berries.
"I wish we were back at the lake." Jim whined.
"Yeah, I'd jump in clothes and all." Eric agreed.
Mike and little John remained silent as if the effort to talk took too much energy.
An expensive looking Buick Electra bustled down the road

toward the lake, raising a deep cloud of dust to the tree tops and shooting gravel in random directions. Suddenly it ground to a halt and backed up.

The boys looked up, startled.

"It's Doc Jacobson" Little John grinned. "Nice car. I bet it's air conditioned. Don't you wish you were him?"

The whir of an electric window sounded alien out here in the country and the doctor's appearance didn't fit either. His suit coat and white shirt bore testimony to the air-conditioned comfort inside the car. "You boys alright? You haven't been fighting, have you?" The doctor stuck his head out into the heat. His thin black tie hung out the air conditioning like a dog's tongue on a hot day.

"No. We're fine." Jim stated. The boys looked at each other questioningly.

"What's that on your faces? It looks like blood." Worry lines stood out on his forehead as he studied them closely.

"Little John held out his pail. "It's raspberries. Want some?"

The doctor looked at the bucket, reached out his window, tenderly picked out two and placed them in his mouth. He closed his eyes and leaned his head back against the headrest. The worry lines disappeared as he loosened his tie and sighed.

"Mmm. Boy, that brings back memories. That's the best medicine I've had in years." He opened his eyes and looked back at the boys. This time a deep satisfying chuckle rolled from his belly as he took in the big red smears on their faces. "You boys must have had a great morning."

They all nodded vigorously.

"I sure wish I was one of you. You want a ride?"

Their jaws dropped. "Really? That would be great."

"I've never been in a car with air conditioning before."

"Me either."

They slid down the road in air-conditioned luxury and the road flew by. Mike sat in the back seat and gazed out the window.

"Mister President?" one of his many aides said.

Riding in the huge black presidential limousine, the President of the United States of America lifted his mind from trying to feed the world, and looked toward Jim Swanson, his aide. "Yes Jim?" he asked in his powerful baritone.

"All these people came out to thank you for ending the war, and bringing our troops home safely."

The President nodded knowingly. He was exhausted. It had been a hard negotiation that probably no one else in the free world could have handled. In the end, he had had to arm-wrestle their President to get him to agree to the final terms.

Now, rows and rows of people stared and waved, as the car drove on taking him to his presidential retreat at Camp David.

The President waved and the crowd exploded with cheers and waved in response.

"Mike... Mike? What are you doin'?" Jim asked.

The boys stared at him as he waved out the window.

"Uh...waving at the cows," he stated. "See they are waving back." He pointed to a small herd under a tree swishing flies away with their tails.

"You're nuts." Jim said.

"Hey, they are!" Little John waved at the cows.

"You're both nuts." Jim shook his head.

The doctor spoke up with his parent voice. "You boys were quite a way from the lake, weren't you? Your parents know where you were?"

"Oh yeah, we've been a lot farther out." Jim stated with authority. Like that time a couple weeks ago when we went all the way to the river looking for arrowheads."

The doctor sucked in a sudden breath, "Did you find any?" he asked excitedly, sounding more like one of the boys than the boys did.

"Not this time."

"I found something I thought was one but the others said it wasn't." Little John said.

"You hold onto *anything* that even looks like it was sharp on one side. The Indians made all sorts of tools for skinning, punching holes, and even hatchets for cutting wood. I have a collection with arrowheads, spearheads, hatchets and skinning knives. They are all beautiful, works of art formed by the earliest sculptors. Art that could save a man and his family's lives. Most aren't worth much but some are. I have one spear head for which a gentleman from Chicago offered me $10,000."

"Wow really?"

"Did you sell it? I would."

"Yeah, wow."

"No, I didn't sell it. I like to collect them. If you boys find any, let me see them and maybe I'll buy them if you are willing to sell."

The boy all grew quiet. Each calculating precisely what they could buy with $10,000.

"Well, here you go." The doctor dropped them off in front of the Swanson's cottage and drove off with a wave.

Stepping out of the air-conditioned car, the heat assaulted them ten times harder than when they had stepped in.

"Wow. Is it hot!" Little John said. "Sure, glad we're back, so we can go swimming."

Little John started trotting of towards his house to change, but looked back when no one was following. They were looking at the ground. "Hey guys aren't you goin' swimmin'?"

They all shook their heads.

"I'm looking for arrowheads." Mike said.

Journal

Dr. Jacobson gave us a ride in his air conditioned car and told us about an arrow head he was offered $15,000 for. We looked but still haven't found one. Tommorrow is the big picnic I can hardly wait. I'm going to have three hamburgers and three helpings of shortcake. Everyone will be there. Maybe Linda's family won't. Something strange happened today. Linda was crying. She ~~must~~ might have been hurt.

Mike paused a long time thinking about it before he continued.

and no one did anything to help.

Chapter 17   Fourth of July Bearies

Mike struggled to keep the picnic table from dragging in the dirt but he wasn't quite tall enough.

"Heavier than it looks, isn't it?" Uncle Vic stated from his end of the old picnic table.

"Yeah," Mike grunted and picked it up again. "How... (pant)... far we... (pant)... gotta go?"

"Just to the clearing between the cabins. Let's rest a minute."

Mike dropped his end, sat down and rubbed the dents out of his hands.

Linda came bouncing out of her cottage. "Hi Mickey, whatcha doin'?"

"Mike! Mike is my name! What's it look like? We're getting ready for the big picnic," he declared in exasperation. Then in a softer voice, "Uh...Are you coming?"

"Sure. Can I sit next to you?" her face glowed with excitement.

"Uhhh..." Visions of the guys' reactions to seeing her sitting next to him made him squirm.

"That would be fine for your family to sit next to ours," Uncle Vic answered. His eyes danced back and forth between the two.

Linda dashed back into the cottage.

"Thanks," Mike said, relieved at his uncles wording and hoping his voice sounded adequately depressed but inside he felt ...what? He let out a long breath that sounded an awful lot like one of his uncles.

As Linda ran back in the house, Uncle Vic grinned at Mike and winked. This just confused Mike even more.

The two of them finished positioning the table. Aunt Lilly fussed over the tablecloth. It was not nearly clean enough or new enough and it would probably be all dirty before they sat down that afternoon.

"Then what you putting it on now for," Uncle Vic grumbled.

"I want to see how it looks." She smiled back at him. "Why don't you two find some nice flowers to put on the table?"

"I got things to do," Uncle Vic grunted.

She patted his arm with a light chuckle, "I know." She looked at Mike.

Mike looked toward the lake. "I, uh… got things to do."

Uncle Vic chuckled and his aunt laughed out loud.

A screen door slammed and Linda drifted slowly over toward the table dragging her feet. She walked toward Mike but looked at her feet. "Mom says we can't come." She sounded close to tears.

"OH, let me go talk to her," aunt Lilly said cheerfully.

Linda looked up hopefully.

"Get her to bring one of her pies," Uncle Vic tossed over his shoulder as he headed toward the shed.

"Oh, what a good idea," she replied.

A few minutes later Aunt Lilly came out. "Mike why don't you and Linda go pick some of those blackberries on the north side of the Lake."

"Me and Linda?" He looked at her uncomfortably. "Why can't I go with the guys? Hey wait! I don't want to miss the picnic."

She walked over and hugged him. "You won't miss it. It's not until 5:00 and it's not even ten yet."

He squirmed away from her embrace. "What do you want the blackberries for anyway?"

"Linda's mom is going to make a pie for the picnic."

"We can go?" Linda squealed.

"Sure you can honey." She put her hand on Linda's shoulder. Mike there are two small buckets you can use in the shed. You better get hustling."

"I… It'll go faster if I get Jim, Eric and Little John. Well… maybe not Little John he eats too many."

"These taste great but they're awful seedy," Jim said dropping another large handful into the bucket.

"My mom puts them through a strainer I think." Linda said.

"The seeds don't bother the bears." Eric grinned wickedly. "My grandpa says grandma was over here picking berries one time…" he looked around to make sure they were all listening closely.

Linda's mouth hung open and her eyes bulged. "What? There's bears around here?"

"Ohhh, yeahhh," Eric nodded.

"Eric..." Mike started. He stood behind Linda, pointed at her and shook his head.

"You really think there's bears around here?" a shaky voice asked almost ready to cry.

Mike looked over to the speaker, who looked ready to run. "No, Little John there are no bears around." As soon as Little John had heard someone was going berry picking, he wouldn't be left behind.

"Sure there is. That's why they call them bearies. Get it? B-e-a-r-i-e-s? Anyway, grandma was over here picking berries and..."

"Eric..." Mike began.

"No, let him go on I want to hear." Linda stepped closer to Eric.

"Grandma was picking berries." Eric restarted.

"You said that," Mike stated impatiently.

"Well, let me finish. Grandma was picking berries with grandpa and she saw a real thick patch like this one over here by little John."

Little John moved away from the patch. "I don't want to hear," he said, slapping his hands over his ears. "I'm not listening. La la la la la la la la la..."

"Be quiet."

"What?" Little John lowered his hands.

"So, Gram goes over to the bush and fills her bucket. Grandpa walks up behind her and without looking she hands the bucket to him and tells him to take it for a minute but he drops it. She turns to holler at him ...and it's not Grandpa."

"No! Don't say it. It's... it's bad luck." Little John slapped his hands back over his ears. "La la la la la la la..."

Eric paused to savor the expressions of his audience.

"Maybe I shouldn't go on," he said looking slyly at the crowd.

"Did it eat her?" Linda gasped.

Jim pushed her shoulder. "You saw her this morning, silly."

"Oh yeah." Linda flushed.

"Well, according to grandpa she jumped straight up into the air about eight feet, somersaulted over the bear, and ran half way round the lake in 30 seconds... on her hands. Then Grandma jumps in and says 'Yes, and I could a done it in less time if Grandpa hadn't been hiding under my skirt shouting, "Hit 'im! Hit 'im!"

"She did not," Jim said rolling his eyes.

"You calling Grandpa a liar?" Eric looked at each of them.

"Then she sees the bear eating her berries and she gets mad. She runs back and hollers at the bear, beating it on the snout with Grandpa's hat. Grandpa jumps in and says, 'It woulda been fine if she had bothered to take it out of my coat pocket first.'"

"What's wrong with that?" Mike asked.

"He was still wearing the coat."

"Really?" Little John's jaw hung slack.

They all laughed.

Jim hit Eric, "That's stupid. I don't believe any of it. Grandpa's always making up those stories." Jim turned his back and went back to picking.

"Come on, he's just making jokes," Mike said and walking a little way away began picking berries. Linda followed, *very* closely.

"What was that?" Little John flew back up to the dirt road.

"What?"

"I heard something."

"Oh, don't you start."

Linda looked around nervously. "I think we have enough berries."

"Don't let Little John scare you."

"I'm not afraid," Jim said, "but I do think we've got enough berries for two pies."

"Are you sure? What if she wants to make three?" Mike looked down into the bucket and something on the ground caught his eye. "Boy, look at the size of that dog's..." He stopped talking when he realized it was *not* the footprint of a dog.

"What?" Linda studied his face and then followed his eyes down just as he stepped forward.

He reached into the pail, "...of that dog gone blackberry." He held up a big one and stepped forward obscuring the footprint.

He glanced around nonchalantly, Eric continued to pick while the other three watched him.

"Come on Mike, let's go." Little John stood in the road and looked up the hill anxiously.

Mike looked at Linda. The bear could be anywhere ready to leap on them. He had read that bears could run fast. If we run, it will chase us. The image of a bear leaping on Linda, attacking her savagely leapt into his mind. What would Buck do? He grit his teeth. It would not happen. He would not let anything hurt Linda. If they got to the road and over the next hill where all the houses were, they should be safe. He knew what to do.

"You guys go ahead; I'll be right there."

"Okay. Com'on, let's go."

"I'll wait and go with Mike," Linda said.

"No, you go with them. I... I just want... to be alone."

She looked at him oddly then, "Oh I know...." she giggled, "Boys pee in the woods."

Mike blushed. "Yeah, I got to go." He did a little dance. "I'll see you in a bit."

She giggled. "Okay. I'll take the bucket."

"Maybe Mike needs the bucket," Jim chided.

Mike's breath came in gulps as he watched them work their way to the road. His eyes darted around the brush. He quickly snatched up some rocks. The weeds were moving there. He wound up but stopped in mid swing as Eric's head popped out of the weeds. Mike watched each of his friends climb the bank to the road, making sure they were to the road before he proceeded. He knelt down in the weeds, sneaking in a low crouch to the next rise, he resumed visual scanning.

The bear frequently heard people in his woods. Normally he quietly ignored them but these people were in his food source. He was hungry; the winter had been hard and long, using up his entire fat reserve. The people who came up here for the summers didn't throw out food in pits behind the cottages anymore. He was forced to live off the land, but humans still smelled like food to him. These days his stomach nearly always cried for food. Animals were hard to catch except the small slow ones. He had eaten a porcupine a week before; flipping it on its back to get to the soft belly. The needles festering in his snout didn't add to his disposition. He moved slowly forward, investigating the people in his berry patch.

The Army Ranger scanned the foliage. Any bush might conceal the enemy, ready to blow him away at their pleasure. There was little chance of returning alive but he knew someone must delay the enemy to allow the friendlies to escape. He had volunteered for this mission knowing full well that he was the only one who could do it. He slowly slithered to higher ground, careful to make no sound, which might betray his presence to the enemy. He concealed himself in the bushes on the slope just below the hill.

Here he could watch his comrade's head up the road toward the hilltop where a chopper would pick them up and still watch the brush where the enemy waited. He reviewed his resources carefully; placing a couple grenades within easy reach where they would be handy if he needed them. He settled back to wait for the attack that he *knew* would come.

The bear knew one small animal remained. People were dangerous. Normally he avoided them, but this one was small and alone at the top of this short hill. He had seen how slow they were. His stomach rumbled again. He knew he could cover the 50 yards as fast as any deer.

The Army Ranger had told them there was no danger. He took one last look at his friends. They were a long way down the road, almost to the top of the hill and to safety. He imagined his friends seeing his body when he was brought back. Would they realize he died to save them? His stomach growled. He *hoped* it was his stomach. He would miss the picnics at the lake. What he would give for one more bowl of sweet strawberry shortcake before he died. He could taste it, drenched in whipped cream, homemade baking-powder biscuits, hot from the oven, soaking up the luscious juice until each glorious bite was a foretaste of heaven.

The bear knew it was better to get closer. Too many things can happen. He crept up the hill slowly. He moved amazingly quietly for such a large animal.

It does not matter if there is a bear here or not Mike reasoned. He wouldn't wait to find out. *Strawberry shortcake* was being served tonight! Mike jumped up and ran up the slope, his feet clawing through the gravel and rocks onto the road, moving as fast as he could, knocking stones down the hill bouncing into the brush. He heard a roar and looked back. "Bear!" He screamed. He didn't run... he flew!

The bear had crept quietly toward the small person sitting on the hillside. He could see him now standing up. A shower of rocks flew down on the bear as the person jumped up and ran. His eyes blinked as several hit him in the face. One of the larger rocks hit right squarely on his sensitive nose on top of a festering porcupine needle. He roared in agony and stood on his back legs. More rocks and gravel showered down upon his sensitive nose.

With all the noise the others made, they never heard Mike until he was almost to them. Linda turned first and saw red faced Mike sprinting up the hill, a bear standing on the edge of the blackberry patch they had just come from.

"BEAR!" She shouted, as Mike passed them all.

If Grandma had been there, Mike would have beaten her back to the cottage… even though the wide-eyed Little John rode on his back, clutching desperately to a bucket of blackberries.

Chapter 18   The Most Beautiful Day Ever

Have you ever seen so much good food? Jim asked.

"Yeah, last year at the same picnic," Little John grinned as he shoved his third grilled hamburger in his mouth. Ketchup and mustard dripped from it onto a paper plate.

"I mean what could be better? How could life get better than this?"

"My folks could be here," Mike grumbled.

"I suppose. Are they coming up at all this summer?" Jim asked

"I don't know," Mike said morosely. "Dad said they would try to make it this weekend but it looks like he had to work again."

The sound of singing cut off their conversation. They turned to see four men gathered around in a circle, singing with broad smiles on each face. The four-part harmony of the impromptu barber shop quartet brought a hush to the rest of the families gathered around.

"Boy, that's neat," Jim said.

"Shhh!" Little John motioned with his hand.

Mike trotted over to the circle and listened in slack jawed amazement to the incredible harmonies and intricacies of sound that seemed too mystical to emanate from someone's dad. He did not know sound could be so sweet. He closed his eyes and the sounds took physical form, gently lifting him by his ears, and carrying him up into the clouds. The chords and emotions were richer than he ever thought music could be. When the tenor hit an incredibly high note, cheers arose from the families and Mike opened his eyes. The music broke amid the laughter and scattered applause. The magic was over, but Mike would carry that music forever. If only he could sing like that...

"Hey Mike, look what I got!" Eric shouted.

"It's just a box of caps." Mike said. "I used to have a cap gun when I was a kid but it broke.

"Com'on back here. I'll show you what we can do," Eric said slyly.

Back behind Jim and Eric's storage barn Eric showed Mike. "See... you stick the pin through each cap and fold the caps back and forth until the pin is sticking though every cap in the roll. This connects all the gunpowder in each cap. Then you carefully pull out the pin and tape this match to it."

Eric inspected his handiwork in triumph. "One regulation Fourth of July firecracker."

"Wow! That's neat. Let's light it off."

"Not here."

"Across the road by the swamp. No one would know who did it. I don't know why grownups are such a pain about firecrackers."

To every craftsman a highly functional creation is extremely pleasing and the firecracker's volume and destructive power was exceptionally satisfying. After Eric left, Mike began his own crafting. He had purchased three and a half rolls of caps from Eric for one slightly used paper shotgun shell Uncle Vic had given him.

Eric had used one roll of caps. Mike's would be better. He used two rolls. Mike got all the caps pierced and folded over but he couldn't get the pin out. It seemed to slide out so easily for Eric but the friction of the powder against the side of the needle of two rolls prevented it from coming out. What should he do? Maybe he should twist it. He held the firecracker in one hand and the pin in the other. About the time his hand began to twist, his brain began to think it might not be a good idea because friction created heat...

He felt it more than heard it.

Explosion! Flash, shocking pain, horror!

His body rocked with the blast but it paled compared to the blast of terror that assaulted his brain. Catastrophe of this sort had never entered his fragile young life. One twist and his world view changed forever.

HE COULD NOT SEE! He could not see! His eyes stung from the shards of explosives tearing into them. He could not see! His hands throbbed, burned, and tingled with undistinguishable pains. The pain was different than any he had ever known, but he knew... he couldn't feel his fingers!

OH GOD!

OH GOD!

What am I going to do? I can't see. I'm blind! OH GOD! I can't read. I can't play football or anything. Oh God. His body quivered and he choked in little sips of air.

Mike blinked and blinked.

Oh God what am I going to do? OH GOD!!!

It felt like gravel and fire cratered his eyes but... maybe... hey! He could distinguish some light and dark patches.

Oh, please God PLEASE, heal me please God! Please do a miracle!

He rubbed at his eyes with his wrists unwilling to touch them with the bloody stubs on his hand. The exposed bones would make it worse.

He opened his eyes. It was blurry and his eyes stung, but he could still see! *Thank you, God!* Maybe he would need special glasses but he could SEE! He needed to examine what was left of his hands but he was afraid to look down.

"Oh God." He prayed unable to think of anything else to say.

If there were still stubs of fingers, he would be able to get by, but without fingers... He slowly rolled over his blackened hands. His shock was complete. His blackened hands stung, his face stung, but everything was still there. *Thank you, thank you God!*

You are so good to me! Thank-you, God. I don't deserve it. *That was really stupid. That was close,* he thought. *I will never do anything like that again.* He gasped in a great lungful of air in relief, walking in nervous circles to burn off the tension.

Silence hung in the woods as even the birds and insects tried to recover from the explosive violation of their environment. He closed his stinging eyes in silent prayer, thanking God for the miracle He had performed.

He opened his eyes; they were gradually getting better.

"Wow." He said out loud in relief. Horror slapped both sides of his face... He was deaf!

Mike stumbled in a near faint. He knew he said something but he didn't hear it. He was deaf. He was deaf. He was deaf. His relief in seeing was forgotten. He was deaf!

It wasn't the woods were quiet. He just couldn't hear the birds and insects. He was alone with his silence. His chest heaved but he couldn't hear the breathing. *Oh God Oh God Oh God help me! I'm sorry I'm sorry I'm sorry. I shouldn't have done it. Oh God God. I'll never hear singing again. I'll...*

What was that? He heard something. He whistled loudly. He

could barely hear it. *Thank you, Lord. I can hear!* Maybe he would need a hearing aid like the one Uncle Oscar wore in his pocket but... He whistled some more. It's coming back! He heard a bird song and looked up as it got louder. As his sight had come, so his hearing returned slowly but it returned like a tender caress to his face from God. The sky was beautiful, the trees glorious works of art. No aria of Handel was more exquisite than the gentle cooing of the mourning dove along the gravel road. It was the most beautiful evening of his life!

"Mickey," Linda called from the two track. "I saved you a piece of blackberry pie."

"That's the most wonderful thing I ever heard," he laughed. "You have the *sweetest* voice I EVER HEARD." Was that a halo around her head? Or was it just the sun behind her, filtered through the mist in his eyes. He grinned hugely.

Her responding smile outshone the sun.

"Hey Mike," Little John called from down the road. "My dad brought up some firecrackers. Want to help light 'em off?"

"Uh... No thanks. I am going have some pie with Linda. Then I am going for a walk in the woods. Aren't the bird's songs beautiful? Look at that sunset. It's gorgeous."

Throwing aside his blackened shirt, he raced with Linda back toward the table. He did not care what the guys thought. He and Linda laughed together as Mike slapped the leaves of the passing trees and then paused to touch the bark of an old birch. Mikes eyes danced to Linda's as he heaped great mountains of whipped cream onto the flakey crust of the enormous slab of blackberry pie that she held for him. Her eyes never left his.

It was the most beautiful day he had ever seen, and tomorrow would be beautiful and then next day too. No day would ever be ugly, no sound, unpleasant. He had discovered joy!

Journal

Blackberries make the best pie ever. Maybe that is because you have to work so hard for them. You taste the sunshine and the dew. You smell the sunny dust of the road that you walked down to get them and you see the stains in the creases of the hands that picked them, holding yours. You put some whipped cream on it and the flavors mingle into pure joy. Today I really saw grains of sand for the first time. It is soft and beautiful. It whispers secrets about where it came from when you rub it between your fingers. No two handfuls are the same. I threw it into the air and the wind shaped it into wild animals, the sunset colored it with rainbows and green ferns framed it in life.

I watched a chipmunk dance on a log stuffing itself on a big juicy strawberry I gave it. I know God gave it stripes for camouflage but why did he make them stripes?

I had thirds on shortcake. Aunt Lil never made it better. Whip cream slides around your mouth and breaks into small tickling sweetness. How do I tell the differences in how things feel? Why does paper feel different than wood? Life is amazing. God is a genius. I think I will spend the night down on the dock watching His stars. Who knows what other secrets he might want to share with me? Ever notice how words have beautiful shapes. Sometimes they even sound like what they mean, like JOY! Even the Y has its hands raised!

P.S. Notice how I spelled every word right!

"Mike!" Uncle Vic called from the darkness in front of the cottage. "Come down here."

Mike set the journal aside and jumped off the old sofa that he used as bed and bedroom. He ran around the cottage toward the lake. "What is it?"

"I want you to see this."

"What?"

A sudden flash in the sky answered for him, as flowers of red and green lights covered the lake.

The pops and crackles of home fireworks being shot off around the lake were interrupted by a huge BOOOMawhoomamawhoom. The echoes rattled around the docks to be answered by oohs and ahhs from the people sitting on their docks watching.

Mike walked down slowly toward the dock sheltered behind his tall uncle. He had a new attitude toward fireworks. His uncle was about to give him an even deeper view.

Aunt Lilly was already sitting on a chair on the dock and Mike dropped to the dock, his legs dangling into the warm gentle water of night.

Another rocket shot off. It spanned Mike's entire field of view engulfing his whole being in sparkling streams of golden starlight. The boooom shook his chest as if to say, 'did you see that?' Then the darkness of night returned making the memory of the light all the greater.

Mike was barely aware of the sound behind him. His uncle's voice was low but solid. "Francis Scott Key was negotiating a prisoner exchange when he was held on a British warship during the war of 1812. All he could do was watch as the British bombarded Ft. McHenry. It was a dark, rainy night and he couldn't see the fort's flag, his people's flag, his country's flag. He wrote down those words."

Uncle Vic took in a deep noisy breath and recited the poem in slow deliberate power. Emphasizing each word with the strength they gathered through the decades of bloodshed for her.

"O say can you see by the dawn's early light, What so proudly we hailed at the twilight's last gleaming? Whose broad stripes and bright stars through the perilous fight, O'er the ramparts we watched were so gallantly streaming? And the rockets' red glare, the bombs bursting in air, Gave proof through the night that our flag was still there. O say does that Star-Spangled Banner yet wave O'er the land of the free and the home...." Uncle Vic's voice cracked. "Of the brave?"

The two men leaned over the railing of the ship. They had been heedless to the cannon balls that threw up splinters from the wooden ship holding them captive. Blood slicked the deck and their feet ground over the sand that had been spread before the battle for traction.

Both sides stopped firing hours ago, but now what had happened? Dark rain soaked their clothes and chilled them to the bone.

"Do you see it, Francis? I can't see anything. Oh God, let them stand," his voice cracked.

"No, I do not see it and the British sent several gunboats to the west to slip around and make a landing. I fear she is lost."

"There, the sky is beginning to light. Do you see it, sir?"

"I cannot tell."

They moved to the stern of the ship to get a slightly better view.

"She held through most of the night, I know it, and that was during a terrible barrage. I could see it in the glare of those vile rocket attacks."

"Those men have taken a beating. God, be kind to them. Give them strength."

"They'll stand. I know those men. They will stand, though it cost them all."

Long hours they had stood there and yet they continued staring in the darkness, waiting, hoping and praying.

Francis sucked in his breath. "THERE!"

"YES! THERE! I SEE IT!" He slammed his fist down on the railing of the British warship. "SHE STANDS!" He shouted. "She stands... proudly." His voice cracked and tears flowed freely down the young man's face. "They will stand," He slapped Francis on the back. Wonder, fierce pride, a resolve of purpose mixed in the emotions of his voice. "And they will stand today, tomorrow, always..."

The fireworks continued but Mike stood up from the dock where he had been sitting, in tribute to the men who could not stand after that battle or any of the many battles in the 200 years since. He looked down to his hands still tender from the firecracker and remembered the horror he had when he thought he had lost them. His mind could see the men who had lost their hands...for him. Men like Buck, who gave up their lives that he should have his. He did not dare to look at his aunt and uncle lest they see his tears, but solemnly stepped off the dock. Once away from the dock he wiped his eyes and quietly ascended the stairs. It was only as he climbed that he dared turn his tear-filled eyes back to the dock and saw his uncle wipe his own eyes.

Mike nodded and ascended the steps.

Chapter 19 To the Dump

After breakfast Mike was picking through an impenetrable tangle of fishing line and hooks wondering if he soaked the mass in water long enough, the dried worm glue would soften so that he would be able to salvage some hooks with a hammer.

"Come on Mike," Uncle Vic called. "We have to take the garbage to the dump."

Mike jumped up and grabbed a garbage can. "The dump! Yay! Can I bring anything back this time?"

"Probably not. Unless it is really small and does not stink. AND I am the one who decides if it stinks." Uncle Vic had learned *this* lesson well.

Mike loved the dump. He couldn't believe what treasures other people brought there, and now he had his fort out at the farm to fill.

Uncle Vic made sure the two silver cans were secure in the trunk and then went back into the cottage.

Mike had been sitting in the car ready for at least two hours, he was sure, before Uncle Vic came back out with a box under his arm. Mike could not figure out why adults took so long to do anything. He assumed the box was more garbage. "You aren't throwing that cool box away, are you?"

"No, I am not and no you can't have it." He slid the box carefully under the seat in the old Rambler. With a long noisy breath he stated, "Last night being the Fourth of July celebration got me thinking about a lot of things. Like how we got our freedoms."

Mike had heard these kinds of lectures before. They usually had lots of meaning for the adults but not too much for Mike. The commentary continued with Mike half-listening and half watching for the pit bulldozed into a field that was the dump. But something caught Mike's ear that he had never heard from an adult before.

"One of the reasons we live in freedom today is because as Americans we have the right to bear arms. No politician can get himself elected with a bunch of fancy talk and then take away all our freedoms. The first thing Hitler did was take away all the people's guns 'to keep the people safe.' Then he started taking other things away ... like their books and their lives. The first thing Lenin did in the USSR was take away all their guns to 'keep the people safe.'" That's a bunch of crap. The reason we are a free country today was because we took up arms against the British. The reason the black man is free is because a bunch of white men and boys took up their guns to free them. The reason no punk on a motorcycle with a Nazi helmet breaks into every house he feels like, is because he knows that he might be facing Samuel Colt's justice. But if you don't know how to use a gun safely, it won't do you any good."

Mike got so absorbed in this he had not even noticed they were at the dump. Now he jumped out of the car into a smell even more overpowering than the opossum he found last year. Uncle Vic parked the car and they dumped out the cans. Mike began looking around furiously. He knew his time was limited, so he had to search systematically. Mostly he saw plastic bags filled with typical household garbage. The smell of rotting food was enough to make even Mike lose his appetite. He knew he had little time before he would have to leave this great treasure store. He picked up a rock and threw it at a glass jar. It broke with a satisfying crash. Some old broken chairs caught his attention. He ran over to examine them and tripped over something buried in the ground. A tire!

"Hey we could make a tire swing!"

"You got any rope?" Uncle Vic asked.

"Uh...no. Um... do you?"

"Nope"

Mike ran to another treasure, cast it aside and ran to another. Uncle Vic took care of the garbage and then busied himself with the box.

"Mike, come here."

Mike ran back to Uncle Vic who held something cradled in his hand.

Mike stopped short in amazement. It was a .22 semiautomatic pistol.

"First rule you have to understand, what was a gun made for?"

"Uh... to shoot things?"

"To kill. Target shooting is practice in killing. Never point it at something you don't want to kill. That is not a pretty way to say it, but you have to understand that it is not a toy. It is not a way to look cool. Guns can put food on the table, protect you and they can kill you by accident. You have to know how to handle them safely. Here watch."

Uncle Vic placed the .22 in his hand removed the 10-round clip, opened the slide in the automatic so Mike could look inside. "Is the gun safe?"

Mike furrowed his brow with concentration and tentatively said, "I think so."

Uncle Vic slid the clip back in and slid the action back and forward. "What about now?"

Mike shook his head.

Uncle Vic removed the clip full of bullets. "Now?"

Mike was starting to get the hang of it. "Yes, it's safe."

"Good." Uncle Vic flipped off the safety and BANG! He fired a round into a glass jar in the dump.

Mike jumped backward at the bang. The shattering glass matched his crash of emotions that an empty gun could fire a bullet. He would have bet his life...Yes. That's the point. He realized his uncle's wisdom. Here was a lesson he would not soon forget.

"Surprised ya, didn't it?"

"It sure did."

"Always, always...always assume a gun is loaded. Never play games with a gun."

"But how did it fire a shot? I saw you take the clip with the bullets out."

"There was a bullet in the chamber. Remember that," he said. Though he knew the boy would likely never have to be reminded again. He might have just saved a life.

The next twenty minutes went smoothly with Uncle Vic explaining the weapon, its maintenance, and how to shoot it.

A man who had been pushing the garbage around with a plow on a tractor walked toward the garbage pile he had made with a burning rag on a stick. While still several feet away he threw it at the pile. It flared into flames with a "woof" and enough speed to indicate the pile was drenched in gasoline.

Uncle Vic looked at the black smoke rising from the mound of flames.

"Well, it's time to leave."

"Why? Can't we watch the fire, for just a little?"

"Get in the car." Uncle Vic said in a commanding voice.

"Hey, what's that?" Mike pointed at a movement in the pile of rubbish.

The fire spread to other mounds and began to throw off a low rumble.

"Hey, there's another." Mike pointed a little ahead of the first dark shape.

"Just get in the car," Vic ordered.

Mike remained rooted to the ground in fascination as the piles of garbage began to writhe and move like a wave in front of the flames.

"Now! Get in the car." Uncle Vic grabbed Mike's arm and pulled him toward the car.

It was only now that Mike realized hundreds of black brown objects were running straight at him.

"Rats!" Uncle Vic stated as a command.

"But we have a gun." Mike protested as he hustled into the car and rolled up the window regardless of the heat.

Uncle Vic mashed down the gas pedal and the spinning tires of the old Rambler threw gravel like a Saturday night hot rod. He didn't waste time on words until they were on the black top.

"Yes, we have a gun. Here is today's test. How many shots in that gun?"

"Ten."

"How many rats did you see?"

"A gazillion. Oh..."

"Fancy firepower doesn't always win. I think they are just beginning to learn that in Viet Nam... What's that?" Uncle Vic motioned to something at Mike's feet.

"Oh, I was going to ask you about that but ran out of time in the hurry to get out of the dump. Can I keep it?"

"Do you know what it is?"

"No... I thought it looked like a space gun."

Uncle Vic let out a long sigh. "It is just an old ornate table leg."

"Oh... but isn't it cool?"

Chapter 20   Into the Swamp

It was a dark cool overcast morning. Mike had just finished breakfast and now walked back toward the cottage from house 22. The ground around the cottage was strewn with shrapnel of green leaves, premature acorns, and branches from the storm the night before.

"Hey, get out of there!" Harold shouted next door.

The screen door flew open and Linda shot out of her cottage. Though Mike wasn't sure, it looked like her dad swung at her.

She came out sobbing but when she saw Mike she looked away, wiped her face and headed down to the dock.

"Linda?" Mike called, "Linda, where ya going?"

"The dock," she murmured without looking back.

"Ya wanna do somethin'?"

She turned red eyes toward him. "What?"

"Uh..." he bit his lip, and winced at his options. He had spoken before he thought. He spoke out of emotion not out of rational decision. It was too nasty out for most things; it even looked like it might storm. I was thinking... The guys were talking... about...that is..."

She perked up and began to walk toward him.

"We thought we would go... to the swamp looking for arrowheads and I thought you might want to come." He punched himself internally. He had never invited her along with the guys and didn't like the way it would sound but...

"Really?"

"Yeah, I was just on my way to get Little John."

"Sure, I'll go." She swiped at her face. "Should I bring anything?"

"Uh, no...Let's go get the guys."

With the weather too cold for swimming or boating, it took little convincing to get them to go out searching for adventure. Especially since Doctor Jacobson told them about his $10,000 spearhead.

The outing had a remarkable effect on Linda's attitude. "What do arrowheads look like? Where do we look for them? Have you found many? What do you do with them? I want to make mine into a necklace."

Jim, the intellectual, was quick with answers for every question.

Mike just remained silent. He had said too much today already, but he made a show of studying the ground with a knowing look.

They came to a Y in the road. Left would take them around the lake; right would take them to the swamp. Are you sure you want to go to the swamp Linda?" Jim asked. "There's lots of scary stuff there."

"Sure, she is," Mike said. "Tink is tuff." Inside he kicked himself. What was wrong with him today?

Linda glowed.

The other boys looked at Mike. "What?"

"Never mind." Today, for some reason, Mike didn't care what they thought.

"What kind of scary stuff?" Little John asked with a furrowed brow.

"Let's look here," Eric said, pointing into the swamp.

"Why here?"

"There's an animal trail." He pointed to a small path in the weeds that led into the soggy ground.

"You sure we can find our way out? I've heard people can lose their direction in a swamp and never find their way out." Linda commented with at furrowed brow.

"Sure, we won't go very far off the road. I've been in here a million times," Jim said.

They parted the weeds and headed in.

"Just like we didn't get lost going to the river?" Little John said glumly and followed them in.

"If this is a trail, how come we have to crawl?" Linda asked.

"Cuz animals aren't as tall as we are."

"There. We can straighten up here."

They continued down the trail. It branched and then branched again. Several times they crouched down to get under low hanging branches.

"What was that?" asked Little John.

"Oh, don't start."

"No, I'm serious. What was that?"

"A frog."

"How long are we going to keep going?" Little John whined.

"What makes you think there are arrowheads in here?" Linda examined the black goo sticking to her shoes, as if expecting something to crawl out.

"Cuz there are animals in here and Indians hunted animals." Jim said knowingly.

"Oh, like that one?"

They all stopped dead in their tracks gaping at the scene before them.

Gasp.

"Run!"

"No. It's cool."

"Wow!"

"Neato! That looks like a whole skeleton." Eric stepped forward and picked up the deer skull.

Great debate occurred among the company as to how the deer had died and whether it might be contagious. The general consensus was that they should wash their hands before they eat or pick their nose.

They explored some distance further and came to a drier section of the woods. Here the trees thinned and there were some grassy areas.

"Hey, this is cool! We could have a picnic here. "

"Or maybe camp overnight," Jim said.

The other boys did not respond to his suggestion lest they be forced to act upon it.

"Hey, a turkey feather," Eric hooted.

"How do you know it's from a turkey?"

"It looks just like the one Paul McCurry has."

"Hey, look! There is some old chicken wire fence by those weeds. Do you think this used to be a farm?"

"Uh... I think that's marijuana," Mike said.

"It looks like chicken wire to me," Little John said.

"No, I mean the plant. It looks just like the posters you see in the store in the mall in Grand Rapids."

They each looked at it closer.

"I thought that came from Mexico," Eric suggested.

"You can grow it in Michigan too," Jim said with an arrogant smile.

"We should tell someone. It's illegal," Mike said.

"My cousin says it's no worse than beer and wine," Little John put in. "Why don't we…"

They heard a tearing sound and turned. Linda grabbed a handful of the plants and pulled them up by the roots. Then she flung them across the field, and grabbed another handful.

"Let's just leave," Jim said flatly.

Mike walked over and stood next to Linda.

Tears ran down her face as she grabbed another plant. Without looking at Mike she murmured, "Just like beer and wine."

Mike reached down and grabbed two handfuls of plants and pulled.

Soon they all joined in and the air was filled with plants flying across the open field.

An hour later they stumbled back onto the gravel road and Jim boasted, "See I told you I could find our way out of the swamp."

The rain came as they started for home. Mike looked at his hands. The cool rain felt good on his flushed face and they walked home in silence with their heads bowed to the rain, except Linda's. She held her head high, a triumphant fire in her eye.

Journal

We went to the swamp and found some cool bones. Swamps are neat. I wonder why? They smell funny, they are kinda gross, kinda scary, mysterous and confusing. Sometimes with all the weird stuff around you, yor mind begins to spin. You have to be careful where you step. You feel lost even when you know where you are. Come to think of it, swamps are like girls.

Chapter 21   Barn Flies

There are too many things to do Mike thought lying in the hammock. His thoughts raced. Summer is going too quickly and I haven't found an arrowhead, seen a pheasant, a shooting star or the northern lights.... or learned to swim, he added reluctantly. I can milk a cow now though, and I learned to paddle a canoe by myself and I have seen a bear and made my own firecracker. He wasn't sure who he could tell about the last one though.

He put down his cousin Buck's 10-year-old copy of Boy's Life and hopped out of the hammock. Maybe Mister Vanderkooi knows where there are some pheasants.

He and little John found the farmer down in a well pit beating on some pipes.

"Hey what'cha doin'?" The ever-cheerful little John asked.

"Tryin' to make this no good..."

Mike and Little John tried to follow his comments but many of the words neither boy had ever heard before. Mike tried to remember some of the better sounding ones for future use.

"Doesn't your pump work?"

"NO!" Stated the farmer. This was followed by another string of nonsensical words.

"Anything we can do?"

The farmer's beat red face looked about to explode. He glared at Mike and then collapsed onto a concrete block like a balloon releasing its air."

"No." He shook his head looking at the brown sand at the bottom of the pit.

There was an awkward silence. "Why don't you buy a new one?" Little John squeaked out.

"I can't afford it. It's been a bad year...again. Medical bills are expensive."

"Medical bills?" Mike asked.

"For my wife's cancer," he said mechanically.

Mike was just about to say 'I didn't know you were married,' when he realized the farmer was not...anymore.

The farmer sighed, "I got a loan at the bank that is due. I can't pay it without selling my cows. But if I sell my cows..."

"You don't have any milk to sell," Mike finished sadly.

The farmer just nodded.

Mike's stomach hurt. "I got six dollars you can have."

"I've got $4.77 you can have and I bet I could get more," Little John added.

The old man forced a tight-lipped smile. "Thanks, that... that means a lot."

"That pump looks really old. You've lived here a long time, haven't you?"

"I've lived here 68 years. There have only been two nights in my life I didn't sleep in that house. Sure would hate to sell it now. Tell you what, I'll let you go up in the hayloft and throw down any hay left up there. I want it to look good for the sale. But ya got to be careful. It is awfulyl shaky. I got to go in the house a minute. I think I got some of this sand in my eye." The old man rubbed his right eye.

The boys went up into the hayloft, took off their shirts, and started tossing down bales. That is... after doing a very thorough search for spiders. Mike mentally mapped the spider webs. Flies loved the old barn filled with manure and so the rafters contained the most complete collection of spiders Mike had ever seen. Though they were very interesting academically, Mike's interest level changed radically if he thought one happened to come threateningly close, like within 8 feet.

Little John had known Mike for a long time. Consequently, Little John waited until Mike was in the middle of tossing a bale of hay from the ledge of the loft to the floor 10' below. Then, reaching out slowly with a single long stalk of hay, he dragged it artistically down the middle of Mike's back.

Lying on the barn's floor the boys argued about exactly how they got there, when a voice from underneath the hay made them jump.

"I know exactly what happened if you really want to know," the farmer offered.

"I just happened to walk in through the door directly below you boys the instant that you," he pointed to Little John, "touched Mike's bare back." The old man tried to sit up pushing hay, manure, and boys from his lap.

"I looked up just in time to have a bale of hay land in ma right eyeball. I swatted it away but it knocked me back into the manure drain. My ankle twisted on the dang blasted curb and I sat down. From there I watched as Mikey flew through the rafters like a hoot owl. Of course, that woke up the spiders pretty good, they jumped on his back and he seemed pretty excited to have them along. He made one big loop through the rafters and came in for a landing in the pile of hay back in the hay loft."

"I just jumped to grab a rafter and swing to the floor but the floor was too far away so I swung back up." Mike protested.

"Then why did you do a second lap?"

"I landed on a pitch fork," Mike mumbled.

"His second lap through the rafters knocked John outta the loft and on ta my head, but don't worry boys, the concrete curb under the manure cushioned the impact," he said disgustedly. "I noticed that when Mike finally landed, Johnny boy was so worried about him that he laughed himself into a coughing fit."

"Yes, I noticed too, and I was concerned about his health," Mike said.

That's not why you were pounding on my back," Little John protested. "He wasn't concerned about my health, he was hittin' me," Little John hooted picking hay and manure out of his hair.

"You deserved every punch. I would have hit you harder if I hadn't broken my arm when I fell."

"You didn't break your arm. That was the pitchfork that you heard snap."

"Well, it feels like it."

"Look on the bright side. You got to fly. What did it feel like?"

"Like a fly in a spider's web."

"Quit your bellowing, would you?"

"That's not me, that's one of them big cows," Mike said and pointed at the big cow in the large corner stable.

"She's calvin'," the farmer sighed. "Oh, my achin' back." He stood up slowly leaning on the metal cow-restraining rail.

"But Calvin is a boy's name. Is it a boy cow?"

"What?" Mike asked.

"She is having a calf," the farmer explained.

"Oh. Can we watch?"

"Sure," the farmer smiled for the first time that day, and rubbed his aching back.

The boys shuffled their feet in the dust as they made their way home in the failing light.

"That was incredible. Farmers have the greatest job in the world," Mike said. "Wow! When I grow up, I'm going to be a farmer."

"Yeah, it was cool." John said unenthusiastically wiping his face, again.

"The best part was when the calf appeared and Mister Vanderkooi told you to pull it out."

"Yeah, and I got covered with slime ...very funny."

"And highly educational. That was so cool. And the calf sucking on my thumb. Let's go back tomorrow. Do you think Mister Vanderkooi knew you'd get slimed?"

"I would guess by the way he was rolling around on the ground laughing he might have had some idea it was going to happen."

"What a great day!"

"Right."

As they were walking down the long driveway to the cottage, Uncle Vic took one look at the boys, shook his head and pointed down toward the lake. As they passed, by he tossed down a bar of soap from the wash stand on the porch.

Chapter 22   Deadly Storms

Mike tossed uneasily on the sofa he used as his bed. He loved sleeping on this screened in porch. It was like sleeping outside. He usually slept well. Tonight, he sat bolt upright and wide eyed as an explosion echoed through his skull. It rattled the windows of the cottage and then rolled around the lake. A flash of light and droning of rain on the roof clarified the source of the explosion. Another boom a boom-a-room-a-rum-a-bum slid around the shoreline of the lake. Mike snuggled down deeper under the covers but there was no hope for sleep. The wind was strong enough to blow the shades over the screens up and Mike was getting rained on. The sound of the rain and running water made him realize he had to go to the bathroom, or more accurately to house 22. He was not about to run 75 feet through this downpour to get to the outhouse. He didn't want to get struck by lightning. He hated thunderstorms. He heard a noise inside the cabin. Another flash illuminated Uncle Vic. He stood on the enclosed porch next to Mike's bed looking out the large windows toward the lake. He was completely dressed.

"You're not going out there, *are you?*" Mike asked incredulously. He sat up and looked toward the lake.

"I was planning to. Isn't it glorious? Gad!" He exhaled deeply, the sound of the air going in through his nose seemed as loud as the thunder. Another flash outlined the sky with excitement. "I love it."

"Wow!" Mike said. "That was..." his sentence was interrupted by another window shaking boom.

"You wanna go down to the lake with me?"

Mike looked at him in shock. "Won't we get struck by lightning?"

He leaned down close to where Mike's face hid in the old

frayed quilt. "If I thought so, I wouldn't go. The trees obscure most of the view here."

Mike hesitated, "I'll go if we can go by way of house 22."

Uncle Vic snorted a laugh. "Yeah."

His aunt stepped out onto the screened in porch wrapped in a thick old bathrobe. "Make sure he wears something warm. Does he have a raincoat? Let me think, I bet we have some garbage bags that he could cut a hole in and slip over his head."

"Lilly, he'll be fine."

"What about his bare legs. He should wear something over his shorts."

"He is fine Lilly."

With the constant rain and talk about house 22, Mike thought his bladder would burst before he struggled into his cold cutoffs. He slid on a 20-year-old coat over his sweatshirt and an old worn felt hat. Mike wondered what good the hat would do with its many holes but he didn't want Aunt Lilly to waste any more time looking for a better hat. He accepted it in silence. When she finally released him, he exploded out the back door, leapt off the porch door and dashed to the outhouse. Pools of water covered the dirt path. Flashes of lightning held water drops in midair. Each step sprayed water, pine needles and dirt in every direction.

He trotted back to the porch as his uncle came out and headed around the cottage to the lake. They never used the lake side exit. He slowed down to wait for his uncle. Soon he realized there was no point in trying to stay dry. The warm rain on this hot summer's night didn't feel too bad.

It seemed to take forever to get to the lake walking behind Uncle Vic and his flashlight. Mike usually dashed down the steps, but not tonight. He could only see each step by following closely behind his uncle, the light his uncle shown illuminated only the next step. He couldn't see far enough to do anything but step in his uncle's footsteps. This was frustrating but after a few steps he got the hang of it.

"Sure wish the steps were wider," Mike said stepping bent nearly double in his effort to see the steps and keep the rain out of his face.

"Your grandpa was trying to save money. During the depression no one had much. Many of these cottages didn't even have steps."

"Why is it that ALL adults are required to make anything I say into a lesson," he said.

"Maybe it's because you look like you have a lot to learn?"

They made it to the bottom just in time for another flash of multiple chains reaching from one side of the sky to the other. The sound reached inside his chest and shook his heart. He cringed, but immediately afterward he was back up staring at the tormented sky. His face was fully exposed to the hard pellets of dark rain. He moved closer to his uncle for protection from the wind.

His uncle put his hand on Mike's shoulder. "Makes you feel pretty small, don't it."

"It sure does. It's scary, but…cool."

"I'm sure God appreciates such high compliments on his fireworks."

As if in answer, a close flash triggered huge boom, sending echoes rattling and rumbling around the lake like congregation's amen to the preacher's statement of God's glory.

"I could stay out here all night," Mike said, leaning against the diamond shaped bark of an old pine tree.

Mike loved this old pine tree. At times he wondered how old it was. Age had rotted its center but it was the image of the perfect tree in Mike's mind. He pictured early America filled with trees such as this one. It was the largest old pine on the lake. Aunt Lil had picked the property, in part, because of this majestic old pine, lifting its head high above the others. It was a soldier, standing tall, guarding the forest. It was, without a doubt in Mike's mind, the most beautiful of the forest. Like most things in life its greatest asset was its greatest weakness.

"Let's stand over in the clearing a little further." Uncle Vic stated flatly.

They moved away from the tree into the beach clearing. The storm continued to build with flashes so frequent, Mike couldn't tell when it started and when it ended. The rain flowed furiously in heavy drops seemingly one continuous stream from cloud to earth. It had rained this hard once before, and then Noah and his family were the only ones to survive.

"The tree kept us drier," Mike protested. "Let's go back over there." He took two steps toward the tree.

Time held its breath. The earth paused in its rotation and held still in the heavens. The fusion reactions within the sun halted. Electrons stopped their orbit around the atoms. Eternity loomed on the horizon, heaven above, hell below but nothing here. Nothing.

Nothing. In that nothing a single mote floated. Mike. Alone.

Then one electron shuddered. It bumped another, which pushed still another. It released an avalanche of movement, unleashing time. God sighed and the world moved. The very breath of God slammed Mike to the ground. His ears stung. He lay in the mud quivering, one more dust spec blown to the ground in the storm. A worm that lay twisted and covered in bark, pine branches and debris, Mike lay dead.

If he was dead, why did he hurt all over? Why did his skin tingle? What happened? Was he hit by lightning? Was he dying? He could not breathe! Panic! Horror! He couldn't breathe! His stomach muscles were stuck. He curled up in a tight ball unable even to groan. He managed a tiny breath, the merest sip as from a thimble. It wasn't enough. What could he do? Oh God! He tried again and got two thimbles of air. He sucked in this meager breath and savored it. It was the most precious air in the whole world, well worth a million dollars. He took in another three thimblefuls, and then a juice glass full. He rolled up onto his back with a groan and crawled slowly toward the steps, bits of bark and debris falling to the ground, washed off into the darkness.

The flash, which exploded the old white pine tree, was bright enough to stun a blind man in daylight. In the moonless dark of the heavy rain, he was plunged into blackness so thick it pressed against his face. His skin tingled. He heard himself scream something but he was so far removed from his being that he couldn't tell what he himself had shouted. He scrambled up the steps half by feel and half by terror. He slammed his calves and forearms into the cruel corners for the concrete steps multiple times before he made it to the top. Near the top the light from the cabin became visible enough to reassure him. Once at the top, the light of the cabin showed him he could indeed see. He was ashamed that he had scrambled up without any concern for his old uncle. He looked back but it was too dark to see down to the beach.

He called down, "Uncle Vic! Are you alright?"

"Yep, "groaned a voice behind him.

He turned. His Uncle Vic stood on the porch. "Let's watch (pant) from inside (wheeze) the cottage for a while.

They sloshed into the brilliant light of the kitchen, soaking the newspapers that Aunt Lil always spread across the floor during a rain. It quickly became a ripped up mass of pine needles, mud and water, exposing the linoleum below. Aunt Lilly hugged them tightly. She looked near tears. "I'm so glad you're back safely. It sounds horrible." She grabbed Mike's jacket and hung it up. "I've got hot water on the stove. Would you like cocoa or hot tea? We don't have marshmallows for the cocoa...Oh!" She sucked in a breath, "...dear God!" Her hands went to her mouth as she stared at his legs.

Mike looked down. The normally light-colored floor was covered in puddles of bright red blood.

As he watched drop after drop fell from his left hand. His eyes followed the drops down to the bloody red mess that was his legs.

"It doesn't hurt." Mike said, but even as he said it, he became aware of the throbbing.

In retrospect Mike wished he would have taken a picture of it. It wasn't nearly as bad as it looked. The rainwater took a little blood, kept it from clotting and spread it everywhere. Mike made a mental note to remember that for the future, as it rendered great effect on the audience and caused little additional discomfort. Next time he got a cut he would make sure to accidently spill a glass of water on it. As soon as Aunt Lil wiped off his legs the bleeding stopped. Likewise, a bandage on his finger took care of that. How he would love to have Jim or Little John see all the blood. Eric would not have been impressed. Eric was always bleeding from somewhere. He had actually been to the emergency room twice. Mike was very jealous.

It was just as well that the day was rainy. Aunt Lilly wouldn't let Mike go swimming until his legs scabbed over well. Mike could hardly wait. He loved to pick at scabs. He picked up the old copy of Huckleberry Finn he found at the cabin and lay down on the old sofa to read and listen to the sound of the rain on the board roof. Aunt Lilly was taking advantage of the poor weather to stay inside the kitchen and make homemade rolls and cinnamon rolls with brown sugar topping. This was going to be a <u>great</u> day. Not to mention the story he would have for the other boys. He had already been down to the beach in the rain, collecting souvenir pieces of bark to show his parents.

Journal

Disasters are really neat if you live through them. I'm going to go outside in every lightning storm from now on.

He paused in thought, gently rubbing the sores on his legs. Then he continued writing.

Well, maybe once or twice.

"I'm leaving', leavin'…." Mike sang to the radio with the gusto of someone who thinks no one can hear.

Aunt Lil gave him a hug as he walked into the kitchen. "Buck used to sing that song all the time. I never listened to the words," She paused with a swallow "…until he was gone." She shook her head and hugged Mike tightly, "It's good to have you here to hug."

Mike didn't mind hugs as much as he used to. He picked up a steaming hot yeast roll. Heedless to the molten butter running down his hand, he finished it in two bites.

"Don't you want some honey on that or maybe some strawberry jam? I think I have some strawberry jam in here." Aunt Lilly poked through the small refrigerator moving one thing aside after the other.

"Mthis is fime." Mike had picked up another roll without any butter on it and quickly finished it also.

"Oh here, have some apple juice." She pulled out a large can.

Mike couldn't resist. The only thing better in the world than Aunt Lilly's rolls were Aunt Lilly's rolls with apple juice.

"Save some room for the sticky biscuits," she cautioned.

"I'll have room."

"You go through rolls just like Buck. I have a hard time keeping either of you filled," she said still poking through the refrigerator. "Here. Here's some cheese. Do you want some cheese on them?" She handed him an unopened bag of cheese. "I think we have some ham in here too." She bent back over for a more thorough investigation.

Mike wondered if the lady ever sat down. "No thanks Aunt Lilly, I don't need anything on them. The rolls are great just the way they are."

She jumped at the sound of the buzzer and opened the oven door. Mike reached over and closed the refrigerator door before looking back at the rolls, lightly browned and swirling with fragrant cinnamon.

She set them aside to cool a bit before attempting to flip them over so the butter and brown sugar in the bottom of the pan would soak into the rolls.

"How many can I have?"

She laughed. Her laugh was more music than speech. It seemed at times every paragraph was sung. Her face was merely the frame for her smile. She was so different from Uncle Vic; he couldn't understand how they ever got together.

"You can have as many as you want."

"Really?" His eyes grew almost as big as the cinnamon rolls.

She laughed again, and then looked him up and down. "I guess I better limit that."

His countenance fell

"...to eight."

Mike's mouth dropped in disappointment.

"...of each."

He grinned. "Oh, I don't think I could eat more than six of each."

"Well, I want to take some over to Linda's family."

"I'll take them," Mike said quickly.

"That's all right; I want to talk to her mother."

"Oh," his face sagged.

Aunt Lilly stopped her cleaning, and looked sidewise at Mike's face. A sly smile crept over her face. "Come to think of it, I would appreciate it if you could carry the rolls for me. She rubbed her wrist. My arthritis has been acting up and the Bufferin isn't doing as good of a job as it used to."

"Sure, I'll do that!" he said a little too enthusiastically.

Her smile broadened and she gave him another hug. The short woman's shoulders were only a little higher than his were.

"Let's go right now while the rain is stopped and the rolls are warm." She heaped several rolls on a paper plate and slid them into a plastic bag. Then she did the same thing with some of the sweet sticky cinnamon rolls.

Mike watched her put each one on the plate like a hungry dog, hoping she would stop soon.

She punched Mike in the shoulder. "Don't worry if we run out, I can make more."

"Maybe you could teach me?"

"Oh, what a great idea! But not today."

They soon stood at the door of the neighboring cottage. Though it was a hot day with the mugginess of the rain, the door was closed. Aunt Lilly pulled open the screen door and knocked.

Linda opened the door. "Hi Mickey!"

Mike made a show of rolling his eyes.

"Mom, Missus Malloy is here."

A moment later her mother appeared at the door with a hanky over her mouth. She coughed once or twice and said through the hanky, "I'm so sorry I can't invite you in but I've been sick."

"Oh, I'm sorry to hear that. We made some rolls and I thought you might enjoy some."

"Oh, they're beautiful."

Mike handed her the two plates. She took one and set it down and then took the other and set it down. All the while, she held the hanky over her mouth.

"Wow! They look great." Linda said. "Can I have one now?"

"Now is when they're best." Mike stated with great authority.

"He had about ten, I think," Aunt Lil shook her head.

Mike glowed.

"Thank you. You are..." she paused. "That was so nice." Linda's mom said a few more things that Mike didn't quite catch. Her voice seemed to fade. Her eyes looked like she was about to cry. They said goodbye and the door closed.

"She must be pretty sick," Mike said, "What do you think she's got?"

"I'm sure I don't know," his aunt snapped abruptly enough to make him look at her.

He had never seen this sweet lady with an anger filled scowl on her face before. He half expected her to say, "I'm mad enough to spit." Like his mom said when she argued with his father. The expression on her face could pickle a watermelon whole.

Whenever he saw his mom with that expression it was time to become scarce. Still, he was reluctant to leave the house full of rolls, so he didn't want to go too far. Even though he was sure the frog pond would be over flowing and he really wanted to see it. He just headed down to the lake for a few minutes.

He sat down, watched the rain dance on the lake for a while, half the time looking over at Linda's dock to see if she might just happen to wander down to the lake. After all, it looked like it was brightening up over on the other side of the lake and the rain was probably going to stop any time. The only consistent thing about Michigan weather is its sense of humor. It poured.

Mike dashed up the steps and ran around the side of the cabin. He could hear his aunt and uncle arguing through the screen window.

"It's none of our business Lilly," his uncle said in his end-of-conversation voice.

To Mike's amazement his aunt Lilly replied with fire in her voice. "It is everyone's business to love your neighbor."

"We can't just step in."

"We can't just sit back."

"This is not about giving them food or money. We could endanger our own safety. Everyone is responsible for his own family."

"Harold is out of control."

"How do you know? He is going through tough times. Anything we would do would have no lasting effect anyway."

"I don't like it."

"Me either, but I am not going to destroy my family to try and save theirs."

His aunt slammed something on the table and Mike heard her working in the kitchen. The sound of a long in drawn breath from his uncle told him the conversation was over. Still, he was reluctant to go back into the cottage so he headed out to the outhouse to read. It didn't smell very good but the atmosphere in the cottage didn't smell good to him either.

Chapter 23 Lessons, Life, Death and... Fishing

Mike was still mulling over his uncle's comment, when it finally stopped raining. Uncle Vic came and said, "It's time to fish."

"What? It's the middle of the afternoon I thought you said..."

"Rain changes things; it washes worms and insects into the water. The overcast sky draws the fish out of the places they hide from the sun."

So, pretty soon they were out at the drop off down by the bend. Just like Uncle Vic said, the fish were going nuts. Mike hated it when the grownups were right.

"Hey, I got another one!" Mike hooted.

"Well reel it in. Don't just talk about it."

Mike turned the crank as the pole danced. "It's not tugging very hard. It's a small one."

He looked over the side of the boat to see if he could see it yet. A flash of white caught his eye. Sure enough, it was fairly little. He followed its path up toward the boat. It was too small to keep but they had enough for dinner anyway. Suddenly a much bigger flash appeared; his pole bent nearly double then popped back up. The little fish popped out of the water still attached to Mike's line.

"Wow, did you see that?" Mike shouted.

"Sure did," Uncle Vic chuckled. "You almost had yourself a pike."

The small fish swam in circles along the top of the water. Mike reeled him in reluctantly, hoping the pike would come back, but he didn't.

Mike pulled the small fish out of the water. "Look! There are teeth marks on it." He held it up for his uncle. "Is it gonna die?

Should I just kill it anyway?"

"I don't know. Put it back. It might grow into the biggest fish in the lake. 'The injured ones are the smartest and the toughest,' Uncle Abner used to say."

"Who's Uncle Abner?"

"My mother's oldest brother, Uncle Abner. He was in the Civil War."

"WHAT? That's impossible! That was back in the slavery days a hundred years ago. He couldn't be your uncle."

"Do you know how old I am?"

"Uh...*Old*, but not 100."

Uncle Vic chuckled, "I was born in 1901. My mother was from a large family. She was the youngest born in 1865. Her older brother Abner was 17 when he went off to fight. He was probably born around 1846."

"But that was before the gold rush. *Your uncle* was born before the gold rush?!" History flashed through Mike's mind like the lightning that blew into the old pine tree's heart. Images flew past his eyes; images of covered wagons and Indians, miners then men in blue charging up a hill. Here was a man that had talked to history. *Talked* to history? Come to think of it, he was history. What moments before had been mere dates on a flat page of a boring history text exploded into real living breathing people, flesh and blood that could be touched, felt, and smelled by a witness of it.

Mike's jaw hung open while his heart pounded. "Did he talk about the war? What did he say? Did he live around here? Did he know the Indians? Was he a trapper? Did he pan for gold? What did he have to say?"

Uncle Vic chuckled. "Well, I'll tell you if you let me." He took one of his long noisy breaths. "His folks had a farm and he thought it was boring. He said he would go away to become a hero. He came back a year later..." His uncle looked hard at Mike "without his right leg. I remember him talking about the war when I was a teenager. He said the most significant thing he learned from the army experience was how wonderful his mother's food was, how wise his father was, and how sweet it is to live on a peaceful farm and watch the summer clouds drift across the blue sky in peace.

"He also learned how much easier it is to work with two good legs. He had loved to play baseball but when he came back, he would only hit and pitch and he wasn't very good at that anymore.

He was still in pretty good shape when I knew him. His arms were bigger than your legs. He used his arms where other men used legs. He was a tough old cuss. Yep, he used to say, '*the injured ones are the toughest and smartest.*' After meeting him, I believed it."

"Were you in any wars?"

"Nope too young for the first, too old for the second. Guess that's why I'm not too smart." He winked.

They finished in silence for a while.

Mike had always played army, but never imagined himself coming home... permanently damaged. He tried to picture Buck coming home with some serious injury. What would they do together if Buck couldn't hunt or fish? What if Buck couldn't get a job? That made him think about Linda's dad.

"Is something wrong with Linda's dad? Is Linda's family going to... starve?"

His uncle looked at him. Mike heard the long inhaling breath that always announced a significant story, but this time his uncle remained quiet. The silence worried Mike. Adults were always silent when they did not want say something bad. Finally, when he spoke, he said, "They won't starve. They get some money from the state and neighbors will help them."

His uncle picked his words as though he was picking his way through a minefield at midnight. He leaned close to Mike. "Linda's father and I have a very different opinion of how to take care of our loved ones." His words were hard as bricks. "He is..." His uncle's lips disappeared and his face burned red. He took a deep breath and started again. "A few years ago, I might have talked to him about it, but now...He's been listening to too much of this shi... *doo* about doing what you feel... this '*be true to yourself*' crap you hear everywhere these days. A man is responsible to take care of his family *no matter* whether you like it or *feel like it*. That means you do everything and anything you can to protect them. And he is *destroying* them. I... yes, there probably is something wrong with him. But he doesn't need a doctor or a psychiatrist. He needs a good licking....but don't tell anyone I said that. My ideas are old fashioned I guess."

Mike took off his shirt. "It's getting hot out here now."

"Yep. And the fish aren't biting anymore. Might as well go back and get something to eat. We've solved the rest of the world's problems." Uncle Vic flashed a conspiratorial smile. "It is time we received our just reward. I bet aunt Lil's supper is coming out of the oven."

After dinner Mike walked out to the gravel road. One of their neighbors was walking off in the distance. The man limped and the rake over his shoulder almost looked like a rifle.

Mike turned away from the memory of the war. He looked toward the setting sun. It was beautiful. Mike kicked a large stone with his right toe and watched it fly. He kicked it with his left. He jumped and spun. He faked left. He faked right. He sprinted till his legs burned and savored the burn. Then he slowed and hopped, skipped and jumped. He crouched at an imaginary scrimmage line.

There were only seconds on the clock and the football player had 50 yards to go. Only one player had any chance of making the game winning touchdown. The goal line was in sight…

Chapter 24   Ultimate Power

"Okay Mike," Jim whispered. "You run past Billy around the tree and then cut back. I'll hit you with the ball when you're even with the corn."

"That's dandy, but keep the ball away from their tomatoes." Mike rubbed a red smear on his cutoffs for emphasis. He looked back toward where the football lay in the middle of Billy's front yard. It was the only grassy area around large enough to play football. It was hemmed in by the house on one side, and the vegetable garden on the other side.

"You coulda had that one if you tried. It's hard to get the pass over Little John."

"You boys gonna play football, or do you want me to ask ma for the cribbage board," Billy asked from the sidelines with a wink.

"We're plannin'," Jim called back.

"Didn't take God that long to plan the universe," Billy drawled.

"Yeah, but he didn't have to work with Jim," Mike shouted back.

Jim pushed Mike toward the line. "We're ready."

Mike got down on the line and growled at Little John.

The chubby faced boy just grinned back.

"Hut one hut two HUT."

Mike snapped the ball back, bumped into John as a token block and shot along the predetermined course toward Billy's garden. Eric was toe to toe with him the whole way. The only advantage Mike had was he was taller than Eric.

He looked back to Jim to see the ball was already in the air. The wobbling pass would land right behind him. He spun, caught the ball and headed in for a touchdown.

"And the crowd went wild!" Mike shouted.

"That was a pretty good move, Mike, but I especially liked the expression on Eric's face when you cut. You went one way and your jock strap went the other. Poor Eric didn't know which way to go." He slapped the armrest on his wheelchair with a chuckle.

"Yeah, that was a pretty good move Mike," Little John said.

"I wish you could play." Mike tossed the ball to Billy who caught it with his lap.

"What? And get all dirty an' smelly like you?"

"That's just my tenna shoes. I been down at the Vanderkooi's farm."

"I hate to be the one to tell you, but with all that sweat, I don't think it's just the shoes." He tossed the ball to the other boys who started a game of catch.

Mike stood next to the wheelchair. "How come you're always so happy? You laugh all the time. You're about the happiest person in the world."

"Why shouldn't I be happy? Everyone else is at work and I get to sit out here and watch you make fools of yourselves," his grin broadened.

"No really. How can you be so happy sitting in that wheelchair?"

He leaned close to Mike and in a whisper of conspiracy said, "Because I have *ultimate power*. I have more power in this little finger than in an atomic bomb."

"Right."

"You don't believe me? Watch this. I can make a glass of water appear right here, out of thin air." He waved his thin hands.

"*This* I got to see."

He turned to the boys throwing the football. "Hey Jim, go get me a glass of water, would you?"

"Sure."

Jim trotted up to the door and disappeared inside the house and reappeared a moment later with a glass of water.

"Thanks." He turned to Mike. "See...ultimate power."

"Anyone can do that."

"Oh yeah? You try."

Mike turned to the other boys who continued to throw the ball ignoring the conversation. "Hey Eric, go down to the lake and get the canoe paddle for me."

Eric trotted up to Mike. "What?"

"Go down to the lake and get a canoe paddle for me." Mike glowered down on Eric who was several inches shorter.

Eric scratched his chin shrugged his shoulders and in one swift move swooped down, grabbed Mike's ankle and lifted it over his head.

Mike sprawled across the grass in surprise.

Eric sat down on Mike chest and beamed, "Get it yourself."

Billy laughed so hard he started coughing and his mother came out to see what was going on.

Finally, Billy said, "See I told you. Only I have ultimate power."

Mike dropped his head back on the ground and laughed loudly. "Where did you learn that, Eric? That was cool."

"Paul McCurry showed me some wrestling moves. Watch this."

Soon the front yard was a flurry of flying elbows and knees as the two boys rolled around on the ground.

"That's not how you wrestle," Little John said. "I saw it on TV." He ran toward the two.

They both stopped wrestling, looked up in horror, just in time to see Little John soaring into the air above them.

"Nooo!" they screamed, just before his famous belly flop crushed all the breath out of them.

"Ohhhhhh!"

"What's the matter Mike? Looks like someone dropped a baby grand piano on you." Billy said.

"More like a baby elephant," groaned Eric.

Little John flung a handful of pine needles at Eric in reply. Soon pine needles filled the air like javelins of laughter.

As it started to slow down, Mike said, "It's not fair that you can't be involved, Billy."

"Who says I can't?" He flung the magic glass of water on three of the boys, and was rewarded with three quite satisfying screeches.

Mike stopped laughing long enough to take a deep breath. He turned to Billy. "Why do we laugh?"

Billy wiped his eyes. "It's reflexes."

"You mean like when the Doctor hits your elbow and your arm jumps?"

"Yep. It's like a yawn; your brain needs extra oxygen to stay awake so you yawn. You laugh to keep from suffocating in sorrow," Billy postulated with a lopsided grin.

Billy's mom came out "Sorry boys, but it's time to go. Time for Billy's supper." She quietly pushed Billy into the house.

Mike stood watching his mother take the handles on Billy's wheel chair and back him through the doorway in to the house. "...and that's why *you* laugh so much," he whispered to the door and bit his lips.

Chapter 25 Horsing Around

"Mister Vanderkooi, Mike looked around excitedly, "Do you have any horses? It would be so cool to ride a horse just like John Wayne."

No, I don't have time for any horses. I have tractors. They are a bit stronger and don't bite or kick me quite as often. My daughter had a horse, she named Donalda." He chuckled. "Named it after her English teacher she said. After meeting her teacher, there was a resemblance, but the horse had a better figure. Now that one horse took up more time than any hundred cows."

"What?" Mikes asked wrinkling his forehead. "How is a horse different than a cow? They eat, drink, and poop. What is the difference?"

The old farmer rubbed the stubble on his chin. His mouth slid into a melancholy smile. "Well, a cow is just an animal but a horse is a big dog. The horse has to be trained, washed, combed, hooves cleaned and main braided. You have to pet it, tell it you love it, kiss it and fuss and then you have to trailer it to the shows..." long pause. "...a lot of shows." His eyes trailed off to an empty coral with peeling white paint, as if he was seeing something that wasn't there.

In a husky voice he said, "Yep. Horses take a lot of time." And then a little quieter murmured, "So do little girls." His lips tightened and he became quiet. After what seemed like several minutes he looked down at the boys with a big grin. "I just happen to have some time to teach you a true manly sport! I have a real cowboy rodeo sport for you. You ever hear of bronco busting? The man that stays in the saddle the longest wins. That there is a man's sport. Course not ever' one is tough enough for that."

Mike and Little John stared with slack jaws and eyes like saucers. "Wow! Really?"

He looked down on the boys with pity and shook his head. "No, on second thought it might be too rough for you. Of course, I did it, and even my panty waist brother tried when he was finally old enough but... you boys grew up in the city." He wrinkled his nose. "So, I can understand that you probably are not quite up to this." He looked away as if tossing aside the idea. Then cut his eyes slyly back to the boys.

Years later Mike would play that scene back in his mind and see the Machiavellian glint in the old farmer's eyes and hear the maniacal laughter of a sadistic torturer about to strap someone into the pit with a pendulum swinging lower on every stroke. There is an evil that lies dormant just under the surface of every farmer. Why else would they have children and sentence them to a life of forced labor waist deep in manure. But we digress...

Mike knew he was destined for this ride into glory today. Nothing would get in the way of such a masculine event. The ride would be told and retold to generations yet unborn. Angels would sing his glory! Too bad Linda wasn't here to faint at the mere prospect.

Mike and Little John sat on the top fence rail, their feet on the lower rail. Mike forced a hard look of mild disinterest as his right leg shook uncontrollably. "Remind me, uh... just how we are supposed to this?" This was just like the water skiing. Once again, he knew, *he knew* he was facing certain death. At least with water skiing there were girls in bikinis. He looked at the ancient leather skinned farmer in his baggy, manure splattered overalls and sighed.

"Well, wait until a medium sized one comes close you. Here, I will give you some food pellets. That will bring them in. Then just jump on its back and grab the ears. I will time how long you stay on. The one that stays on the longest wins."

Mike swallowed hard as a medium sized black and white... pig came around him snuffling for the food pellets. Mike dropped them into the dirt where he judged he wanted the head to be when he mounted his steed. The hog got into position pretty much correctly. Mike grit his teeth and jumped.

"I shoulda mentioned, he is not going to be very happy about it," the farmer slapped his leg. "WEEEEEEE!   HOLD ON BOY!!!"

Ultimately it did not matter that Linda was not there to see it, she probably heard him from 2 miles away.

"Hmmm... two seconds. Not very long."

Little John studied Mike lying in the muck. "What was that sound you made?"

Mike sat up, wiping something disgusting from his face, and stated in his best haughty voice, "I very clearly shouted 'Yeeha!'"

"It sounded like a little girl screaming EEEEEEEEEE!" Little John threw his hands up in the air and waved them wildly for affect.

"I don't see you riding anything!"

"I'm just getting ready."

The farmer studied little John. "Actually, we better get you on one a little bigger than the one Mikey rode. I call Mike's, Tiny. He was the runt of the litter and has been so sickly I had to hand feed him for months." He winked at Little John.

He pointed to the next pen over where the pigs were a bit bigger. "Now Cyclone here, could bear your weight. Yeah, he would be a good ride." The farmer rubbed his nose to hide the smile and winked at Mike.

"Okay, he can't be any worse than those linemen I faced last year."

Mike studied Cyclone. "I didn't know pigs got so big."

The farmer said, "These are all babies," and he pointed into another building where the boys observed a hippopotamus nursing a litter of piglets. In the pen just behind that they could see an even bigger one.

"Oh my..." the jaws of both boys dropped.

The farmer continued. "DO NOT EVER go near any of the pens in that barn. I'm serious. They could kill you. And then... they would eat you. Ready Johnny boy?"

"They'll WHAT!?"

The farmer studied his watch. "I don't know. I think it was a tie. You are going to have to do it again."

"HE WON!" both boys shouted in unison.

The farmer slapped Little John's back and chuckled. Then looked at his hand and wiped it on his pants. "Actually, I think I have to give it Johnny boy. He screamed louder."

"Yeah, which time? When you pushed him, when he landed on the pig, when he fell off the pig or when the pig chased him around the pen biting at his butt?!"

The farmer laughed out loud. "Each time actually got better. So, are you done with bronco busting?"

"Yeah, I think so."

"You want to try the "Hay Toss Competition?"

"I think that may be more our speed."

Chapter 26   A Sailed

Mike studied the little fiberglass sail boat. The hull was a simple construction. It had a red top and a white bottom clamped together by a metal bead that went all the way round the outside of the boat. The mast dropped into a cup holder in the center of the boat. A brass ring went around the mast and attached to the actual aluminum rods that held the sail. There was a pulley to pull the sail up and a rope at the end of the sail closest to the stern. It looked really complicated. "Are you sure it is okay?" Mike asked.

Jim gave Mike one of his you-are-such-a–little-boy looks. "Yes. Mister Nelson said we could use it anytime we want. He said we did not even have to ask. Just stow the sail and pull it up on the shore when we are done."

Mike looked at the sail boat and then at the wind ruffled lake. The waves were not whitecaps but the wind was sure blowing hard today. He wondered how on such a beautiful blue skied day there was so much wind. Mike bit his bottom lip as he looked at the far side of the lake and wondered how far he would have to swim if something did happen.

Jim watched him look things over. "You can bring your life jacket," he said shaking his head. "But the boat floats even if it tips."

"Tips? What do you mean it tips? It tips *over*?"

"That's the best part!" Jim said excitedly. He explained the joys of getting a sailboat going as fast as possible without tipping it. He told of how one person would steer and the other would operate the sail. If they felt like they were about to tip over, they would just let out a little sail. "I will even let you control the sail so if you feel we are over too far you can control how far we go."

Mike nodded, accepting his death sentence once again. He had to die someday, after all.

Jim looked at him. "But you are not going to *wear* your life jacket, are you? It looks really stupid."

An hour and a half later a laughing Mike had to admit to Jim that this was one of the most exciting things he had ever done. "I LOVE THIS!" Mike shouted over the wind.

"Told ya you would. Pull that rope a little tighter. I think we can get some more speed."

The boat leaned over a little further as both boys stuck their toes under the cockpit and leaned back as far as they could try to keep it balanced. "Ohhh, ohhh ohhh…"

"Omygoshomygoshomygoshomygosh. Let out some line!" Jim shouted over the wind just as a new gust hit.

The sail touched the water and over they went. Mike scrambled to keep in contact with the sailboat while Jim jumped clear.

Jim quickly surfaced and started shouting orders. "Don't let it turtle! Don't hold on that side! Get over on this side! "

"Turtle? What's that?" Mike asked as he dog paddled around the boat.

"Right now the sail is keeping it from turning completely over. If it turns completely upside down it will be nearly impossible to get upright. Get over here now!"

"WHY DIDN'T YOU TELL ME THAT BEFORE!? Ratfink!"

Even as they started pulling the sail was sinking further into the water.

"Come on! Get more leverage on it. Stick your butt out as you pull on it."

Mike adjusted his body and sure enough the boat stopped sinking over and slowly started to come back up. "Ha! We got it." This was nearly as fun as sailing itself.

Soon they were back up and sailing and Mike had no fear of tipping the boat. They had proved they could deal with anything. They continued sailing for about half an hour. As Mike got bolder, they went over a couple more times but each time they were able to quickly right the boat. "This is sooo cool!"

They were heading back toward the Nelson's dock, and Jim said, "Let's do another lap."

"Sounds great!" Mike practically cheered.

As they came about in the turn, Jim pointed to the southwest corner of the lake.

Mike looked casually in that direction and saw a distinct line of nearly black clouds. "Whoa! We better go back."

"We got time. Besides the wind is picking up!" With that statement the boat shot forward like a torpedo and they flew across the lake. The clouds were moving fast and by the time they were three quarters of the way across the lake the sun disappeared. Mike was going to say something about going back but as he looked back at the wake of the sailboat, it looked like the wake of a motor boat. "I bet we could pull a water skier today. WOW!" He shouted.

His shout was answered by a flash of lightening followed way too soon by the crack of thunder.

"Oh crap!" Jim shouted and without a word of instruction, both boys went through the motions of turning around or "coming about" as Mike learned it was called. Now the angle was right that they could very easily watch the fury of the incoming storm.

Mike wrapped the rope around his hand another time as it became harder to hold. The lightning came more frequently now and it was obvious that when the real storm reached them it would be something. Mike looked at the aluminum mast sticking up above their heads. "At least the lightning will strike the mast and not us!" he shouted.

"You are two feet from that mast, idiot! Do you think that will make a difference to either of us?" Jim shouted back. Then, "Oh Lord." And he pointed toward the rough rippling of the water a couple hundred yards away. "That has to be a huge gust of wind coming!"

"Oh no! You're right." Mike had spent enough time on and around the water to know what that ruffling meant. He hurriedly began to unwrap the rope from his hand. Time slowed down and so did Mike's ability to move.

Both boys watched the ruffling of the water as the monster gust approached. It grabbed Mike's eyes and he could think of nothing but how far over they were already and when that hit, he better be able to let out a lot of line in a hurry, but how much? Letting out too much would just tip the boat over backward and they would be just as dead in the water as they would be if they went with the wind. He had a sudden insight into the vector and forces that he would not learn the name of for many years. "Turn into the wind!" He shouted to Jim in a rare demonstration of command.

"You're nuts! Wait. Yeah!"

But it was too late. The gust slammed the sail into the water. Mike let out line. Jim tried to turn but the rudder was lifted out of the water.

"Too late! Yeeeeee!"

"OHHHHH my…"

CRACK!

They both fell over backwards into the churning water. Frantically they scrambled to get hold of the boat and right it as they did so many times before, but they were in for a surprise. The boat *was* right side up and the sail lay in the water.

"What?"

"It must have fallen out of the cup thing. Stick it back in and let's go!" Jim cried scrambling back into the boat.

Mike grabbed at the mass of sail, booms and mast. His mind could not wrap itself around what he saw. The mast was in the cup thing. The cup thing was secured to the top of the sailboat but the sail was in the water. He looked back to Jim who tried to sit down but there was something wrong. "The top of the... the sailboat has peeled off from the bottom. Look!" Mike pointed to the bow where it was very evident. The entire front of the sailboat had the top layer, along with the piece that held the sail peeled back like a banana.

"Crud! We're screwed," Jim said wide eyed staring at the damage.

"What will Mister Nelson say?" Mike said.

"It doesn't matter if we are dead."

To emphasize the point, lightning flashed with the enormous bang you only hear on the water where there is nothing to obstruct the sound and… when the lightening is close, very close. While the wind had died down after the initial gust it was still intense. The waves became whitecaps and a stinging rain pelted down.

"Whattawedo?"

Both boys looked around the boat, in near panic.

"Pull the sail in so we don't lose it! It will slow us down anyway.

"Can you paddle with the rudder?" Mike asked.

"That will take forever." With no better ideas, Jim pulled out the rudder and paddled like his life depended on it. "This is getting us nowhere."

"The wind will blow us in eventually. Hey, maybe we could hold up the sail."

"That's nuts! You're too short to do any good."

Mike ignored the comment and picked up the sail holding it as high over his head as he could.

"Hey, the wind is so strong --- that's doing it! Great job!"

Lightning slammed into a tree hidden along the shore. Mike shuddered. "Here, you stand up and grab some. We will double the area and move faster."

"No, I have to steer. Besides I would rather let the lightning strike you." Jim grinned up at Mike.

"POTLICKER!" Mike shouted but he grinned down at Jim. Lightning could strike him. He didn't care. He was doing a 'great job.' It would take lightning to peal that smile off his face. It was the first time anyone told him 'Great job.' GREAT JOB! He rolled it around his mind.

With a shudder the foresail mast came down falling across the deck and killing five of the ships most experienced hands. The captain pointed up in terror, "Stow the main topgallant, man... she will never hold in this storm. She will pull us over and drag us down to the bottom with her. We're as good as dead." The captain shook his head. No man alive could climb to the top of the mast in this storm.

Lightning danced from the top of the maintop, but someone had to do it and he was the only one who could. Mike flew up the ratlines to tie down the flapping sail but the ropes were near worn through. His bare feet balanced precariously on the rope under the boom as he desperately tried to remain in place in the tossing sea. He must hold the sail in place or it would tear off. He tried to hold on to the boom while the rain tore at his skin, lightning flickering around him. He never felt so alive. The captain was shouting something. What was it? Could it be? "Great Job!"

"That was so cool watching you hold up that sail with the storm blowing all around you!" Linda said. "I would have been terrified."

"It was no big deal." Mike shrugged. "What I was really afraid of was what Mister Nelson would say, but he was funny!"

"What?"

"We were very apologetic to him. He looked at the sailboat and put a hand on each of our shoulders. He put on that enormous grin of his and said, 'Don't worry about it guys. It wasn't your fault. What a shame, that old, old sailboat finally died a glorious death. Now I guess I have to tell Missus Nelson I just *have* to buy that 16-foot catamaran I have been wanting for ten years.' He winked, slapped us on the back and went back up the stairs whistling."

Chapter 27   Slick

"Oh look!" Linda pointed across the barn yard to where a very large dark shadow crept noiselessly along the edge of the corn crib. "There is another cat. That is at least four I have seen today. Can I hold it? How many cats do you have?"

"Uhhh... I wouldn't try to hold that cat." The farmer stopped walking, pulled the John Deere cap off his head and wiped the perpetual sweat above his brown leathery face. "You see, I don't own any cats. They just live here."

Linda looked at him confused. "But you must feed them, right?"

"In a manner of speaking I do. I grow food. The mice and rats and the da... dern deer eat some of the food I grow. Way too much. And the cats, blessed cats, eat the rats and mice." He looked toward the woods and mumbled, "I wish they would eat the deer."

"You never feed them?" she asked incredulous.

"Nope don't need ta. Them cats are amazing. You watch 'em."

"Look pretty lazy to me." Mike said scornfully, as one lay down in the shade and began grooming itself fastidiously.

"Come out here at dusk or early morning and they look as sly and vicious a hunter as any ol' lion or tiger from Aferca. Although, in midday I have seen them take birds or snakes."

"SNAKES! You have SNAKES!!!"

The farmer stared at her a moment. "It's a farm... I sure do!" He looked down in consternation at this hopeless city girl and shook his head. That anyone could conceive a farm without snakes was just silly. Then he looked at the boys and laughed. The boys stood wide- eyed and slack-jawed, vibrating with wild excitement. They looked about ready to wet their pants.

The farmer tried to calm them down. "Well, not many snakes, because of the cats but the snakes like the mice too. All of nature preys on the mouse. You don't ever want to be a mouse."

Mike thought back to the many times he felt like a mouse and vowed to never again be a mouse.

"This is sooo cool," said Eric, "Let's go find a snake!"

"Look over there by the road." He pointed to the end of the driveway. "They like to crawl out from under the corn crib an' lie the in sun this time a' day."

The boys were off like a shot. Linda watched them go. "But why did you say I can't hold a cat?"

"Hmmm.... there might be a couple that would let you hold them, but they are not used to people and are really wild animals. That big one you just pointed out is the only one we named. My daughter calls him 'Slick.' If he was a human he'd wear a leather jacket, slick his hair back and carry a switch blade. You look at him close, and you will see that half his right ear is gone, his left one has multiple slits and there are scars all over his face. Every night he heads out into the woods to pick fights with raccoons and mountain lions, but he always comes back here for an easy meal and some..." he stopped abruptly, looking down into the innocent eyes of the young girl. "Uhhh.... Some time with his girlfriends."

He changed the topic quickly. "He's getting old too. Yep, he is one of the smart ones."

"How can you tell?"

"Dumb cats don't live very long. For example, did you know, a cat can go through a fan in one direction but not another?"

"WHAT?" This was a day of crazy talk for poor Linda.

"I've seen it myself. I got a fan up in the loft to help keep the girls cool, but it doesn't have any guard over the fan blades. When the fan is on the blades are nearly invisible. For a while, I was finding a cat with a gash in its head facing the front of the fan. So I started watching and if a cat walks into the fan from behind, it goes right through, but from the front, he doesn't make it. The old ones, they know that."

"The farmer rubbed his nose. Now you see that cat there?" He pointed to the roof of a small building by a tree where a tiger striped cat crouched watchfully. "The birds pick up the spilled grain on the ground there, and then fly back to that tree for cover. The cats will wait and watch on that roof. They know they will survive the fall of twelve feet, but they don't go to that higher roof right there even though there is more birds up there."

"How often to do they fall?" Linda was just about convinced the old man was crazy.

"Why every time! You don't think they can fly! They got to grab the bird with their paws. What are they to grab anything else with?" The old man was just about convinced the poor city girl was crazy. "Oh! Watch right now." He grabbed her shoulder and pointed.

The sparrow fluttered to slow down its flight into the tree. Just as it was about tuck into the tree, the cat launched. Cat and bird dropped to the ground noiselessly. The cat tried to adjust its hold and the bird flew away.

Linda gasped.

The old farmer grinned down at the slack jawed girl. "I bet you thought farming was boring."

The cat got up, shook itself, licked its paws and with a disdainful glance at Linda, glided away. She could almost hear the cat say, "I meant to do that. I am not really hungry right now. That bird was too skinny. I will catch a bigger one later. Right now, I need to have my nails done and take a nap."

Linda walked down the drive toward the boys. After *this* afternoon, maybe that would be best thing for her to do too.

Chapter 28   Fish Towel

"Why don'cha just grab the fish?" Linda protested.

"This is easier." Mike chewed his lip in effort and studied the fish wiggling on the end of his line. He grabbed it with a gray and brown towel in his hand. Its mottled colors implied it might have once been white but that must have been so long ago that other colors might not have been invented yet.

"It's his lucky fish towel," Little John explained from the front of the boat.

"I always take it with me when I go fishing. It's more important than bringing bait." Mike stated with the confidence of any experienced fisherman.

"And that way he doesn't have to touch the fish." John grinned.

"Yeah, fish are slimy... like girls." Mike sneered in jest at Linda and plopped the small bluegill back into the water. He dropped the fish towel into the boat, and began the tricky procedure of lacing an acrobatic worm on his hook.

Linda picked up the fish towel with two fingers. She made a face. "It's awful smelly, just like boys." With the word boys, she threw it in Mike's face.

"Oh man!" Mike snatched it off his face and wiped at the fish slime. Of course, his face was now coated with worm goo.

"Aww." Little John laughed.

Mike glared at little John and snapped his angry face back to Linda.

She flinched and threw her arm in front of her face. "Don't hit me," she whimpered.

Instantly Mike's face dropped. "I... I wouldn't hit you," he said, puzzled.

"I'm sorry Mike," she whispered looking at the bottom of the boat. "I'm sorry. I'm sorry. I'm sorry."

"That's... Okay Tink. You're right. It does smell like Little John." He threw it at him and Mike and little John both forced a laugh.

"He's never been washed either."

"You mean you never washed that fish towel?" She asked.

"Nope."

"Isn't that disgusting?" Little John made a face.

"Ick."

They turned at the sound of someone walking out on the dock.

Aunt Lilly shouted out. "You youngsters going to fish all day? I just took fresh sticky rolls out of the oven."

Little John had the anchor in the boat and Mike was rowing before she was done with her sentence.

The boys beat her up to the cottage's kitchen where the fragrance of cinnamon, yeast and butter blended into the world's most powerful bait for young humans.

Linda walked up the hill more slowly with Mike's aunt. "Aunt Lilly, would it be all right for me to wash Mike's fish towel?"

"Oh, yes dear," she said. "You can wash all of Mike's things if you'd like. I have to pry the shirts off him with a crow bar. I haven't yet figure out how to wrangle those horrible ragged cutoffs from him. He wears them every day. Why, just yesterday a pair of his socks walked up to me and begged me to wash them or put them out of their misery. I felt so bad for them I dropped them right in to a bucket of hot water. They were so repulsive the water jumped out." She hugged Linda. "I have a bag of rolls for you and your...family."

The next morning Mike rowed out to the drop off and Little John dropped the anchor. Mike's first cast barely hit the water and he had a strike. Linda cheered.

"Wow, lookit it go!" Little John hooted.

"It's a pike!" Mike cheered.

"What's a pipe?" asked Linda.

"It's a Northern Pike! Like the one my dad caught." Mike glowed.

"Keep the pressure on it!" hollered John.

"I know."

"Don't let it get away."

"I know."

"Keep it from going around the anchor line."
"I know."
"Don't..."
"I know. I know. I know. Help me get it into the boat."

Little John hesitated, his hands over the pike splashing next to the boat and in a monumental show of courage; he thrust his hands into the water pinning it to the side of the boat and sliding it up with both hands.

"Don't tip us!!"

He flew back basically flipping the fish into the boat.

"Wow, lookit all those teeth!"

"How do we get the hook out?"

"Where's the fish towel?"

Linda peered out from under her eyebrows. "Here it is Mike. I washed it for you... but it kinda fell apart."

Mike stared in horror. "You washed it!"

"I guess it was really old. I fixed it but I needed a patch. I used a piece of my favorite doll blanket from when I was little."

Mike looked at the cleaned frayed white towel with the strip of white blanket with printed yellow flowers and pink ribbons. "But it was my lucky towel! I never washed it!"

He looked at the fish and he looked at the towel.

"But you ain't never caught anything like that," Little John said chuckling.

Mike looked at the girl, looked at the towel, looked at the fish, looked back at the girl and grinned. "Thanks!"

Linda shrugged, "I guess I added some more magic to it. Tink can do that."

"Uh...." Mike looked at the fish and looked at the towel. "Say Linda, would you be willing to uh... wash the towel again... tonight?"

"Oh Uncle Vic, you should a seen it! It was 24 and 1/4" inches long. Aunt Lilly took a picture of it."

Uncle Vic put the bag of groceries down on the kitchen table. "Did I miss the part where you shout," then he spoke in a squeaky voice, "Uncle Vic, Uncle Vic, what do I do?"

Mike felt his face burn.

"...and you *love* every minute of it." Aunt Lilly punched Uncle Vic's shoulder.

Uncle Vic nodded with a wide satisfied smile.

Mike's mind flashed as if all the synapses in his brain fired at once. When Uncle Vic picked on Mike, it was how he *played*. Just like Jim teased Mike, Uncle Vic teased in *his way*. It was *Mike* who interpreted it as a put down. Uncle Vic really did *like* having Mike around. He was playing with Mike just as Mike played with the guys. Mike felt a warm glow envelope his being as if the whole world hugged him at once. Mike's grin grew to record size.

Uncle Vic leaned close to Mike and squinted. "So, where is this monster fish? Pike is good eatin'. …or is this a typical fisherman's story."

"I gave it away, but aunt Lilly took a picture. I'm going to have it framed."

"You *gave away* the biggest fish you ever caught? What kind of fisherman are you?"

"The finest kind," Aunt Lilly said strongly. She stood on her tiptoes and kissed his forehead. "I think you've grown this summer."

The next morning, Linda bit her bottom lip as she held out the fish towel, "Here's your towel Mike. I washed it more carefully this time. The pike tasted great. Thanks."

Chapter 29   August   Summer Sneeze Feels Fine

The early morning danced between the branches of the fir trees around the cabin. Mike cracked his eyes open and sneezed. He reached over the side of the bed and grabbed a Kleenex. Before he got it to his nose he sneezed again. He got the Kleenex to his nose just in time for the third sneeze. He dropped the soaked Kleenex and grabbed another. Soon a small Kleenex mountain began to form at the base of the bed.

Aunt Lilly walked up to the bed wrapped in a faded and tattered bathrobe with a glass of apple juice in one hand and a pill in the other. "Good morning and welcome to hay fever season."

"Couldja hold it down. You'll scare the fish," said Uncle Vic strolling around the outside of the screened in porch with his fishing pole and tackle box.

"Imba cubin." Mike stammered. Jumping out of bed, he ran, gathered his things and still beat his uncle into the canoe.

"Don't you want some Kleenex?" Aunt Lilly called.

Mike cringed.

Uncle Vic stepped onto the dock and chuckled. "You better go get it or she will carry it down and insist on you puttin' some Vicks on your chest too."

Mike dashed up the stairs two at a time, pausing only to sneeze, grabbed the box with a quick, "Thanks."

"Do you want some cough drops too? I've got some here somewhere. Just a minute."

"No, I don't." He shot back down to the canoe before it was untied.

They paddled quietly toward the drop off. Every time Mike sneezed the canoe rocked softly.

Uncle Vic stopped paddling. "Maybe I should put you in the back facing toward shore. Then with the jet propulsion I wouldn't have to paddle. As it is, I think we are going backward every other stroke."

"It's not that ...Choo." Mike sneezed again. "I don't think it's as bad on the water. Why did God have to make allergies?"

After fishing in the morning, Mike went back to the cottage for lunch and his allergies flared up again. He vowed to spend the rest of the summer out on the water where he didn't sneeze quite so much.

"Hi Mike," Buck's girlfriend Grace trotted down the steps with something in her hand. "I thought you might want to hear part of a letter Buck wrote me."

Unconsciously Mike cringed. There was something about the excitement in her voice that reminded Mike a little too much of his mother telling him about an "opportunity to build character." He wondered if he should run.

She sat down on the dock next to Mike and opened the letter. "I won't read you all this boring stuff, but half way through he says, 'It's funny the little routines I miss. I am sorry I can't swim across the narrows with you this Labor Day. That has been a fun tradition. Why don't you get Mike to swim it with you? He should be able to handle it by then. Mom says he is spending the whole summer up there, swimming every day. He should be in awesome shape by then. Tell him *Ooh Rah!*'" She didn't read the next two lines, one of which was, 'Make sure he doesn't wear that *life jacket*.'

She put the letter down. "I have been swimming across the narrows every Labor Day since I was younger than you. It's kinda as a way to say farewell to the lake. A few years ago, Buck started swimming it with me. So, what do you think?" She leaned into him so that their shoulders bumped. "Are you willing to be Buck's substitute?"

Mike was absolutely certain he could never do that. So he did what any self-respecting male would do... he lied. He made a great show of studying the narrow part of the lake to the east where the lake bent to the south bringing it closer to the far side. "I don't think my mom would let me be so far from shore."

Grace did what any self-respecting female would do, she called his bluff. "We can call your mom from our cottage if you'd like. We have a phone. My dad rows a boat alongside of us. If there is any trouble he will reach out with an oar, and I am a certified lifeguard."

He bit his bottom lip, "I will if I can wear my life jacket."

She shook her head, "Then it is not swimming. It is floating. You might as well be in an inner tube."

That sounded more like it to Mike, "Can we take inner tubes?"

"No." She hugged him. "Nothing can happen. I'll be right there. We can practice together before the big swim. Okay?"

"I'll think about it." He would think about it until he came up with an ironclad excuse and then he would say 'NO!'

"You'll say yes. You can do anything. You remind me of Buck."

Mike's stomach hurt.

She sprung up heading toward the steps.

Mike let out a long sigh.

She turned, "I'll stop by tomorrow and we can practice."

After she left, Mike lay on the dock reading a Charlie Brown book. He felt an awful lot like Charlie Brown today. A box of Kleenex sat by his side with a small mountain of white tissues mimicking the mountains of white clouds in the brilliant blue sky. The afternoon sun baked his sinuses making him feel like a person again. Dennis plodded around in the water as usual looking for minnows and crayfish, occasionally pausing to plunge his muzzle into the water. Typically, he came up empty.

"Dennis! Here boy."

The dog looked up the hill to where Uncle Vic stood calling.

"Com'mere boy. Come on," Uncle Vic called in his urgent hunting voice. The dog charged up the hill like his tail was on fire.

"What is it?" Mike called up.

"Something's under the cottage," Uncle Vic called down.

The boy charged up the hill like *his* tail was on fire.

Mike arrived at the top of the stairs just in time to see Uncle Vic squat down by the tiny crawl space access door. He fumbled with the latch while Dennis whined and trembled with excitement.

The door was barely open six inches and Dennis shot through with a howl.

"What's going on?" Linda asked running over, her black curls bouncing in excitement.

"Dennis is chasing somethin' under the cottage."

"Under there?" She bent over and peered into the gloom. "What is it?"

"I don't know. Do you Uncle Vic?"

The crawl space was the area below the floor and above the black earth the cottage had been built on. Uncle Vic used it for storing scraps of lumber and odds and ends that were mostly junk but he didn't want to part with. Rusty pieces of steel and splintered planks were draped in cobwebs, and decorated with mouse droppings. The entire area crawled with spiders and crickets. Mike wouldn't have gone under there for any money. Occasionally Uncle Vic would pull out a piece of lumber that he could get out by reaching through the little doorway but no one went into the crawl space. Mike even hated grabbing the pieces of lumber. He shuddered when Dennis charged into the refuse.

They all leaned closer to hear what was going on though they didn't need to get any nearer. The noise of the ferocious chase carried well. Boards clattered and metal rattled amid a chorus of snarls and growls. Here and there a glass bottle rattled. It all stopped with a sudden yelp followed by a whimper. They could hear Dennis working his way out to the door. He was almost there. All three leaned over to see what he had.

It sounded like he was close but Mike still couldn't see him. He got down on his hands and knees as close as he dared to the spiders. He knew they were watching him. They longed to jump on his neck. Spiders are especially fond of tender young boys and it is well known that necks and backs are the most delicious parts. The noise came closer and Mike got a glimpse of the dog's white fur a few feet away, but something was wrong. It sounded like an animal was still whimpering far within. Maybe Dennis had injured something but that made no sense. Why didn't Dennis just drag it out?

Mike remained on his hands and knees but pulled his head back from the opening and looked up at Uncle Vic. "Uncle Vic do you think it is stuck under one of the...." Mike stopped talking. His uncle's face underwent a spasm.

Mike had never seen a heart attack or a stroke but this must be what it looked like. What should he do? "Aunt Lilly!" he shouted. He turned to Linda but her face showed the same attack. It occurred to Mike that it might be something contagious coming from under the cottage. He looked at the doorway. The scene two feet from his nose burned so deeply into his retina that it seemed to burst out the back of his head and propel him several feet into the air. Bigger than he ever imagined, a skunk waddled out from under the cottage. He was huge. Mike's body launched itself into the air, without even bothering to ask his brain. His legs were running before he hit the ground.

Linda shouted up from her dock. "Is it gone?"
Mike looked down from the tree. "Is it gone Uncle Vic?"
"I think so," said a voice from above him. "He headed out behind the outhouse."
"What if he builds a den out there?"
"Well, maybe it would smell better."
"What happened to Dennis?"
"We better go look."

The sounds of a noisy misery came from under the house.
Aunt Lilly and Uncle Vic were trying to discuss what to do, but the constant whimpering was so loud it made conversation impossible.
"Would you two kids quit whimpering! I know the smell is bad. It must have sprayed under the cottage. (Cough, bork)... but we got to... (whew)... figure out what to...(cough)... to do here." Uncle Vic said holding his stomach.
"Let's head back by the outhouse where we can breathe," Aunt Lil suggested.
"We can't until we get Dennis out. He must be caught or injured," Uncle Vic said.
"Oh, poor thing," Linda murmured.
The three of them crowded around the tiny door. Mike was awful glad he didn't have to go under there. Even the dog should not have to go. He shuddered to think of Uncle Vic crawling with his face in the dirt into such a tiny hole filled with spiders and mice. It seemed too miserable a chore even to save Dennis.
"Maybe he'll work himself free," Mike suggested hopefully.
Uncle Vic stared in the hole. He shone his flashlight as far as he could. He poked at the sides of the opening. He looked down at his waist. Then he stood up shaking his head. "Mike, do you think you could fit in there? I'm too big."
"Uh..." Mike's heart dropped through his stomach, blew through his knees and rattled around his ankles. He looked around for an escape and saw Linda. Her eyes shone with delight and pride.
In the entire male experience, nothing is more gloriously painful

than being watched by a female. "Sure," he squeaked and then more boldly, "Sure," he said courageously, casting a look of disdain at the door crawling with spiders, and disappointed they weren't tarantulas. It really was too bad there weren't any snakes. A thought slapped his brain. *Maybe there are!*

He looked from Vic to Linda. She gave him the biggest smile he'd ever seen and his doom was sealed.

Mike buttoned up the old coat tightly around his neck. He was already sweating and the scratchy winter coat made it ten times worse. He double-checked the handkerchief tied around his mouth. The sweat on his hands made it hard to hold the old chrome penlight. The only way he could tell it was on was to shade the bulb with his hand and look directly into the bulb. Normally, on a bright sunny day this wouldn't bother him, but he was already two feet under the house and he was surrounded by darkness.

The Green Beret soldier crawled 50 yards down the long enemy tunnel and tension was high. It was scarcely higher than a casket and he knew booby traps lay triggered all around him. He moved with the caution of one who knew his life depended on carefully checking and rechecking every movement. Fortunately, he was wearing the latest technology flak jacket to protect him from enemy booby traps. He coughed into his gas mask and cursed the Cong. They had used one of their vile gas grenades on their way out of the tunnel and his filter was leaking. His eyes watered, mixing tears with the sweat running down his face. Dust from the tunnel stuck to the moisture and itched, compounding his misery. He wanted to back out, but he could not. Someone depended on him. One of their own was still alive down here. He could hear him in the distance. He sneezed and his mask filled with slime which stuck to his face with every breath. He sped up his pace. Itchy dirty sweat, made it feel like insects were crawling over every part of his body, but he pressed on. He needed to get out soon, before the gas overcame him. He sneezed again. Fortunately, he trained himself to be immune to the effects of various gasses. He saw the soldier. He appeared healthy, merely tangled in some wire. He was a mite panicky however. The Green Beret was forced to crawl on his elbows forward, his face practically buried in the dirt. When he reached the prisoner, the only way to untangle the captive was to support himself on his elbows and use only his hands to try to unravel the booby trap that held the soldier. He almost had him freed but in his panic the other fellow climbed right on top of Mike's face, scratching Mike's face and neck. The soldier twisted and turned in desperation, knocking the gas mask off Mike's face. He tried to jump over Mike but flung himself across Mike's face in the process. Mike couldn't breathe. The poison gas had saturated the soldiers clothing and now Mike's face was covered in it. Mike knew he must free himself quickly or they would both die.

"Wow, Mike!" Linda gasped. "That was amazing. I never saw anybody throw up so much before. I didn't know you could hold so much in your stomach."

"You got out of there pretty quick," Uncle Vic said admiringly.

Dennis walked over, sniffed the vomit and began to lap it up. A fresh wave of nausea rolled through Mike and his stomach heaved again.

"Even more?" Linda asked excitedly.

Mike felt like he had the flu. Chills swept over him and his stomach churned. He had absolutely no strength left. He rolled on his back to be prepared for his burial. Even if Aunt Lilly were to call him for some of her fresh rolls he would say, "No thanks. I'm just going to lie here and die." He had absolutely no energy. Even if he were helped to his feet he would fall over for sure.

His Uncle Vic reached down and brushed Mike's jacket.

"Whatsa matter?" Mike mumbled.

"Nothing. You had a spider on you."

Mike leapt to his feet, threw the coat to the ground and flew down the steps three at a time. He dove under the water without taking off his shoes. He popped up and wiped his hands furiously over his body and his hair and dove under again staying as long as he could hold his breath.

"Oh, I guess it's not." Vic said with a light chuckle to Aunt Lilly and held up the stick he had picked off Mike.

She slapped his shoulder lightly. "Oh you!"

"You can sleep over at Jim and Eric's tonight. Uncle Vic and I will just sleep through the smell," said Aunt Lilly. "I'm glad we all have hay fever. I can hardly smell it now."

Mike blew his nose, expecting to see the Kleenex black with skunk smell.

"Yeah, I suppose I am thankful for allergies today," Mike said grudgingly. "But I would rather never see a skunk again."

"Well, at least you got to impress Linda today. You are number one in her eyes."

Mike squared his shoulders with a barely discernible smile.

"Yep, no one can vomit like you." Uncle Vic winked and slapped Mike on the back.

Chapter 30   Not a Ghost of a Chance

Early morning sunshine shone on the four, sun-browned backs heading down the road. The boys had all taken their shirts off in the morning heat. The corn next to the road creaked in the wind.

"I wish the corn was ripe," Little John said.

"We must be getting close to the farm. You can smell it," Eric said.

"Nah, you just got behind Mike. You can still smell the skunk," Jim said.

Mike pushed Jim toward the water filled ditch beside the road. This, of course, started a shoving match, but it abruptly ended in a shout.

"Hey! Look!" Little John pointed.

They all looked to where he pointed.

There, in the middle of Mister Vanderkooi's yard, was a sign. It said "For Sale – Farm Realty."

"What's that mean?" asked Little John. "Is he selling some cows?"

"No stupid, he is selling realty," Jim said. "He is selling his farm."

"He can't do that."

"He said he was low on money. He must have to sell the farm."

"Oh man!"

"Whaddowedo?"

"We can't let him lose it."

They stood in the road and stared. A small dust cloud appeared on the road in the distance and the boys moved out of the road to let the truck pass. As they watched, a pickup with the windows rolled down slowed to a stop in front of the farm. A man and woman sat in the front seat looking at a piece of paper and then at the farm.

The boys didn't know what to do. The woman got out of the car. "Have you boys ever been in that house?"

"UH... no," Mike stammered.

"But we been in the barn," Jim said.

"And the fields," Little John said.

"And the manure pile," Eric added.

The lady smiled at Eric's comment. "What can you tell me about it? ...Other than the manure pile."

They looked at each other.

"It's *real* old," Mike said.

"Yeah, real old," added Jim.

"Parts is fallen apart," said John. "We can't go near the barn because it's falling over."

"And there is a ghost," said Eric.

The woman stepped back. "Ghost?"

The boys all stared wide eyed at Eric.

Jim's face relaxed and took on the conspiratorial glow that Mike knew all too well, "Yeah... the ghost. He drowned here back in the 1800s and so he haunts the place at night. There was a terrible storm and he was trying to save his...favorite... pet pig." He nodded mournfully and sighed. "It was very tragic." He looked like he was about to cry for the sheer memory of the fateful event.

Mike was really proud of Jim's acting. No doubt with a little more preparation, Jim would have been able to work up a few actual tears. This, he had done on one other occasion, but that time, the high probability of a good licking added a few deposits into the tear bank. Still Mike wondered if he should accidently punch Jim and so trigger some tears.

"Drowned? Where?" The lady asked, "This is the top of a hill."

"Uh...uh... see the swamp down the hill. That's where he drowned."

"Doesn't look very deep."

"Well, it is. The whole area floods every spring. "

"At the <u>top</u> of this hill?" she said dubiously.

"Artesian wells," Jim said with a knowing nod though he had little idea of what they were.

"Oh." The lady nodded. "Well, thank you for your help." She got back in the car and the couple drove off.

"Oh man, that was close," Mike whispered.

After dark, Mike zipped up the fly on the old two-man tent and crawled down into comforting warmth of the sleeping bag.

Eric squirmed around. "Boy, it's crowded in here. Move over."

"You're the smallest, you don't need as much room," Jim said with a punch.

Eric punched him back but both of the bigger boys just glared back at Eric. Eric lay back on the sleeping bag and studied them a moment longer.

"Hey Mike, why don't ya leave the flashlight on for a while," Eric said a calculated tremor in his voice.

"Why?"

"Just in case there are any ghosts around here. You know like…like at the farm."

Long silence. "You are the one who made up that story. How can it scare you?"

"I…I don't know, but just leave it on."

Longer silence. "That's stupid," Jim said and turned it off.

They lay there in silence for five incredibly long minutes.

"What was that?" Mike asked, turning on the flashlight.

"What?" Jim asked.

"I didn't hear it."

"Listen."

"There."

"That's frogs."

"No not that…There."

"That?" Jim asked

"No, not that... That!"

"That?"

"No wait….That!"

"That shlrp?"

"No, the whooommppp!"

"I didn't hear it."

"Shhhh."

"That?"

"Yeah."

"I *heard* it."

"What is it?"

"I…I…don't know," Jim said. "That's weird."

"Maybe it's a ghost."

"No such thing."

"Little John said…"

"Quiet!"

176

"Maybe it's aliens," Mike whispered.
"Like on…"
"Yeah."
"Oh… man…"

Mike's eyes tried to bore a hole in the heavy canvas of the tent. His ears strained to identify the culprit.

Finally, he slid his hand up to the tent flap and opened up just enough for one eyeball.

Missus Swanson yawned as she sat up in bed. Rubbing the sleep out of her eyes as they tried to focus in the bright morning sunlight, she stepped out of bed and screamed.

Two boys jumped nearly to the rafters without leaving their sleeping bags. Later Mike figured he must have jumped with his butt.

"I'm sorry boys," she apologized. "I thought you were sleeping out in the tent not on our bedroom floor. I didn't know what I stepped on."

"We...we got cold out in the tent," Jim said.

"Where's Eric?" she asked.

"They got Eric!" Mike cried, jumping to his feet.

Both boys dashed out of the kitchen and out to the tent. Jim flung back the flap.

Eric shielded his eyes from the light. "Go away."

"You're okay?" Jim asked.

"You slept out here by yourself? Weren't you afraid of ghosts?" Mike stated incredulous.

"There're no such things as ghosts. I fell asleep easy after you guys left and I had some room."

Jim pounced on him.

Mike calmly reached down and undid the ties. The tent collapsed on the two squirming figures. He would sleep in his own bed tonight.

Chapter 31   Missing Life

Friday was always the longest day of the week. Mike could hardly wait. The boys had been gone all week but could not come up for the weekend until after their mothers and fathers got out of work. He swung in the hammock and read but his mind was on other things. It had been a boring week and he had great plans for the weekend while the boys were here. There was a whole mess of frogs pouring out from everywhere. He knew they were the bait to catch some monster bass.

He heard the crunching sound of a car driving up the two track to the cottage. He dropped his magazine and sprinted around the cottage to meet the boys.

Uncle Vic and Aunt Lil stepped out on the back porch. The car stopped but the doors did not fly open. Instead of the boys flying out of the car as they usually did, they remained in the car looking uncomfortable. Mister and Missus Swanson slowly got out of the car carrying Uncle Vic and Aunt Lilly's mail.

Missus Swanson's eyes were very red.

Mister Swanson's brow furrowed as he walked toward the couple. He held out the stack of mail to Uncle Vic. To Mike he looked angry but when he spoke his voice was quiet and shaky.

Mister Swanson bit his bottom lip and said, "A...a... telegram came for you today."

Aunt Lilly's face fell into her hands. Missus Swanson steadied her with an arm around her shoulder. This quickly became an embrace and both women sobbed together.

Mike looked from face to face. Trying to figure out what happened but the made no sense of it. "Is it from Buck?"

Mister Swanson shook his head in a short choppy movement.

Uncle Vic slowly and deliberately opened the telegram. He took one of his deep noisy breaths. His voice cracked as he said, "Says he's missing.... doesn't say he's... gone." He rubbed his wife's back and she *flung* herself on him, sobbing and wallowing in his embrace.

Uncle Vic swallowed and wiped one eye with his hand. "He'll show up." He swallowed loudly.

"What does that mean?" Mike squeaked.

Mister Swanson placed his hand gently on Mike's shoulder and spoke carefully, "It means that when all the other soldiers came back from a battle, Buck... did not." Mister Swanson explained softly. "They don't know if he was captured or...or what happened to him."

"Maybe he just took the week off and went camping." Mike suggested, meekly though he knew it was a lie.

"Maybe," Mister Swanson whispered. "Mike, why don't you come spend the night with us." He turned to Uncle Vic. "If you want us to drive you or Mike home or if there is anything else we can do, let us know."

Mike looked from face to face. He never thought the war on the other side of the world could reach all the way to northern Michigan... all the way to him.

Missus Swanson took Mike by the hand, and led him away. Hot tears streamed down Mike's face but he made no sound.

Jim and Eric set the tent up again. The absence of their usual bickering added to the heaviness of the night. Mike crawled into his sleeping bag, but after they went to bed, Mike crawled back out of the sleeping bag and headed down to the dock. It was a clear night with no moon and the stars were the brightest he'd ever seen. The Milky Way was flung across the sky like a glowing veil hiding the face of God.

Mike sat on the dock and watched the stars. His mind wallowed in the dark pit of his cousin's fate. Was some godless communist beating him? Was he dead or was he lying wounded in some muddy rice paddy waiting and praying for the release of death.

Mike let out a long sigh. Buck's life was so short.

He heard steps on the dock behind him.

"What... you doin'?" Jim asked softly.

"Thinkin.'"

"I figured. Want some company. I can't sleep."

"Sure," Mike mumbled.

For about a half-hour they sat on the dock occasionally shifting positions, neither saying a word A large fish jumped close to shore.

"Whoa! This must be when we should be fishing," Jim said.

"I don't know. It's pretty late."

"What time do you figure it is?

"I don't know. Maybe midnight?"

"I wonder if fish sleep."

"I wonder if death is like being asleep?" Mike half whispered.

"Nah, you go to heaven or... the other place."

"You ever think about how old you might be when you die? You know like what things you'll wish you woulda done."

"No, I guess I just figure to live to be old having done everything."

"It seems like Buck had already done everything. You think he's alive?"

"I don't know. Yeah, I think he is alive. I heard my dad say they found some Japanese soldiers just a couple years ago who didn't know the war was over."

"Really?"

"Yeah."

Mike's voice lowered. "But most of them that didn't come back were dead. It musta been pretty rare for them just to be lost or somethin'."

"I bet it's not all that rare. We almost got lost coming back from the river and all of Vietnam is a big swamp."

"But Buck never got lost... Well, except that time he took me over to Picnic Lake and ...and ...that time over ta Bear Swamp...and... well I guess he did get lost a couple times."

"Sometimes the lost are found."

"Yeah, but it's pretty rare."

At that moment, a meteor burned its way across the sky brightening up the whole lake in its fiery death.

"Wow!" Jim shouted.

"Man! Did you see that!"

"That was incredible! You could see everything like daylight!"

"You think that's a sign? But what kinda sign?"

"I don't know but we just got to see something pretty rare. Rare things do happen," Jim said thoughtfully and yawned. "Come on, let's go to bed."

"I'll be up in a minute," Mike said.

Mike cracked open his eyelids. The last star was fading, a

gentle robin's egg blue filled the sky, but the sun wasn't up. Something wet touched his hand. He jerked it away and realized it was just the dew on the dock. He heard a soft boom of someone stepping onto the dock two cottages down and watched his uncle slide the canoe smoothly into the water.

He stared in admiration as the old man paddled noiselessly over the water. Each stroke appeared to touch the water without breaking the surface, with little more ripple than a spoon in a soup bowl.

Uncle Vic pulled alongside the Swanson's dock. Without a word Mike stepped in just as his uncle had taught him. He stepped in as gently and smoothly as if the canoe were made of glass. Mike picked up the paddle Uncle Vic had placed in the front and softly caressed the water as though he was comforting a small-injured child. They were the only two people in the world and yet neither spoke.

The mournful cry of a loon carried across the lake and Uncle Vic headed in that direction. As they approached the bird, the loon dove and disappeared from view. The bird reappeared, but each time they got close, he disappeared under the water. Sometimes the loons cry seemed a mocking laugh, other times it was a lonesome wail. They never got very close. The loon flew off toward the sunrise as they approached the other side of the lake. Water lilies embraced the shoreline in this little cove, cups of yellow and white amid the large saucers of lily pads that Mike was sure hid world record bass. He never saw them, but they *must* be there. The lake seemed to hide so many things. They slid in among the lily pads with a soft whish as the pads slid along the bottom of the boat. He reached down and touched the tender blossom of a lily. The lake didn't always hide things. Sometimes it made them beautiful like the lilies. He saw a flicker of a shadow and turned to see the sun gliding up. The light sparkled on the lake surface.

They sat there a long time. Neither said a word. Finally, as the wind began to pick up Uncle Vic picked up his paddle and pushed them off toward the cottage.

Mike put out his hand to catch the dock and they slid to a soundless stop. They pulled the canoe up and turned it over. As they headed toward the steps to go up, Uncle Vic rested his hand on Mike's back. "I'm glad you've been up here Mike. Your aunt and I talked it over and we are going to stay here rather than go home. If you want to go home though, the Swansons will take you."

"I... I want to stay here." Mike's voice cracked and he hugged his uncle.

Uncle Vic squeezed him back then pushed him toward the steps. He swallowed hard. "We better get ready for breakfast."

Mike trudged up the stair. His uncle blew his nose behind him.

Aunt Lilly was hustling about the kitchen as if she expected company.

It was the biggest breakfast Mike had ever eaten not because he was hungry, but because she had made so much. Then they all went back to bed.

Mike did not go with Aunt Lilly and Uncle Vic to tell Grace. Mike thought he was supposed to say something when they came back but all he could do was stand and look awkwardly at the couple shuffling back to the cottage. In response to his questioning look Uncle Vic said, "She's a gem. Said ...he'll be home by Christmas. He smiled but the words came out with a husky scratch.

The week dragged on in quiet routine. Aunt Lilly would start crying for no apparent reason. She and Uncle Vic spent a lot of time just sitting together quietly in the swing, holding hands and watching the lake. To Mike, they looked really old. They had always looked very old but now they seemed to age before his eyes. How old were they? Uncle Vic was a teenager during WWI. He had seen the biplanes. He said he was born when this century was just a toddler, but that just seemed impossible.

Mike knew his aunt was much older than his mother who was the baby of her family and his uncle was much older than his aunt. Buck had been born late in his aunt's life. After all, his uncle was retired and his cousin just out of college. How old was he? The question suddenly seemed vitally important. He didn't want his uncle to be old. He wanted to keep coming up here with him forever. This just made him sadder yet.

One afternoon, Mike screwed up his courage and found his way over to Grace's, telling her that he would be proud to swim across the lake with her. Inside, he knew he would drown in the attempt but it no longer mattered. He felt so bad that when she hugged him, he even hugged her back. He thought it would make him feel all noble telling her this but somehow it just made him feel worse, it seemed like he was living a lie. He did not want to be around anyone.

In the days that followed, he tried to avoid the cabin and spent more time by himself. He went for many canoe trips solo, having become quite adept at steering the canoe and paddling long distances by himself. He even ventured to fish in Turtle Bay by himself, but only during broad daylight, of course. Secretly, he hoped the turtle would attack so he could get revenge on something.

The buzzing of the cicadas in the trees was all the company he wanted, but even their humming reminded Mike of an old man standing around waiting for something. Gloom hung around the cabin like the dark shadows dwelling under the huge old pines.

He knew he had to go on with his life. Buck would want him to be strong and encouraging to Uncle Vic and Aunt Lilly. He needed to cheer himself up. The brightly, cheerful farm fields filled with the smiling faces of Black-eyed Susans around the lake beckoned to Mike, and he found himself walking out to Mister Vanderkooi's farm.

"No, I haven't sold the farm yet. Why? You gonna buy it?" Mister Vanderkooi demanded.

"No." Mike stammered. "I...I wish I could. Then you could stay here forever."

The farmer slapped the boy on the back with a sigh. "Well, everything changes. Ain't nothin' certain."

"That's fer sure."

"Anything new on young Buck's missing...?"

"No." Mike turned away and swung the hay bale into the growing pile.

"If you're selling the place, how come you're puttin' up hay?"

"It ain't sold yet and I got ta take care of ma girls. Besides, whoever buys a farm will want hay so he'll be more likely to buy it with hay."

"I suppose."

"It's the uncertainty that makes life, ma daddy used to say. Hoeing a dry dusty field of beans becomes a lot more interesting if you think you might starve this winter."

Mike grinned weakly.

The farmer continued, "Life never turns out like you expect it. You don't know what is good or bad you just take it as it comes. My nephew broke his leg. He was convinced it was the worst thing that ever happened to him. Now he'd have to wait for months to go overseas and join his outfit to fight in WWII. He got the news while he was still in the hospital. Ever' last one of them was killed on D-day. A shell hit their landing craft. Not a one made it. That broken leg saved his life."

The farmer looked at Mike and sat down on a hay bale. "It's just like that with your cousin. You don't know. He might be hidin'. Yeah, fightin' some secret war? Do ya think? I don't know an' neither do you nor anybody. That's life. That's what keeps us from dying of boredom. Makes it worth living. You might turn over a lump a ground tomorrow and find a fortune." He stood up and kicked a lump of manure. "Me I only find sh... cow pies, but who knows, one-day... maybe I'll find a treasure." He winked at Mike and his huge gnarled hands grabbed the twine around a hay bale and flung it up onto the elevator.

Mike's insides glowed. *He is fighting some secret war.* Buck would do that.

Billy carefully worked the dial on his ham radio. His fingers ached. He knew he was squeezing it too hard and he wished for the 100th time that he was back home in Indiana where his antenna was about twice as long and had a lot more range. He had only had the right atmospheric conditions a few times and now the voice was fading. "That's right," he said overly loud into the mike. "I'm looking for information from any Marines that saw Buck Malloy on his last mission."

Chapter 32 Life Saving

The thick green jungle brush was too dense to even see through. They parted the branches carefully with each step, never too sure of what was on the other side. More than once they had come across spiders of the size of a large dog that could have taken off Mike's entire leg with the smallest bite. Rumors of snakes, the diameter of a Volkswagen abounded. This was the darkest of the Dark Continent, Africa at its wildest. No one came here except one man and his daring team of animal hunters.

The leader of the safari cocked his hat back and gripped his machete. "Everyone be careful. The place was crawling with crockigators yesterday. The zoo is will pay us $100 a piece for them, but only if they're alive."

"And if we are too," said the beautiful lady photographer trailing behind the men. "Are you sure there is no quicksand?" she said peering down at the water seeping up from the ground around her $200 high heeled hiking boots.

"Nothing is certain here. Be on the watch, there might be paranoias in the water."

"I'm not afraid of a few paranoia fish," Eric said.

Jim rolled his eyes. "You mean piranhas."

"Never mind." He took a step closer to the River of Death.

The water boiled as alarmed alligator's shot off the bank into the water.

"Dang. You scared 'em off."

"Not all of them. Look. There's one!"

"I see it. Stand back. Let me show you how it's done." In a mighty leap the daring naturalist threw himself on the back of a huge crockigator all alone. He pinned the mighty beast to the ground by wrapping himself around its legs. He had to keep it from getting into the safety of the water or hurting any of his frail companions.

"Help me. It's getting away." Mike shouted.
The four boys and one girl swarmed around the one small frog, finally plopping it into the pail they had brought. They all huddled around the pail and watched it try to jump out. Satisfied the beast was safely subdued, they moved on.

The river narrowed and became shallower.
"Ah, here is a good place to trap them." He motioned his capture team forward then turned to the beautiful female photographer. "You better wait up on the high ground, and keep a sharp look out for the Zamboni tribe. They swore vengeance on us for capturing their sacred Rock Rhino."
"What will they do to us if they find us?" Linda asked.
"Torture us, kill us and eat us." Mike sneered.
"With no French fries?" asked Eric.
"That's part of the torture," said Little John with a faked shudder.
"Well, we're safe!" Jim exclaimed. "By the time they got done with Little John they'd be too full to eat for a week."
"I'll feed you to the crocks first." Little John pushed Jim into the water at the edge of the swamp.
"Yikes." Jim stood in knee deep water and peered around in alarm
"Great. Stay there. We'll herd them toward ya."
Ten minutes later. "Maybe you should try herding them toward us."
Five minutes later. "Linda, maybe if you get over there."
Three minutes later. "Quit letting them get away."
One minute later. "Hey, you flung mud on me."
0.0001 seconds later. "Stop....Stop I give!" A tornado of mud, water, and flying frogs swirled through the air powered by a rebel band of Zambonis.

"What a great day." Mike said.
"I can't believe you ate that frog, Eric," Little John said in awe.
"Hey, six million fish can't be wrong. You want to try one." Eric held up the bucket with about two dozen frogs in it. "They taste good when they're fresh and little."
"Really?" Little John studied the bucket dubiously.

"That one right there looks good," Eric said pointing to a small one and licking his lips.

"He palmed it," Jim said.

"What?" asked little John.

"Like magicians. They make it look like they put something in their mouth but they hold it and hide it in their palm. Here, I'll show you."

"OH MAN!!!! Why'd you tell him! He was going to *eat* one," Eric snorted.

"It's like this." Jim picked up a small frog and locked its back leg down with his little finger. He opened his mouth wide and brought it up to his mouth. The frog excited by the event, committed an indiscretion in Jim's hand. Jim flinched. The frog hopped free...into Jim's mouth. Jim, being startled did the natural thing and inhaled. He coughed and hacked. His friends tried to help as best they could, by laughing like maniacs. Eventually they thought of trying to help dislodge the frog, by slapping him. Sometimes the slaps even landed on Jim's back.

Little John collapsed into the gravel road. "Stop! I'm gonna pee." Of course, that helped. Suddenly all were aware of the need. Mike ran off into the brush.

Finally, Jim coughed it up looking quite as green as… a frog.

"Watts matter Jim, (gasp)… hee… hee...got a hee… hee... frog in your…" Eric couldn't get the last word out. Whether because he was laughing so hard or because Jim's hands were around Eric's throat was difficult to say.

Jim's sobriety helped them calm down.

When everyone finally calmed down enough to talk, Eric shook his head and said, "You idiot. This is how you do it. You hold the frog like this and you open your mouth and…(wheeze)…(cough.)"

Two frog legs sticking out of someone's mouth is funny anytime but to see it a second time in less than five minutes and to continue breathing was near impossible. They were all rolling in the road, tears coming down their eyes with laughter, all except Eric, of course.

The large wet spot on Little John's shorts only made it worse.

After supper Aunt Lil said she wanted to go for a ride to see if they could find some seedpods. She wanted wild sweet peas to plant by the road of the cottage. Mike elected to stay back at the cottage to avoid the stress of such an exciting adventure. Uncle Vic hinted that his arthritis was acting up and that maybe he should stay at the cottage with Mike but Aunt Lil hugged Uncle Vic's waist and proclaimed she couldn't venture off into the wilds without her big strong man.

Mike watched them drive off and headed to the hammock with an old Popular Mechanics magazine. He was reading about the flying cars that everyone would be using in the year 2001, when he heard a noise on the back porch. He got up and trotted quietly around the side of the cottage. He was careful to be quiet lest he surprise a nosey skunk. Maybe it would be a porcupine. He desperately wanted to get some quills. Eric had told him how to get them without getting poked, but Uncle Vic said not to worry, Dennis usually brings a few quills home every year.

He peered around the side of the cottage but to his great disappointment it was only a human.

Linda's mother jumped, "Oh…hi Mike. I…I was just seeing if I could borrow something, but your aunt and uncle don't appear to be here."

"They went for a ride. I am sure they wouldn't mind if you borrow something."

"Thank you. I wouldn't normally but…"

Mike looked at what she had taken from the case that Uncle Vic left on the porch. Two bottles of beer? That was odd.

She continued awkwardly backing off the porch. "It's his medicine… you see. He has terrible back pain and without it he gets…." her voice trailed off.

"Uh…that's fine. My dad gets backaches too. I don't know what he does."

"Thank you," she said so quietly that Mike barely heard it and she walked quickly back to her cottage.

That was weird, Mike thought and chewed on the event in his mind. He went down to the lay on the dock and watched the sun settle toward the white birch trees on the western side of the lake. Their interchange left him uncomfortable and evening always made him a bit melancholy anyway. The orange and reds cast by the sun on the clouds contrasted with the blue sky and white contrails from jets. It was deliciously sad watching the sun disappear. Another day gone forever. How can something be so beautiful as it dies?

The darkness settled over the water and sank into it. It reminded him of the night Cousin Buck took him snorkeling in the dark.

Buck's big waterproof flashlight cast a narrow corridor of safety for the two intrepid snorkelers. Tall weeds grew like columns on either side of the light.

Buck had a pretty big flashlight but not big enough for Mike's taste. He moved closer to Buck as much for security as for warmth in the cool of the night. Buck pushed him aside in the course of moving his arm to swim. Mike looked around nervously, but outside of the cone of light loomed an impenetrable wall of blackness. The weeds sucked in every glimmer of the light, as if vacuuming up the dirty light contaminating the water. Mike's breathing was always labored as he swam with Buck, trying to keep up to his muscular cousin. Now his breath came even harder as he wrestled with his sanity to refrain from running for shore.

A movement on the mucky bottom directly underneath him caught his eye. He tried to pop out of the water and run along the surface but just succeeded in shrieking like a girl. A painter turtle methodically paddled along the bottom beneath his legs.

His cousin's hand shot out and grabbed at it but the turtle slid into the weeds and disappeared.

Buck stood up, his fins sinking into the mucky bottom raising great clouds of silt. "You are just fine. There is nothing here that can hurt you, is there?" He said in a slow deliberateness designed to calm.

Mike shook partly from cold partly from all that he couldn't see in the water. "N…n…no," he stammered out. "I was j..just s..surprised."

Buck grinned, "It's the surprises that make it fun." Enthusiasm bubbled from him as he slid back into the water.

They had only gone a little further when they saw it. Mike shivered in the heat of the setting sun even now, two years later, to think of that night. Mike had begged to carry the flashlight for a while. They had gone a little further out. While this put the mucky bottom further away from accidentally plunging one's hand or foot into it, the blackness of the deep water seemed to stretch away like the bottomless pit reserved for Satan and his demons. Mike tugged on Buck's arm to lead him back toward the shallows. Buck pointed and even as Ebenezer Scrooge trembled when the last spirit pointed a dark bony finger towards a gravestone, Mike shook with a mighty fear. For there, only a few feet away, was the meanest looking creature Mike had ever seen. Two feet of muscle and teeth, the Northern Pike, for all the world looking like a freshwater barracuda, ready to slash huge slabs of flesh from anyone that dared venture into his world after dark. Mike stared unable to move. The long under-hanging jaw dropped rhythmically working its gills to show off teeth, that could probably bite a finger clear off.

Mike shot toward shore shrieking and stood up as soon as he could run clumsily toward the nearest dock. He only succeeded in stumbling in a slow walk as the flippers resisted the water, grabbing sand and seaweed.

"Mike! Mike come here," Buck had commanded. He stood still, waist deep in the water. His voice was calm but commanding. "It is already gone. It was afraid of you. You are much bigger than he is."

It was pure logic, but the fish had teeth.

"Come on Mike it was nothing to worry about, was it?"

Soon Mike was back out there swimming next to Buck. Mike had been afraid, but Buck was there. Buck hadn't belittled him or called him names. He just quietly urged him on. There was nothing to fear. He was not alone…then. But now he was.

Was Buck alone? Mike wondered what the sunsets looked like in Vietnam. Was Buck dead or was he being held captive in some communist prison camp with no good food, no exercise, no daylight. A tear ran down his cheek.

Mike wiped the tear away and looked back at the cottage. The white bucket holding the frogs glowed in the fading twilight. He picked up the bucket and gently set it in the water allowing the frogs to swim out.

"Darn Communists," he said to the lake. He looked back down at the frogs. "Go home to your families, eat flies and watch sunsets."

He heard a noise and saw Eric watching him from the bottom of the hill.

Jim came trotting down the steps carrying his fishing pole. " Hey Mike, give me the frogs, I'm going fishing."

Mike held out the empty bucket, his eyes looking at the ground.

"The frogs got away," Eric said casually.

"Oh man!" Jim scowled. "I was gonna use 'em for bait." His face changed abruptly. "Hey! Now we got something to hold crayfish in. They're even better bait and I know where there's a

mess of 'em."
"Neat!"
"Where?"
"Let's get Little John!"

In that dead time, after breakfast and before it is warm enough to swim, is the time for exploring or playing cards. Today the boys sat down on the dock playing cards. The beagle lay quietly in the bright sunshine. The boom, boom, bang, on the neighboring dock announced that Linda's dad had finally awakened and was going fishing.

Mike watched him unsteadily drop his gear in the boat.

"Looks like he's already drunk," Jim said to nobody.

Mike studied his cards, played an ace on the discard pile, then looked over at Linda's dad rowing the aluminum boat out to the drop-off.

The boys continued to play cards. They had been done fishing for a couple hours but it was still too cool for swimming.

Mike watched as Linda's dad tied an artificial bait to his line. "Didn't you give all the leftover crayfish to Linda's dad?"

"He wasn't up yet when I stopped by," said Little John. "So, I just put 'em in his bait cooler so I could bring the bucket back."

The man cast his artificial lure out into the water and reached down behind the seat.

Eric played a five and stated casually, "He doesn't have a bait cooler. He has a *beer* cooler."

"Yeaaaaheaaaahahahah." Linda's dad jumped up in the boat and swung his hand back and forth. The large crayfish attached to his little finger was easily visible even at sixty yards.

The beagle jumped up and ran to the end of the dock, eager to be part of the excitement.

Little John played a ten of hearts.

"Hey, that's the big green one I caught," Eric said.

Jim looked up. "Oh yeah, you're right....Gin."

"Yeeeeeeehaehhehaehheha." Her dad slammed his hand against the side of the boat. The banging of the aluminum boat echoed off the trees.

"Boogers! You won again."

"He's not gonna catch anything if he scares the fish." Little John shook his head sadly.

"I wouldn't mention you gave those to him if I were you," said

Jim. "Whose deal?"

Harold rowed the boat back to his dock about noon. No one was around but that stupid dog without the teeth. His head hurt, his hand hurt and he hadn't caught anything.

He left his tackle and pole up in the boat and struggled up onto the dock. He lifted the cooler onto the dock and stared at the crayfish crawling over his remaining cans of beer.

"I hope you die." He sneered and left the cooler in the sun on the dock for the crayfish to bake in the summer sunshine.

Dennis plodded through the shallow water searching for minnows and crayfish. Every once in a while, he would pounce. Seldom did he get one. He heard a noise and looked at the cooler on the dock next door.

"Dennis!"
No answer.
"Dennis!" Uncle Vic set down the bowl of dog food and started toward the beach.

"Dennis! Here boy com'on. Geet 'em boy." He called in his hunting voice, guaranteed to bring any hunting dog running.

He got down to the bottom and saw Dennis on the dock. He stood there a long time. "Mike?" He called.

"What?" Mike came scampering down the hill to stand beside his uncle on the dock.

Uncle Vic sighed and picked the body of the dog up off the dock.

"What happened?" Mike whispered.

"Looks like he choked on some crayfish. Guess I'm not surprised. Come on, we'll bury him behind the doghouse." They headed slowly up the stairs.

JOURNAL

'Sorrow seems to follow us like smoke follows a liar,' Aunt Lilly said. I know what she means but Dennis lived a good life considering, and he died where he would have wanted.

If dogs go to heaven, maybe he is…

Mike swallowed hard, put the old yellow pencil down and closed the book. He couldn't bring himself to write … *hunting with*

Buck.

Chapter 33   Rowmance

The lake was calm, and the sun sagged low in the sky, supported by a hammock of pink and orange clouds. Mike lay in the cottage hammock reading a Readers Digest that was older than he was. Uncle Vic headed down the hill toward the lake carrying a pair of floatation cushions and a canoe paddle.

Mike jumped out of the hammock. "We goin' fishin'?" He asked excitedly.

"Nope. Takin' my girl for a canoe ride."

"Aunt Lilly never goes canoeing."

"She will tonight."

"Howcome?"

"It's our anniversary. We are going on a date," He winked at Mike and continued down the hill.

Mike sat back down in the hammock dumfounded. Sure enough here came Aunt Lilly in her dungarees (a new word that Mike had just learned) and flannel shirt all set for their date. The dungarees were rolled up at the bottom, exposing her white socks.

When she got down to the dock, Uncle Vic put his arm around her and they stared at the sunset.

What are they doing? Mike wondered. They are just standing there. Maybe he should offer to help them get in the canoe?

Aunt Lilly turned to Uncle Vic and kissed him right on the mouth. Then he held her hand to help her into the canoe. Afterward, Uncle Vic slid into the back seat himself and noiselessly glided out onto the glassy still lake.

Mike tried to think of the last time he had seen his parents hug or kiss and he couldn't remember. He wandered down to the lake to see where they would go. He sat down on the dock and watched. His eyes wandered to and fro but always back to the silent canoe with the two old people out on a date. He kicked at the water. It felt warm and soft. It was a pretty night. The canoe headed toward the bend. They were probably going to Turtle Bay. It was real pretty over there and secluded... if you weren't afraid of Ol' Ironsides or aliens.

Thump. Boom. Boom. Boom.

Mike jumped at the sound and movement of someone walking out on the dock he sat on. He spun his head around.

"Where they going?" Linda asked.

"Just for a ride. Uncle Vic said they were going on a date."

"It's a nice night for one, isn't it?" She sat down beside him.

"Yeah, I was thinking I might take the rowboat out," Mike said half to himself.

"That sounds like fun." She looked at him and said no more but continued to stare at his eyes or at least toward his eyes.

Mike stared at the water in fear. He knew she watched him for some sign. He held his breath as long as he could lest he betray any emotion. Finally, he bit his bottom lip and said, "Let's go."

Her answering smile shone like sunshine on daisies. His fear melted into gladness.

Mike stood up and went to get the cushions and a life jacket for himself. Mike glanced at Linda who stood waiting patiently. They wouldn't go deep. He didn't need a life jacket. Two cushions would do. After all, he had been practicing with Grace. She had even taught him how to hug... now where did that thought come from?

Soon they were underway. Mike rowed while Linda sat in the back.

Mike watched the lake and watched Linda. She leaned back her arms propping herself up with her legs toward him. Her posture reminded Mike of a girl he had seen in a magazine selling soft drinks, but Linda was prettier.

"Uh... here is where we catch all the good crayfish." Mike pointed down to the rocks sticking their heads above the sandy bottom.

She looked down and nodded. "What do you think your aunt and uncle are talking about?"

"Huh?"

"What do you think they are talking about? You said they were on a date. What makes it a date? It's weird to think of old married people on a date."

"I dunno. Stuff."

"Don't you think it is something different?"

"No. I think it's just a man and woman together, alone."

"Sort of like us?" she said with a soft lilt that sounded different from any voice he had ever heard her use before. His mind bore down hard on the word *us*.

"Uh... This isn't...is it? Maybe they do talk different... they must...I."

She ignored his confusion, "I think he is telling her how beautiful she still is and how wonderful it has been being married to her for so long."

"Probably." Mike jumped at the chance to change direction. "Maybe that's what makes it a date. They are talking about each other, not about..."

"Crayfish?"

"Not about crayfish." Mike said softly.

"Let's go on a date Mike."

"Uh...I don't...don't know how, Linda." He licked his lips nervously.

"We talk about each other or about us."

"Uh...I dunno how."

"I'll start...." A sly smile crept across her face.

Mike felt like a small bluegill gasping in air as it hung on a hook.

"Hey Mike!" A voice shouted from the beach.

They both looked toward shore. Jim was waving his arms.

"Wanna build a fire?" Jim hollered out to them. "We have marshmallows!"

"Sure," Mike hollered back to shore. He looked at Linda. She just looked away across the lake.

"You wanna build a fire Linda?"

She didn't answer for a moment but then mumbled "Sure," and smiled weakly.

Mike rowed them to shore.

The fire crackled and threw up a fireworks display of sparks as Little John threw a large log into the middle of the blaze.

"Not too much now, we'll burn the marshmallows."

"I like 'em burned," Little John licked his lips.

"You like 'em any way you can get 'em." Eric said.

"Yep."

Linda sat by the fire with the boys but had said nothing since the boat had docked.

Little John continued. "I got to get 'em while I can. A couple more weeks and summer is over. Football practice starts in a week. I got to get in shape."

"Boo."

"Quiet."

"Don't talk about school."

"Now that you two will be in Jr. High, you guys going out for football?" Little John asked gloating in the glory of being almost a whole year older.

"No. I don't weigh enough. Have you seen some of those junior high football players?" Jim answered.

"Yeah," Mike echoed.

Little John's face lit up. "You should see 'Rhino.' He's almost twice as big as me!"

"What's junior high like?" Mike asked.

"Your classes are all over the school and you have lots of different teachers, which is good, so you're always sure to get *one* teacher you like. And they have dances." He poked Mike in the ribs.

"You go to the dances?" asked Jim.

"Sure. You should see all the food."

"Do you dance?" asked Jim.

"Heck no. Mostly you stand around and eat. You aren't going to dance, are you?"

"You bet," Jim answered smugly.

"With a girl?" Eric asked wide-eyed.

They all laughed.

"No, with a *penguin*, knot head." His brother pushed him.

"Who'd dance with you?" Eric asked looking at Jim.

"I bet Laurie Cannon would," Jim said with a sly smile.

"Oh?"

"Do you know how to dance?" John asked.

"Sure! You just stand in front of a girl and jump around a lot."

"That's not how you dance!" Linda said in disgust. Her first statement since they had pulled ashore caused every head to turn. She had been so quiet they had forgotten she was there, until she spoke.

Linda looked at Mike. "I know how to dance. My mom showed me. Stand up Mike."

A circle of white saucers stared at Mike in slack jawed awe. He stood up slowly with the wild-eyed fear of a mustang with his first saddle slapped across his back.

"Here, put your left hand on my hip and take my hand with your right."

Slowly, ever so slowly Mike moved his hand tensely toward her hip. The earth shifted slightly and his hand made contact. Instantly, Mike's left hand burned with her warmth. His entire being concentrated on the gentle curve where her slender waist curved sweetly to her hip. He hadn't realized under the baggy shirts that she had hips. They were there though and his hand thrilled at the touch. She was saying something but his ears roared with his own thoughts.

"And then we step..."

"What?"

"Not into the fire!"

Mike fell over backward over the log they were using to sit on. General laughter.

"Well, it's harder to do without music," she said.

"Nobody dances like that anymore," Jim said.

"Some still try to," Little John said.

"We'll have to get some music sometime and I can teach you," Linda said sitting back down on the log with a frown.

The marshmallows and talk continued until Little John was called home. Jim and Eric said they should get going also.

Mike stood up, "You going home Linda?"

"No, I'll wait here by the fire for my dad. He is still out fishing."

Mike sat back down by the fire, "I'll wait with you."

"Thanks," her smile glowed in the warm red firelight.

Mike's heart glowed as hot as the fire. Excitement, fear, he didn't understand but he liked how he felt.

They sat in silence gazing at the fire, listening to the sounds of the boys heading up the stairs to their cottage. The fire became the focal point to the world. The rest of the universe faded to darkness, impenetrable black. The only sound in all creation was the lapping of the waves like a shared heartbeat and the sputtering crack of the small fire. The only movements in the world were the soft slow hand and body movements of their quiet conversation. The only world that existed was here. The only two people in the whole universe were Mike and Linda. His heart reflected the glow of the fire.

When there were no more sounds from the boys and the only sounds were the distance laughter of someone across the lake, Mike swallowed hard and spoke. "You know Linda, um... I was thinking about the dancing... and... if you were to hum the tune... it uh... might work. Uh... the uh... dancing that is..."

Her eyes reflected the dancing flames as she stood, and her smile of delight drew the heart from his chest and cradled it in her hand. She seemed to mature as she stood. She knew a secret. A secret that she wanted to share with him. She knew how to dance. What other mysteries did she know? Mike stood stiffly, swallowed hard and glanced around the clearing. Why did he feel like a mouse staring into the eyes of a sly cat?

Her face clouded for a minute. "Mike, if I teach you how to dance, who are you going to dance with?"

"Uh..." Alarms rang shrilly. WARNING: There was a correct answer here and there was a *very wrong answer*. He hesitated. Answer right! Answer quickly! "No one... no one... but you."

She studied him closely, "Hmmm. Ok." The radiant sunshine of her smile returned.

He sighed comfortably and resumed breathing, as a burglar might, hearing the last tumbler click into place. It was the *right* answer.

They resumed the position. It was easier this time.

"Just step when I do." She began to hum.

It was very awkward. Mike tended to take large steps. He wanted to make it an athletic event, but there was no room. Roots were in the way. The fire crowded them and they had to start over several times. Each time they started over, his steps became smaller and he began to think in terms of subtle movement. The humming helped. It was a soothing sound like a woman calming a child.

Linda seemed to relax too. She drew a little closer to him.

Mike's heart thundered. He wondered if she could hear it. *This was weird. I am dancing with Linda and she is awful nice to hold. She even smells good.* He had never thought about the scent of her hair.

His mind was fully on the moment. The warmth of her presence, her hot hand in his, the subtle dance movements, the light of the fire reflecting off her face and twirling in her eyes, the delightful fear of bumping into her body awkwardly, they each held part of his mind frozen in place. Her hair brushed his face gloriously. It struck him that he had missed something in all their 'playtime' games. She was a person just like him. She had hurts and dreams just like his. She liked some things and disliked others. She was not some mystical being either. She was just a person like him and she enjoyed being with him! She enjoyed it especially, when he was nice to her. Wow! The lock had opened but not to let a burglar into the home, rather to invite a friend in for a visit. He sighed and relaxed just a little.

The sound of her humming was the most pleasant sound he had ever heard. It was no wonder he never heard the other noises. The first warning he got was the rough hand on his shoulder, pulling him from Linda and throwing him to the ground. Mike's thigh landed on a large root and he let out a groan, unable to stand.

"What the HELL's going on here!" Linda's dad hollered glaring down at him. "You leave her be. His fist aimed a Mike's face. I don't ever want to see you with her again. Come with me you little slut." He slapped Linda's face. Her hands flew to her face but he grabbed a wrist and dragged her along behind him.

Mike was too stunned to do anything but lie on the ground in stupefied silence. His mind had no experiences or training for dealing with the wild swings of emotion tonight. He had done something terrible... or so it appeared and he sure wasn't going to tell anyone. But... what did he do? And why did her father hit her. It never occurred to Mike that one of his parent's might one day hit him.

It was like those pictures in school where they showed a bunch of items and they asked what doesn't belong in this picture. But in this case, it was like none of the items belonged in the picture. He sat by the fire for another hour. Clouds drifted in, obscuring the stars. There were flashes of lightning in the west.

Aunt Lil came down to get him. "There is a storm coming."

"I know." He answered softly. I want to stay here."

"You don't need any more scars and I don't need any more scares."

But the storm came anyway.

Chapter 34 The Fall

Mike stood on the dock and frowned at the water. On a typical sunny early morning, the lake was calm and clear, fish clearly visible, but today a dark sky, wind and waves obscured any view of what lie below. The night before hung heavy on his mind.

He heard a noise on the dock behind him and turned to see his uncle walking slowly out to join him.

"No fishing today!" Uncle Vic said with a long sigh.

"Lookit all the branches and leaves that came down."

"Yep." Uncle Vic nodded pulling the pipe out of his mouth. "That was quite a storm last night. Looks like it might still be going on off to the north. Watch over there. You might see some lightning. We might get some more yet."

"I saw enough lightning last night. Is that the worst storm you ever saw?"

"No, it was just the first wind of fall."

"But it's still August."

"In a couple weeks is Labor Day. Some of the swamp trees are already starting to turn."

"I know. It just doesn't seem fair. We just got up here and got the chores done. Now we finally have time to do stuff and it's time to go home. It's not fair."

Uncle Vic let out a long sigh. "Nothing is." He looked across the lake to the dark clouds in the north. "Stinkin' wars take all the good men and leave all the lazy bums who don't care 'bout anything except their next drink or drag of weed."

"Why did he go?" Mike whispered.

Uncle Vic snorted. "You know Buck, half adventure and half somebody needs a hand. Like that time, he painted the neighbor lady's house for free or when he volunteered to work at that summer camp instead of working and getting paid. Whenever you do something for someone, there is a cost that must be paid. Buck paid that price for others."

"D'you suppose it is the same for all people in all wars."

A loud noise like something being dropped came from next door at Linda's house. Both of them looked in that direction.

Uncle Vic frowned. "No. Some want revenge. Some are angry. Some want power. I guess it's the motive that makes it right or wrong. It's murder if you are killing someone for your own benefit. It's war if you are doing it to protect someone or some group of people from being murdered. Now Buck, he had to help people..." His voice faltered. "He couldn't turn his back and walk away." Uncle Vic swallowed hard. "...no matter the price." His voice cracked. He cleared his throat and patted his pocket, "Where's my pipe?" He turned and headed back to the steps up the hill to the cottage.

Mike watched him go sadly.

"Ohhhhhhh. NO!" shrilled a voice from the top of the hill.

Uncle Vic and Mike spun toward Linda's cottage. An ominous thud of a heavy weight hitting the floor caused Uncle Vic to take an involuntary step toward the neighbor's cottage. Mike was off like a shot to the top of the hill, running to Linda's cottage.

As Mike jumped up on the porch a high-pitched shriek was stopped abruptly by shattering glass. Linda shot out the back door, and leapt into the arms of a slack-jawed Mike.

"Mike!"

Mike stumbled backward under the impact and stepped off the porch supporting her weight. She nearly tackled him, pinning him against the pine tree next to the porch. She hugged him so tightly he struggled to breathe. Her body heaved with shaky sobs. This was the second time. Mike knew what to do, he thought.

He patted her on the back and said, "It's alright. You're ok." He looked down at her face pressed tightly in to his shoulder." It's ok no one will hurt you."

Something on her face caught his eye. What was *that* on her left cheek?

He twisted a little further. The left side of her face was black and blue. Blood trickled down the side. "What happened?"

"I.... I could," she sobbed. "I couldna."

"What?"

"I couldn't let him hit her again," she sobbed.

Mike's jaw clenched and he glared toward the cottage.

Lightning flashed on the far side of the lake with the low rumble of threatened storm.

The door of the cottage slammed open and Linda's dad stepped out clad only in his underwear and a tee shirt. "Get your hands off ma girl, ya trash! You and your hoods think you own this lake. Well, you don't and I'll show you who owns what. Let go of her and get off my property!"

Mike hadn't realized how big Linda's dad was. Now with him on the porch a foot off the ground and Mike and Linda huddled together standing on the ground, he looked huge. He was a mountain ready to collapse on Mike. His pale sickly face matched the white T-shirt matted with sweat, but it was his eyes that locked Mike's fear. He squinted as if the daylight hurt his eyes, and the tiny, black dots of his pupils darted around in a queer, fearful manner.

Mike kept his arms around Linda but took a step back. His back was against a pine tree where the branches toward the porch had been trimmed. The low reaching branches on either side gave him little chance for a quick getaway. The only way out was back up on the porch. Linda clung to him tighter than ever, her face buried in his shoulder.

"Think I don't know who's been catchin' all the fish out of this lake so a decent man can't feed his family. Yeah, and all you kids stealin' jobs from us skilled labor so's a man can't find a decent job," Harold's hateful glare felt like fire on Mike's face.

I said leggo!" Harold raised his fist to strike them.

Mike wished Buck was here. He wouldn't have hit Buck. Buck would have done some powerful Marine Corps thing. Mike was just Mike and there was no place to go. There were no glorious fantasies here. Her dad was too big to fight back. No alternatives, but he knew what he had to do. He had to protect Linda. He spun them around; Linda still clinging to him so Mike's back protected her.

"Agghhh." Mike grunted, as the first blow struck his shoulder, knocking him fiercely into the tree, a branch tore the skin of his left cheek. The punch would have knocked them both over if the tree hadn't held them up. Pain shot through his upper arm but he shifted to cover Linda better. His face stung and he felt blood running down his cheek.

Linda's head snapped up in fear. "Look out!"

Mike glanced back to see her dad cocking his arm for another blow. He turned back grimacing in anticipation.

Mike heard a grunt. The blow didn't land. Mike turned back. The arm was held back by one end of a shillelagh held by a very large, very angry Irishman.

Uncle Vic leaned forward and spoke in a slow deliberate voice more powerful than any shout Mike had ever heard. The pent-up anger of months of frustration put a growl in his voice, sounding like the very judgment of heaven. "You touch that boy again, and *by God*, I will kill you."

Harold pulled his arm free from the shillelagh and stepped back on the porch, momentarily stunned. Mike and Linda worked their way through the branches, but once twenty feet away, she renewed her fierce hold on Mike.

Neighbors from other cottages came running out to see what was going on. Most stayed back as if afraid to cross the invisible barrier that would get them "involved." Missus Swanson ran up and put her arms around Linda, covering Linda's face. "You don't want to watch honey. Come, let's look at your face. Come with me." She pulled her from Mike and took her to their cabin.

"Hey! You bring her back here. No witch is stealin' my kid," Harold moved toward the steps. Uncle Vic moved to block him.

Uncle Vic stepped up to the porch and stopped, looking about. It was strewn with fishing gear; an unused net, open tackle box full of rusty tangled lures and an empty carton of beer. Two poles leaned against the cottage, their fancy lures dangling free. Uncle Vic shook his head at the mess. "Luann, are you alright?"

Mike watched the pair of men on the porch. He had thought Harold looked large. Now, he realized, it was mostly belly. He compared the two. His uncle stood a full three inches above Harold and though he was old, his life had been hard and decades of sawing wood with a crosscut saw and swinging an axe gave him broad shoulders to back up any threat. Any *sane* man would back down.

Harold was not a sane man. "You leave my wife out of this. Get off my property!" He staggered two steps toward Uncle Vic, but Vic held his ground.

"LuAnn, are you okay?"

"Yes, but I think I broke my arm."

"I take care of my wife. No other... other man does," Harold said, leaning on the fish cleaning station on the porch. "Ya mind your own business. She jus' needs to learn her place. An' keep that boy away from my daughter. She's too good for him. Bring her here now."

Harold's eyes darted around to the people tentatively approaching his porch as someone approaches a wounded wild animal and indeed, he acted like a wild animal. As his eyes shot back and forth to various people, he seemed to flinch from each one.

"What're you all doing here? Ah, I know… the crowd fills the coliseum for the final battle of the gladiators. Well, no Christians will be killed here today. Get out now or I will release the lions."

The neighbors exchanged looks. What was he talking about?

Uncle Vic's knuckles were as white as the bleached wood on the shillelagh. He spoke slowly and controlled but Mike could feel the death threat in his voice. "Here's what I am going to do. I am going to take your wife to the hospital. I will take you too if you like, but you will not get in my way."

Uncle Vic called into the cottage. "Luann, come on out! We'll take you to the hospital."

Harold stepped back toward the house. "Luann! You come out; it'll be the last thing you do. You're not takin' me or my wife nowhere. My wife don't need some other man takin' care of her. Get off ma property now or I'll give you some of this." He took two steps toward Uncle Vic and shook his fist in his face.

Uncle Vic stood his ground and getting his anger under control, he spoke in a low deliberate voice. "You try to hit me, your wife, or that young girl over there again and…" he leaned forward, the shillelagh suspended in the air, "I'll… stop you. You let your wife out now or I am going to get the police."

"Go ahead get the guards and all their spears. You're not man enough to face me alone."

They glared at each other, neither willing to back down. The neighbors murmured among themselves trying to understand Harold's ranting.

Finally, Vic grunted, "If that's the way you want it," and he turned to head to the Swanson's for their phone.

"You'll never get da guards." Harold's hand fumbled for something on the fish cleaning station.

Harold snatched the crusty fillet knife from the tackle box. "My sword will end this…"

Look out!" cried half a dozen voices.

Harold lunged toward Uncle Vic's back but one step forward, he tripped and fell. His legs tangled in the fish line of one of the poles.

"AGH! My leg! It bit me! Get it off."

A small body that Mike recognized disappeared around the corner of the cottage.

Harold gaped at the fishing lure imbedded in his leg. Its rubber skirt of two-inch long legs, danced with his movements.

"Spider! Tarantula! Get it off!" He shrieked and flicked the knife at it. It was covered with fish guts and scales but the blade was razor sharp. The fillet knife sliced his leg wide open.

Mike gasped as blood spurted out. He must have cut a large vessel, for it shot out in little pulses.

Two women turned away.

"Oh Lord, help me! It's killing me." He jabbed at it this time. "EEEEEEE!" He screamed as the knife dug in deep. "It bit me again. Save me! Someone help me."

"Put the knife down Harold." Vic took a step toward the man. "Someone, go to Swanson's and call the sheriff!"

It was unnecessary; someone had already called.

Other men in the group took a step forward but halted when the knife came back up, extended like a gladiator's sword flinging blood on Uncle Vic.

"No! Now I know who you are!" He pointed the knife back at Uncle Vic. "You're one o' them demons. You come back again. You thought you could get me last night! But I'm too strong for you! You're not taking me away yet. It's not my time yet! You think you're powerful?" He swung the knife wildly at Uncle Vic. Uncle Vic jumped back, stumbled over some branches and fell.

"Now I have you!" Harold tried to rise but tangled his feet in the fishing poles and net. The effect tore the lure deeper into his leg. He fell to the ground. The blood all over his legs was covered with dirt.

"EEEEE!" his voice was shrill like a woman's. "Save me! They're gonna take me!" His wide eyes danced wildly from one person to the other. "They are gathering for the kill. Not me! No. I have powers too!" He held up the knife in his blood-splattered fist. He lashed and slashed at the fishing lure cutting large chunks of his own flesh. Each slash brought a horrible shriek of pain but he continued, panting and screaming.

Fish line tangled in streams around him, dangling across his legs, arms, and face. His face contorted as he perceived this new threat. "Not snakes too!" He stared at his arms in horror. "Now you send your demon snakes!" He pulled wildly at his arms trying to wipe off the snakes but with the knife in his hand it was a repeat of the episode with his legs.

There was a final shriek as Vic smashed the knife hand with his shillelagh.

Harold stared wide-eyed and white faced at Uncle Vic as he tried to stand. It wasn't possible.

Uncle Vic motioned to Mister Thorton's boys who were behind the drunk and they jumped on the porch and grabbed him as Uncle Vic stepped forward and pinned him to the blood-soaked porch.

Mister Swanson ran up with a towel while Aunt Lilly ran into the house to see Luann. The porch and the men on it were covered with blood. Large chunks of flesh were missing completely. A large flap of flesh, the size of Dennis' tongue, hung off his calf and lay in the dirt covered in pine needles and moss.

Mike wept. The rain began.

Journal
… They took him to the hospital and when I asked if he would be all right, no one would answer for a long time. Later they told me he hadn't done well on the ride to the hospital. I can't understand what was wrong with his head. Uncle Vic says it was cuz he drank so much. He had ~~diliriuim tremins~~ deleruim tremors I am never going to drink. Never.

Journal
Another boring day. Didn't do anything. Linda and her mom didn't come back. I guess her dad is real sick. She is staying with her mom's sister Missus Swanson says.

Journal
Another boring day no Linda or the guys. Linda's dad is real sick from the dirt in the cuts and he had a heart attack on the way to the hospital. He wasn't very healthy Uncle Vic says.

Journal
I can't believe it. Linda's dad died! I asked if Linda will ever come up again and no one will answer.

The small clean church was pleasant enough. The red brick and white trim contrasted dramatically to the blue sky behind it but gloom clouded every face. Mike and Eric stood outside looking down the main aisle toward the coffin surrounded with beautiful bouquets. Everyone else was still in the church, eating tiny sandwiches that did not satisfy, drinking weak coffee from throw away cups and murmuring comments that left no imprint.

"I didn't mean to hurt him," Eric said hot tears ran down his face. "I just wanted to trip him." He unclipped the tie from his neck and sat down on the curb, his face in his hands.

Mike sat down next to him. "He did it to himself. You didn't cut him; you didn't give him that infection. You just stuck out the fishing pole and he hooked himself and then he proceeded to stab himself with a dirty knife. How many times you stick a hook in your finger? I'll tell ya. Ya done it plenty of times and you cut yourself sometimes but you never stabbed yourself. He was just a stupid, mean drunk."

"I feel terrible," Eric said. He looked back at the small church, where the funeral was still going on.

"You probably saved Uncle Vic's life. Who knows, maybe even Linda's and her mom's. You should be a hero."

"I didn't even tell Jim. Does anyone else know?"

"I don't think so, but you should get a medal."

"You promise me, you won't ever tell I did it. You promise me!"

"I won't."

"Thanks Mike...You promise?"

"I promise."

"You can't ever tell anyone. This is the worst day of my life. I wish I was dead."

Hot tears ran down Mike's face. Mike put his arm around Eric. "You're my hero Eric. You will always be my hero, even if no one ever knows."

Mike rode in silence with his aunt and uncle back to the cottage. It's odd he thought. Linda's dad was a mean, lazy, self-centered man who beat his family, kills himself and at his funeral a bunch of people get together and say nice, meaningless things about him. While Buck, who probably died fighting for the freedom of complete strangers will never have a funeral and every stupid day, stupid people on the stupid news say bad things about him and every soldier over there. Eric probably saved Uncles Vic's life and he wishes he were dead. Life stinks.

Chapter 35 Pheasant Dreams

As soon as Mike got back to the cottage, he took off his church clothes, wadded them up nicely and shoved them into his suitcase. He furrowed his brow. At the funeral he wanted to stand up and shout this is nuts! So much of what we call one thing is another.... He stabbed his brown legs into the faded and stained cutoffs. The scars on his legs from the night of the thunderstorm showed white against his darkly sun-tanned skin. Aunt Lilly said the scars would fade with time but he would always have them. He didn't mind because that was a cool night. She showed him a scar she got from a knife when she was a little girl helping her mother cook dinner. He could barely see it. She said to her it carried a sharp sweetness. She forgot the pain but remembered the comfort from her mother.

The fire in his anger dimmed. He sat down on the sofa that was his bed and wrapped his arms around himself. *Hold me close God. Tell me it will be all right.* The thought came to his mind. *I do that best when you are surrounded by my creation not man's*. Mike smiled weakly and headed out the back door.

He stepped onto the porch and stood in awe of the tall trees, standing like pillars in a cathedral. Choirs of birds sang while squirrels did their holy dance of praise. He raised his eyes to the ceiling painted in an ever-changing fresco of life. Then he made the mistake of looking to Linda's but she wasn't there. He just saw ragged, dark, unholy stains on the porch. Aunt Lilly had done her best to scrub it clean, but even time and nature might not erase those scars completely.

He sighed and walked with no direction in mind, just away; away from the mound of dirt behind the doghouse, away from the site of the telegram, away from the spilled blood. He walked with his head down looking at the dust of the road. He ignored the trees and flowers. Soon he was past where the lake road forked toward town. Meadows opened before him, filled with brilliant wildflowers, but he didn't see them. He looked up when he was near the swamp. The dismal green algae floating on the surface reminded him of Eric's story of the ghost, but he didn't laugh now. A maple, already blood red glared Fall. Swamp trees were always the first to change. Living right next to the water made them change faster somehow. Was he changing faster living by the water? Water was life. Water was death. It made no sense.

This was the first time Mike had been so far from the cottage by himself. As long as he was this far out, he might as well see how Mister Vanderkooi is doing. Maybe he sold the farm. For a moment he basked in the sour sweetness of this new misery added to all the others. It might be the last time I see him. Another misery. Possibly no one ever suffered as much as he was suffering now. He fed it fresh tinder. He relished the suffering, sucking on it while it grew larger in his heart sucking up any last visage of joy. He held it close. When all the rest of his friends deserted him, his suffering would keep him company.

He found Mister Vanderkooi out in the barn trying to fix something as usual. The old farmer didn't see him. Mike cleared his throat, but no response. Finally, he spoke up. "I just came out to say goodbye."

The old man spun around. "Da... Uh... dang you startled me. I thought one of my girls was talking to me for a minute."

Mike grinned in spite of his misery.

"Where is the rest of the troop?"

"Well, some are still at the funeral. Others are home I guess."

"What funeral?"

Mike relayed the story as best he could.

The farmer just shook his head. "If Harry spent his time workin', 'stead a drinkin' he wouldn't a killed hisself. Least wise not with a knife." The farmer straightened up and rubbed his back. "S'pose I'm killin' myself slavin' away. It just takes longer."

Mike ignored the farmer's comment, his own well-rehearsed suffering boiling over. "This has been the worst year of my life. It's been a lousy summer. My parents never came up, and I'll probably never see Linda again. Buck is probably dead and I never got to see a pheasant or find an arrow head, or see the northern lights."

"Why you want to do those things?" the old farmer took of his hat and rubbed the top of his head.

"Cuz Buck did them when he was my age."

"What's that got to do with anything?"

"I want to be like Buck."

"Humfff. The way you was talkin' you sound more like Harry."

"WHAT?" Mike dropped onto a hay bale behind him in exasperation. He could not believe such a slap in the face. Especially to him, since he had suffered so much. How could this crazy old farmer say such a mean thing? This was a punch in the gut.

"Do you admire Buck because of all the stuff he got... or for all he gave? You say Buck was always out doing things with and for others. Harry was just sitting feeling sorry for himself an' not doing anything about it. Here you are just a moanin' like a cow with cramps. You sound like Harold. Now you can choose to feel bad or... get busy. Hmmph," the old man shook his head.

Mike's jaw dropped and he looked at the ground as if looking for an answer and all he saw was... manure. He stumbled through his mind looking everywhere for a quick comeback. But it was true, deeply true. Here was life uncovered. Mike's anger was revealed as more selfishness heaped on top of the manure pile of self-pity. Mike remained silent for a long time, while the farmer continued his work. When he spoke, it was as if to himself. "I guess I *did* have the most fun this summer when I was with others and helping them."

"It looked like you were havin' fun when you were here."

"Yeah, I guess, but you're gonna lose your farm and I'll never get to see you again either," Mike said struggling to regain a grasp on his now slippery sorrow by making it selfless.

"That makes you sad?"

"Yeah, you got the coolest job in the world and you're gonna lose it."

"This has been a tough summer for me without a doubt, but I am glad you were around to brighten it up. I'll miss all you boys and Linda too."

The old farmer looked down at his brown gnarled hands and then at the smooth skinned boy in front of him. He set down his hammer. "I've worked enough for a while. Let's go see if we can find us a pheasant."

"Here?"

"Sure! You watch down by that corn." He pointed across the field to where a gravel road edged one side of his cornfield.

"Really?"

"Yep. Especially around sunset they'll come out to where the corn meets the road to get stones for their crop. They walked in silence except for the crunching of the gravel under their feet. Finally, as they approached the corn the old farmer spoke. "So, Buck saw his first pheasant up here when he was your age?"

"Yeah, and the northern lights and he found a real Indian arrowhead. Dr. Jacobson said he would buy them from us."

"Buy them?"

"Yeah, he has a collection. He even has a spear point he was offered $10,000 dollars for by a man from Chicago."

"Ten thousand dollars! For a rock! And I can't get my da...uh darn pump fixed. What's the world coming to?"

In answer, rooster pheasants shot off like a shower of fireworks. Their long colorful tail feathers trailed behind like the tail on a shooting star. The colors dazzled Mike's eyes. They were sweeter than any exaggerated story Buck ever told.

Journal

I saw a herd of Pheasants. It was incredible beautiful. But there's no one to tell about it to. It's no fun to think about coming up here if none of my friends are here. I wish I could help but I don't know what to do. I hate life... No, I don't. I just don't understand it...I wish you could have seen them mom. I wish you were here. I love you.

Chapter 36   The Tomb

The weather was warm, tall clouds in the distance told him the day could go either way. It might be hot and glorious swimming or the sun might disappear for a catastrophic storm unseen since the days of Noah. He kept his eye on the road. At the first sign of animals lining up in pairs, he would sprint back to the cottage. It was a good day to go see Billy. He always had great stories, and if nothing else, they could play cribbage inside and sip cool lemonade to help with the heat or fortify him for the sprint back to the cottage, whichever it was to be. As he walked down to the large grassy field where they played football, he realized he had not seen Billy sitting outside for a couple weeks. He hoped something was not wrong with him too! Could the man that claimed to have ultimate power be ill?

He knocked on the screen door and peeked in to the living room at Missus Lake who, though she had a magazine in her lap, she was not reading it. She appeared to be listening to something.

"Can Billy play some cribbage?"

Instead of answering she motioned Mike in and put a finger to her lips for silence.

Mike stepped into the room and heard the hiss of Billy's short wave.

"That alright," Billy nodded to Mike and pointed to a chair. The guy on the other end went to get someone." Billy's face did not wear its undefeatable smile. His eyes were red and his face looked like a skull with skin stretched thinly over it. "You can just sit…"

Mike decided to sit here. He had listened for hours while Billy talked all over the world.

Billy's humorous stories were appreciated by more than just the hicks in northern Michigan. He had friends literally all around the world. And, like most short-wave operators, going out of their way to help others was half the fun.

The hissing speaker crackled and a voice came across the radio. It was a rough patch. Billy had explained patches to Mike before. A short-wave operator could patch another radio through his system to reach a radio even further. This then could be patched even further so that a short-wave operator in Michigan could talk to someone in Hawaii or even in say ... Vietnam.

The voice said, "You say you are looking for Buck Malloy?"

Mike froze half way to the seat, his hand on the table.

"Roger that." Billy answered tensely.

There was a definite lag as radio waves bounced halfway around the world.

"I was in his squad during our last fire fight. I just got out of...."Hiss crackle hizzz. Billy's already puckered forehead wrinkled deeper as he adjusted a knob, as though its very touch caused incredible pain. Cuck, hiss, "... were shot up pretty bad. A lot of guys died."

Mike's eyes burned and he dropped to the chair. He balled his hands into fists. A fresh tear broke free and fired down his face.

"They couldn't evac us soon enough... we were overrun. Some of us played dead like I did. They took my watch and ring. Buck was carrying Corporal Hernandez toward the rear and they shot him in the leg. He got back up with Hernandez. The VC butt stroked Buck and he went down. They got him to his feet and made him walk with them. His hands on his head. He was alive when I last saw him."

"Where was this?" Billy shouted.

"Sorry man, I can't say. He's a good man and tough. My prayers go with him. I bet he makes it. He was a rock. Sorry I can't tell you more, I know someone who might be able to tell you more. I'll go get him."

"Thanks a lot," Billy said.

Billy said some other things too, but Mike no longer listened, his ears roared, head pounded. He shot out the door and was out to the road before the screen door slammed shut.

"He's alive!" a voice shouted in his brain. Mike ran.

"Hi Mike." Eric waved from his yard and ran up to the road to catch Mike.

Mike blew past Eric. "He's alive!" Mike gasped.

Eric sprinted behind Mike trying to catch up, but Eric could not keep up. The pounding of Mike's feet echoed the pounding of his chest. He could hear nothing, see nothing. His eyes bleared with tears. The trees blurred into odd shapes like demons reaching out their branches to grab him and hold him back from the telling. The pounding was the thing, pounding, pounding like someone desperate to get in a solid wood door of an old clay house.

"Let me in!" She shouted, and pounded on the crudely cut wooden planks that served as a door.

"What do you want?" a male voice hissed in a low angry voice, then immediately softened when he saw the woman dressed in robes.

The woman was breathing hard, barely able to speak, her cheeks flushed from running. Nonetheless, she grabbed the larger man by his shoulders and pulled him toward her. Her eyes stabbed into his as if she just seen a ghost. "He's ALIVE!" She gasped in to quick breaths. I've just come from there..."

The two disciples jumped past her and ran. The disciple that Jesus loved outran the other and arrived first. He peered into the empty tomb, stepped inside and believed. "He's alive," his intellect pronounced. His emotions had not yet arrived.

Mike flung open the screen door of the cottage.

"Oh Michael...." his aunt's hand went to her mouth and stared at him unable to discern from his red tear-stained face what manner of catastrophe had befallen them now.

Uncle Vic got up from the bed where he had been napping. Eric finally arrived at the porch.

"He's alive," Mike croaked, gasping for breath. "Billy found someone who saw him. He was captured but alive." His words were barely understandable.

"What! What did you say?" Not quite willing to allow herself to believe crystal dreams of false hope.

Mike gulped in air while he bent over his hands on his knees and repeated himself.

Vic and Lilly looked at each other. "Do you think...?" Vic said.

Lilly's lips trebled. Her mouth moved but nothing came out.

"Let's go see," Uncle Vic said. Aunt Lilly was in the car faster than he had ever seen her move before.

Journal
Buck IS ALIVE!!! HE IS ALIVE. He's alive. HE IS ALIVE.

HE IS ALIVE. He's got to be alive. Billy found three guys who saw him after he was captured. Uncle Vic is contacting someone tomorrow. Aunt Lilly kissed Billy a bunch of times. Now she is making him a cake. She is still crying. Why do we cry when we are happy? Maybe we are just getting rid of the leftover sadness and making more room for joy. I am still making a little more room for joy.

Chapter 37   Narrows Escape

The sun wasn't up yet when the executioners rowed up to the dock of Château d 'If, climbed the many stone steps of the ancient tower, and opened the door to his cell. He lowered his head and shuffled out of his prison cell. The executioner walked him back down the many steps toward the boat, torturing him with cheerful, pithy sayings. He bravely endured it but he was close to breaking.

Grace's father remained at the dock in their rowboat. He would row them over to the narrows. There, Mike and Grace would get out and he would attempt to swim across. He had made up several excuses, but Grace refused to even listen to any of them. Besides, this was for Buck.
She told them they had to go early to beat the fishermen and the water skiers who would want to zip through the narrows in their powerboats. It was Friday, but it was still Labor Day weekend and everyone in the world came up to the lake.

The captured soldier swallowed hard as the executioner stepped forward. "Come with me," the woman said pleasantly enough, but Mike knew the terrible fate waiting at the end of the long walk. Why else would the executioner hold his hand, except to keep him from running away? This was a particularly evil executioner. Instead of a black hood over her whole head, she wore a white rubber hood that only covered her hair. Probably to keep blood from splattering on her or so that she could laugh at him more easily, and let him see her laugh. He plodded along wondering what if felt like to drown. Did his lungs burn? Did his chest ache? Would he feel himself settle into the soft black muck at the bottom of the narrows, muscles frozen in death, eyes open to see eternity settle around him. Sorrow covered him in gooey black thoughts.

"Come on, Mike. Cheer up. You will do great. I will be right here with you. You did super in our practices." Grace hugged hum tightly. "Everyone will be so impressed. You don't see the other guys doing it do you? They probably can't."

He brightened. Here was a new thought.

The world-famous swimmer swaggered down to the dock and jumped gingerly into the boat that would take him to the widest part of the Pacific Ocean between California and Australia. He chose this course because it gave him the greatest chance to see a great white shark. He had always wanted to see one.

He would conquer the water. He would not taste defeat. He waded out into the shallow water to his knees. His squad commander nodded her head. She tapped the top of her white helmet in their agreed upon 'okay' sign. He nodded back and stepped to the edge of the continental shelf. Here the sandy bottom gave way to a drop off and tentacles of long seaweed reached up to pull him down into the depths where the crayfish could eat him at their leisure. But he had mastered the weeds, earlier that summer. If he swam on his back, they couldn't grab his arms and pull him down to their evil masters. He sailed like this for a while until his commander shouted back to him.

"Okay, do the crawl now. You can do it! Float on your back only if you get tired."

"I'm already..." water sloshed in his mouth and he coughed as he rolled over onto his belly. He would have to cover distance faster now if he was going to reach the enemy shore and plant his charges before the patrol boats came at daybreak. The sun was already threatening the distant trees.

The rush of the water filled Mike's ears. His legs ached and he gasped in huge quantities of air but he couldn't get enough. Instead of the smooth continuous strokes he had practiced with Grace, he slapped the water in erratic panic. He rolled back over on his back. *This is stupid. I'm no soldier, no great swimmer. I'm just a kid. A kid who is about to drown.* He took rapid shallow breaths.

"Relax Mike." Grace side stroked gracefully next to him. "Take a rest."

Mike took long thankful breaths on his back. He attempted to look at her, lifting his head and inhaled water. Great sputter coughs, he choked hacked, gasped. The boat was awful close. He could just about grab it.

Grace appeared to hover above the water in her smooth treading water. "Dad, move away a little, I think you are crowding him." She winked at her dad and he moved off, out of Mike's reach.

"Oh God." Mike gasped, *Help me God. Help me God.* Mike said in his mind. It was about the same pace as his strokes. He said it again, *Help me God. Help me God.* Actually, it felt like a pretty good cadence. *Help me God. Help me God.* His strokes felt smoother more deliberate. *Help me God. Help me God.* His breathing was even. He was recovering. *Help me God Help me God.* For the first time that morning Mike smiled. It was a cadence like the Marines used when drilling. Buck taught him one.

Hey, hey, here we go, Hey, hey, here we go.
Down the road, Down the road
Long road, Long road
All the way, All the way
Can't quit, Can't quit
Never quit, Never quit
Not me, Not me
Feelin' good, Feelin' good
Feelin' fine, Feelin' fine
Marine Corps, Marine Corps
All the way! All the way!
OooRah! OooRah!
OooRah! OooRah!
Yeah! Yeah!

Well, now he was swimming and not panicking, but he felt silly swimming on his back. He felt like a tiny child or an old grandmother, and he was surviving, not really swimming. He was making little distance, but he continued listening with his mind to Buck call the cadence. Buck was swimming beside him pulling the diving raft behind him. Mike replayed an event from last summer in his mind. The anchor rope to the diving raft had broken during the night, leaving the anchor on the bottom. Buck talked to Mike while he pulled it and Mike swam alongside in his life jacket.

Buck paused in his stroke and treaded water, "I will always be grateful to the Marines for teaching me the breast stroke." He glided forward, the rope tied around his waist. "Here you should learn it too."

Mike rolled over and pulled himself forward with a simultaneous frog kick.

"That's right," Buck said. "You can pull or carry great quantities of equipment that way."

A dreamy smile curled up in the corners of Mike's mouth.

The Marine glided forward toward dimly lit beach, pulling a pack filled with Willie Pete and grenades. This would be one morning no one would forget.

Mike ran out of mind games. The swim took forever. He continued his battle across the narrows for what seemed hours. Exhaustion filled his being until he no longer pretended, no longer thought, no longer felt. He would not defeat the water. He might survive. No, the lake would win. The lake always wins. It is there forever. Mike was passing through and would soon be no more. In the forge of pain, quenched in water, hope disappeared. There was no hope because there was no future. No future meant no dreams, no dreams, and no fantasy. With no future, life was over. Life demands hope, requires dreams, begs for unrealized joys. The future is the fountain of creativity the passion of the powerless. He was too exhausted to think, feel or dream. Stroke. Stroke. Eternity folded in upon itself in a Mobius strip of pain. Yet, he still endured. He endured because it was more bearable to live than die in the water, but soon enough... endurance shattered.

Pain. Someone stabbed his left calf. A knife so barbarous that he could not will any muscle to do anything but react. He curled up to grab his leg and... sank.

"Mike!"

"Mmmk!" Mike heard underwater. He jammed his hands into his calf and the pain subsided but his lungs screamed. *Who cares?* he thought. He made a halfhearted gesture with his arms, surprised when he felt something grab his arm.

An angel appeared, cradling him in her arms, white halo over her head.

"I'm dead," He murmured.

"No." Grace answered. "Do you have a cramp? Can you float on your back another ten feet?"

"Cramp gone. I... float... forever," he said in a dreamy voice.

"Just stroke gently like you did at first."

She was rewarded with slight movement of his hands. A few

moments later she said, 'Now stand up."

He stood. The bottom was mucky, but HE STOOD! His legs buckled then rebounded when his face hit the water. Yesterday he would have recoiled in horror of what might be in the ooze to bite him. Now he didn't care. He took a couple stumbling steps, feeling the slime seep up over his feet covering them completely. Hidden things, like last year's tree branches poked the bottom of his feet and slimed up his calves.

There was no crowd. No explosions of fireworks or grenades, nothing but granite hard accomplishment. Here was reality. It was satisfying, yet a letdown. He waded over to Grace's dock and lay his head down on his arms still waist deep in water. The usual fantasies didn't come. He was too tired to dream. He stayed that way while Grace rubbed his back and then sat down next to him.

"Ya did good Mike," Grace's father said as he slid the rowboat back into its berth.

Grace patted his shoulders again. "Buck would be proud. No..."She stammered "Buck will be proud."

He patted her arm back as a little strength came back.

Buck. That's what he wished. A vision of Buck appeared on the dock. Buck stood on the dock in his Marine utilities, the classic boxy green cap on his head. "Oohrah. That was outstanding! You did a super job, Mike!" He snapped the cap off his head and tossed it to Mike. "You earned it, Marine."

Mike grinned and then frowned at himself. Buck isn't here. Stupid day dreams. Won't I ever grow up... even after this swim?

"Now listen," Buck said putting on his Lieutenant voice. "Nothing happens here," he pointed down to the dock below his black spit polished boots, "that doesn't first happen here." A deliberate, hard finger tapped his forehead right between the eyes. "Keep *dreaming*, and you will keep *doing*," he stated with all the command and authority of a Marine Lt.

Mike nodded and smiled. He rubbed the blur of water out of his eyes but the image of Buck didn't quite go away. It changed but...

"Good job Mike," his Uncle Vic stated.

Mike looked harder. He didn't realize until now, just how much of the father was in the son. The young marine faded into an old woodsman but the iron remained.

Uncle Vic looked at Grace and grinned, "Buck said when you finished the swim...not *if* you finished, but *when* you finish...that I should tell you Oohrah and give you this." He tossed an object into the air toward Mike.

Mike's eyes were still a little blurry but it didn't take much effort to determine what the boxy green object was before he caught it. He stared hard at the Marine Corps emblem on the front and bit his bottom lip and nodded. Yep, there was no crowd. No fantasy filled with reporters. Here was reality. It was *much better*.

Chapter 38 Labor Day Weekend A-Head

Mike sat on the dock. The maple, two cottages down, on the lake was starting to turn. He had been watching it the last week, cursing every new red leaf as a traitor to summer. He found himself thinking more and playing less. Maybe because no one had been around the last week, or maybe things just made him think. Maybe he had been pretty selfish in wanting everything to happen his way instead of accepting life as God brought it. He thought of what Mister Vanderkooi had said. Life really was more fun when he did stuff for other people. Well, not more fun always, but more… well…satisfying.

"Mike, would you fill the water bucket and help Uncle Vic move the picnic table?"

"Yep." He jumped up and ran the steps to the top of the hill. Uncle Vic wasn't in sight so he went to the water pump and started working the handle. The squeaky complaint gave way to the gush of water and the bucket was soon overflowing on to the ground. He picked up the pail and sloshed more onto the ground in the same spot it sloshed every day for the past three months, washing away a little more dirt each time. He stopped in his tracks. It couldn't be!

He set the bucket down and stared. Ever so slowly he bent over and pried the one-and-a-half-inch long flint rock out of the dirt.

"It's… It's an arrowhead," he said out loud. He had wondered if he would recognize one, but this… There was no question. It was a work of art. Look at the symmetrical taper to a sharp point, the notch for tying it to a shaft of wood. How the owner must have grieved its loss. He turned it over slowly in his hands. There was one dark stripe in the creamy color. Mike wondered if it was a bloodstain. There was no doubt it could have killed something. He pictured an Indian hovering over the rock and working for hours to form this magnificent piece. It must have added to the calluses and scars on the Indians weathered hands. Perhaps it had supplied his family with several meals before it was lost. How could there be such beauty in something designed to kill?

For a brief moment he wondered if someone had just recently dropped it there, but he had to pry it out of the earth. It had been there for a while. He had found one! He laughed out loud. "Uncle Vic!"

"What? Well... I'll be.... It's a dandy. Where did you find that? Lilly, come see."

"You gonna sell it to Dr. Jacobson?" Uncle Vic asked.

"No way!"

Uncle Vic chuckled. "You been saying you were going to sell it all summer, but I don't blame you."

"I was thinking I'd make it into a necklace."

"You gonna wear it to school?"

"Uh... it's not for me."

Uncle Vic nodded solemnly and placed a hand on Mike's shoulder, "I've got some new leather shoelaces that would work nicely for that, if you're interested."

Mike nodded. "It's funny. I went all over the world looking for something that I walked right past every day."

.

The rest of the day was a mixture of sorrow and joys. Every cottage on the lake was packed, every cottage but one. Everyone was up celebrating the holiday and making preparations for closing the cottages for the winter. Some people were already out in the water bringing in their docks.

Mike sat on the picnic table watching the road. A lone car drove by, its dust clouds lingering for moment like a ghost, but none pulled into Uncle Vic's drive or Linda's.

"Lil," Uncle Vic called looking at Linda's cottage. "Do you think we should close up Luann's place?"

"What if they come up?" Mike jumped to his feet in alarm. "They wouldn't have any water."

"Well, we'd wait until Monday but it will be worse if we don't turn off their water and it bursts the pipes this Fall. Who's gonna take care of their place now? Harold didn't do a great job but he did keep it from falling completely apart."

Mike listened to the proceedings intently, "You don't think they'll come for Labor Day? They'll miss the Sunday picnic!"

"They've been through a lot, Mike."

Mike lowered his head and walked down to the beach. He thought about taking out the canoe, but with all the people up, the lake was a turmoil of water skiers and pontoon boats. He looked over at Linda's dock and thought about what Uncle Vic said.

Mike walked over to their property. The dock had some boards with no nails in them. Others places there was a large gap where no boards existed at all.

"I nailed all the loose boards, but now I need some wood." Mike said to his uncle.

"That's very commendable. The only spare boards we got are under the cottage in the crawl space." Uncle Vic said. "You're welcome to use those."

Mike made a face. "Those are the only ones?"

"Yep."

Mike stared into the darkness under the cottage. The spiders sneered back. He thought he saw one pull out a switchblade and pick his teeth.

Mike had three boards that looked like they would work but he needed one more. He couldn't reach it unless he actually crawled into the crawl space.

He hunkered down in the dark, feeling the outlines of the board with his hands. The opening was just a blinding square of light beyond the musty cobwebs. He pushed the last board out from under the cottage. A pair of hands helped pull it out, leaving his hands free to crawl.

"Thanks," Mike said and wiggled out.

"You're welcome, Mickey."

"LINDA!"

"Uncle Vic said you're fixing our dock. Oh! There is a spider on you!" She hopped back.

Mike slapped it like it was a mosquito and continued talking. "Yeah, I thought... I mean...I was hoping you'd come up. I got something for you."

He ran in the cottage, grabbed a Kleenex, and wiped the spider goo off his arm. He then glanced in the old mirror and wiped his face really quick, ran his fingers through his hair, grabbed the old cigar box full of fishing tackle and dumping tackle and dried worms on the dinner table. He pulled out the necklace from its secret location and placed it in the box carefully picking out half a dried worm. He glanced around the cottage and his eyes landed on the Sunday funny paper. He wrapped it up in that and ran back out.

He slowed to a walk and casually strode around the side of the cottage with his best swagger. "I was afraid I would have to send it to you."

She stood waiting patiently just where he left her. "A present!"

As she lifted up a corner of the paper carefully, she asked excitedly, "Is it another clay statue."

He shook his head.

She opened the box and gasped. "You found one! Is it real? It's beautiful."

Mike studied the ground. "I didn't do a great job on the necklace part but I didn't have a lot to work with here at..."

She leaned forward and kissed his cheek. "It's perfect Mike."

"UH...Uh...uh...Where are you love... uh living now." Mike's face glowed fluorescent red.

"My mom has a job! Well, it's not for sure but almost. Right now, we are living with my uncle and aunt, and my uncle's company was looking for someone with bookkeeping experience and that's what mom used to do and so she interviewed Thursday. My uncle said they were really pleased with her, so she thinks she has it."

There was a slight pause as Mike still tried to get his brain back in gear from the kiss. "Um...where are you..."Oops, he already asked that. "Uh... so...so you don't have to sell the cottage?"

"Mom said she wants to keep coming up here no matter what happened." Linda's eyes sparkled. "I was *really glad* to hear her say that." She licked her lips and smiled.

Mike grinned back.

"I like Labor Day picnics better than Fourth of July picnics." Little John said shoving the last of a second hamburger in his mouth.

"What? Are you nuts? It means summer is over." Mike slid a little away from him in case insanity was contagious.

"But Labor Day has corn on the cob," John said grabbing a fourth ear off the serving plate.

"Yeah, but no strawberry short cake," Mike moaned.

"MMMFF," added Jim.

Their debate was interrupted by the pooka pooka sound of a tractor on the road. Mister Vanderkooi waved from on top of his tractor pulling his hay wagon. The boys and a few adults went out to the road to greet him.

"I came to offer the boys one last hay ride but it looks like ah interrupted a party."

"Come have something to eat Axel. We owe you some favors."

Linda grabbed his arm. "And you have to come meet my mom."

Mister Vanderkooi grinned down at her. "That sounds real nice sweetie. Say… that's a pretty necklace you got there."

Linda glowed. "Mike found an arrowhead and he gave it to me."

Mike rushed to say, "I was going to give it to you Mister Vanderkooi so you could sell it to Dr. Jacobson, but I didn't think it would be enough to save the farm."

He squeezed Mike's shoulder. "That's alright son." He reached under his tractor seat. "I brought you boys a present too." He pulled out an old shoebox that looked like it had held Ben Franklin's first tennis shoes. He handed it to Mike.

The boys gathered around. Mike was afraid to take the lid off lest something jump out. When he did, the boys sucked their breath in unison.

"Wow!"

"I don't believe it!"

"Where…"

"You got to sell 'em." Mike said. He set down the box so he could pick up one of the two dozen arrowheads in the box.

"They're beautiful." Lilly said picking up a small one.

"Quick," Mike said, "while he is still up here, go take 'em to Doc. Jacobson and see how much he'll pay you."

The farmer grinned. "Shucks, them's *just a few* of the ones he *didn't* want."

Even the adults gasped at this statement.

"When I was a boy, it was my job to follow behind the tractor, pick up the stones from the field an put 'em on the skid. Ever' year more stones would work their way to the surface. Drove me nuts as a boy. Well, I would keep the stones that looked like arrowheads and such. It became a habit and I kept doing it as an adult.

"There must a been some big ol' battle on my fields cuz sixty years of picking up stones filled a lot of shoe boxes." He chuckled. "I thought the ol' doctor would need a doctor himself. He nearly fainted when he saw them. Said it was the finest collection he'd ever seen. *Museum* quality, he called it. I thought he was going to kiss one of the spear points. Cradled it to his chest like a little baby. He pulled a book off the shelf and showed me a picture of one just like it. He was breathing hard and carrying on so I didn't know what to make of it at first. He was talking a mile a minute. He said he couldn't buy even a tenth of them all but that he would arrange the sale of them if I'd like. He wrote me a very nice check for the ones he could afford now. He said he would have to make some arrangements before he personally could afford to buy any more."

"So, you're not going to lose the farm?"

"Nope. Thanks to you." He patted Mike's shoulder like he would a young bull.

"Come on out next spring when I'm turning over the fields. Who knows what you might find." He winked at Mike.

"I can't wait."

Journal

This is my last entry. The writing is bad because I am writing in the car. It is packed so full I can hardly move. It was a great summer. I wish you could have been here at least a little. I don't want to go home but I wouldn't want to stay up here all winter alone. I love it here, but I know, it is not here that I love. It is the people here, and they are all going away.

It's odd. I spent all summer looking for an arrowhead but the best part of finding it, was giving it away. I never got to see the northern lights but I guess I don't have to do all the things Buck did. Everyone is different. I bet I even did some things Buck never did. Maybe I'll see the northern lights next year. I bet Linda would like to see them.

The car hit a bump as it left the gravel road and coasted onto the paved road toward town.

At the bump, the pile of things on the seat beside Mike tumbled to the floor. There was a light crash.

"Oh! Careful Vic. Is everything okay Mike?"

Mike scampered around in the back seat, checking all his treasures, but it sounded like something broke.

"Vic? What's that smell?"

Mike hurried, screwed the lid back on the old peanut butter jar filled to the brim with fresh manure. The top must have been loose and rolled off making the noise. Mike tightened the lid extra tight.

He didn't want it to dry out and go bad. It would lose its wonderful fragrance.

Chapter 39   A Shot at the Future

    Mike and Uncle Vic drove up to the lake in the morning to close up the cottage for the winter. They drove past fields orange with pumpkins, green with rich fall hay and brown with standing field corn. Each field was a picture framed with red maples and gilded with gold beech trees. Here and there a deer watched warily as though it knew hunting season was coming.
    When they arrived at the cottage the first thing they did was go down to the water's edge. "It looks different without any docks out," Mike said in a funeral home voice.
    "It is glorious! I always liked it better without docks cluttering up the lake. It looks like it did when I was your age," he finished wistfully.
    "It is beautiful. I was just saying it's different."
    "It's one of the things I like about the lake. It looks different each day. It is different here than it is over there. Here we have clay and there they have sand. Here we have hills. There they have marsh." He shook his head. "I love it so. I will hate…" His voice trailed off. He looked at Mike and whispered morosely, "Don't ever let them put me in a nursing home."
    Mike bit his lip and shook his head wordlessly.
    "Well, if we want to hunt, we better get to work."
    They went from room to room to make sure everything was secure and no unpleasant surprises. But there was one surprise.
    "Hey, there's a picture of me up here! I didn't even know she took it!"
    "Yep. When I was up here with your Aunt Lil a couple weeks ago, she said it was important to put that up. Is it acceptable?"
    Mike made a big deal of studying the 3X5-picture thumb tacked into the wall next to a banner from the 1933 Chicago World's Fair.
    The picture showed a shirtless 13-year-old boy in cut off blue

jeans and a Marine Corps cap hammering boards into the neighbors' dock.

"Your Aunt Lil said you wanted a picture of you with a mess of ducks, but we liked this one, and she said if we get a bunch of partridge today, we can put that one up too."

Mike thought of the black and white picture of his mom pouring concrete." This is fine," he said. "As long as we can still put up one with a bunch of birds."

Uncle Vic nodded with a sly grin, not mentioning that a copy of the same picture was posted in the kitchen at Linda's cottage.

Thankfully, the cottage was in good shape. Mike was afraid they would spend all day working on it and not get to go bird hunting. After draining the water system and covering the screens with plywood they finally had the cottage sealed up tight. The power was off and all the chores were done. It was time to play. They drove out past the now quiet frog pond, and past the swale where they found the deer skeleton. The dirt two track was narrow and brown dried ferns rattled against the car's side. Mike closed his eyes and he could see Buck and Billy chasing the raccoon down this road. Uncle Vic hoisted up his shotgun and they set off. They hiked through the woods for an hour or so and then headed back toward the car.

"Kinda hard bird huntin' without a dog," Uncle Vic scowled. 'Tell you what, you pretend you're the dog and rush into that brush and see what jumps out." Uncle Vic pointed to the thick tangle of briers next to the old two track and readied his shotgun.

Mike looked at the impenetrable mass and then back at his Uncle Vic. He looked back at the briars took a deep breath and started in.

Uncle Vic chuckled. "No, I was just kidding. I just wanted to see the look on your face."

Mike sighed and shrugged. "That's all right I think I can make it through." He took a step and...

Boooooomawoom. A partridge jumped up. Bang. Uncle Vic shot. He missed and struggled to rack another shell into the chamber but it was too late. The bird was gone.

"Hey! I don't think it went too far." Mike pushed into the brush a little deeper.

"That's alright Mike. Come on back. It's getting late."

"Yeah, I suppose. We sure saw a lot of birds."

"And I missed them all, you're gonna say next."

"No! It was great fun. I don't know when I jumped more. When the birds take off or when you shoot."

"There was a time when I would have gotten most of them. It's getting too hard to use this old pump shot gun."

Mike hung his head at the thought of his uncle getting old.

They walked slowly down the two track. Each in their own rut. From time-to-time, Mike would trot off to investigate some interesting bush only to scamper back to the two track. His uncle rubbed his shoulder. Mike watched his uncle's slow deliberate movements with concern.

Mike piped up, "Maybe if we practice next summer, you will get them all next year. I could throw those clay disk things for you."

His uncle emptied the shells out of the gun. "I'm getting too old for lugging this heavy gun around anymore." This fall Vic's life was filled with dark days and cold emotions, attempting to choke the very life out of him. Looking into Mike's eyes, he saw the sparkling joys of summer. In Mike's face radiated wonder and excitement. Vic sighed, slowly letting bright light from Mike's eyes warm him and chase away Fall's darkness. The chill of Fall melted silently into the dust of the two track and he stood a little straighter.

Mike's chest tightened as Uncle Vic seemed to stagger. He had watched his old uncle deteriorate this summer and he didn't want their time together to be over. He had asked his parents and found out his uncle was almost 70. That sounded way past old to Mike.

Uncle Vic continued, "I am getting too old to take care of the cottage, and with Buck not around..."

Oh no! Here it comes. He is going to tell me he is selling the cottage.

Uncle Vic stopped and stared at the sunset over the farm pasture beyond the car. "Gad, it is a beautiful Fall. We walk in God's art gallery." He inhaled deeply, and placed a weathered hand on Mike's shoulder "The summer is over, but we'll have the memories forever." He let out a long sigh. "I always wanted to build a small barn at the cottage but now I'm too old."

No. Oh please God, don't let him say it. Mike winced. Please God. Oh please no.

Uncle Vic continued, "I'm wondering if you would come up to

the cottage next summer and help me build a small barn. You would have to do a lot of the work. I can't do it by myself."

"Wha...Why sure!" Mike couldn't believe he was hearing this. Thank you, God. Thank you, thank you.

Mike wanted to cry in joy. He closed his eyes and it was next year. He was standing on a ladder, wearing a stiff leather tool belt, a nail in the corner of his mouth. "Hand me another shingle, will you?"

His body glistened with sweat adding definition to his bulging muscles. His breath came hard in the sawdust atmosphere, but he would work until the barn was right. He resolved to work all day and into the night.

"What are you waiting for, get the garage done so we can have dinner!" a fair voice cried.

"Quiet *girl*." It was his favorite insult.

"Hey," the girl exclaimed, "my mom's calling, I've gotta go."

"Then help me, girl."

Linda handed him the shingle.

He hammered it in place in a tight line with all the others like the scales on a dragon's back, but he made sure these scales were going nowhere. Yep, he nailed that dragon 'fur sure.'

"You sure are a good carpenter. When will you build *me* a house?"

Uncle Vic's voice broke the daydream, "...But I can't pay you much."

"What? Pay me? Why would you pay me?"

"So that you can buy shotgun shells for hunting. You'll be old enough next year."

"Yeah, but I don't have a shotgun."

"It would please me... to give you this one. Here." He handed Mike the unloaded shotgun with the casual air of one man handing a hammer to another man. "'Course you gotta clean it first."

Mike's mind exploded with a mixture of emotions, "But...but you should give it to Buck. He'll come home." he said in a panicky voice. "You got that letter saying he's alive in that prison camp and doing fine."

Uncle Vic placed his hand on Mike's shoulder and took a deep breath. "When he comes home, I'll buy him anything he wants." He bit his lip. "But I want you to have this one. Besides, it gives me an excuse to buy a new lightweight 20-gage semiautomatic. It won't weigh as much, has less kick, and I don't have to wrench my shoulder working the pump." He winked at Mike. "Whenever you want something for yourself, make sure you tell the womenfolk it is for some noble purpose. You got to start learning how to deal with women." He nudged Mike's shoulder and the corner of his mouth turned up in a conspiratorial grin.

Mike grinned back. His own gun! He couldn't believe it. This one had been Uncle Vic's and had been all over. It shot that deer last year and those partridge and....

"...And now I don't have to carry it back to the car," Uncle Vic said playfully. He reached down with a grunt and picked up a cane-sized stick. "Shall we strut?"

Mike nodded and slung the heavy gun in the crook of his arm as he had seen his uncle do so many times. He commenced to strut.

His uncle started singing, then stopped. He nudged Mike, "I need some harmony."

Mike joined in shakily.

They sang together and strutted down the two track, red and gold maple leaves fluttered down like tickertape, just as the timeless characters in one of Uncle Vic's stories that would live forever in the summer of his life.

The entire world stopped and stared. He just walked on; his head held high. The glory of the universe shone on him. He knew what it was to strut. God winked, and angels gaped in awe. Mike grinned up at his Uncle Vic. The smile on his uncle's face matched his, but his uncle's eyes were closed and the crowd cheered their elegance.

Epilogue

I am sitting in a rickety green lawn chair on the wobbly dock, with my eyes closed, feeling the last rays of the summer sunset attempt to bore through my eyelids. The waves lick rhythmically on the beach, in time with the beating of my heart. It is over, I think with a melancholy sigh, and the dock shakes as I hear the footsteps behind me. I find myself rubbing my hands together as if they were cold.

A musical voice interrupts my reflections. "Grace says that she and Buck will be up next weekend to close the cottage for the winter. Sorry, but time is up. We are meeting the kids at the restaurant by the orchard. Our summer is over," she said with a courtroom finality.

I gently reach up and her small tender hand completely disappears in my rough brown spotted hand. I stand. The slow, deliberate maneuvering reminds me of a documentary demonstrating the docking of an aircraft carrier.

On standing, I stare into those magical brown eyes. I feel the heat of the summer sunset on my face, and, with a soft chuckle, I hug her tightly, rocking her from side to side. "Oh Tink...,"

"My name is Linda... Mickey." She laughs and kisses my cheek.

"Oh Tink, our summer is never over."

The End